A Stone In My Pocket

A Stone In My Pocket

❧

MATTHEW
MANERA

thistledown press

© Matthew Manera, 2006
All rights reserved

No part of this publication may be reproduced or transmitted in any form or by any means, graphic, electronic or mechanical, including photocopying, recording, or any information storage and retrieval system, without permission in writing from the publisher or a licence from The Canadian Copyright Licensing Agency (Accesss Copyright). For an Access Copyright licence, visit www.accesscopyright.ca or call toll free to 1-800-893-5777.

Manera, Matthew, 1949-
A stone in my pocket / Matthew Manera.

ISBN-10 1-897235-03-8
ISBN-13 978-1-897235-03-4

1. Port Credit Region (Ont.)--Fiction. I. Title.

PS8626.A555S76 2006   C813'.6   C2006-900505-2

Cover and book design by Jackie Forrie
Typeset by Thistledown Press
Printed and bound in Canada by Marquis Book Printing Inc.

Thistledown Press Ltd.
633 Main Street
Saskatoon, Saskatchewan, S7H 0J8
www.thistledown.sk.ca

Thistledown Press gratefully acknowledges the financial assistance of the Canada Council for the Arts, the Saskatchewan Arts Board, and the Government of Canada through the Book Publishing Industry Development Program for its publishing program.

 Canadian Heritage / Patrimoine canadien

 Canada Council for the Arts / Conseil des Arts du Canada

Acknowledgements

The writing of this novel depended to a great extent on historical research. I would like to thank Rowena Cooper, Reference Archivist for the Region of Peel (Ontario) and Anna-Marie Raftery, Historian/Advisor for the Mississauga Heritage Foundation for their help in this area. I also relied on several histories of Port Credit and Clarkson. Among them were: *Port Credit. A Glimpse of Other Days* (1995) by Verna Mae Weeks; *The Families of Merigold's Point* (Mississauga Heritage Foundation, 1984) by Dorothy L. Martin; *Rattray Marsh Then and Now* (Rattray Marsh Protection Association, 1990) by Ruth Hussey and Judith Goulin; *Credit Valley Gateway. The Story of Port Credit* (Port Credit Public Library Board, 1967) and *At The Mouth of The Credit* (The Boston Mills Press, 1977) by Betty Clarkson.

I would also like to thank my editor, Harriet Richards.

A red-tailed hawk might look down on it from a pale winter sky, might look down on a silvery black crack vibrating through the trees, across the meadows, finally splitting open into a shallow bay hanging like a pouting lip from the profile of the lake. The creek, born of meltwater and spring rains. Creekwater, always looking to give itself up into something greater. And the great lake, like a deep watery sigh in the bosom of the land. A refusal in the face of time to be still, to be of one nature. Child of the glacier, mother of the clouds, father of the rain, it is curious and serendipitous, seductive and mournful. Its language is fishes and stones and seaweed and gulls. The waves from the bay collapse one upon the other, incessantly, over the end of the creek until the sandy weight of a thousand and million folds are pressed together to slowly and finally separate the bay from the lake. The folds petrify and their brittle ridges crackle and shatter into shingle. The creek and the lake are forced apart and no power of heaven or earth can remember them back together. A hundred and a thousand years and the bay relaxes into a marsh.

But the storm. The storm sucks the frustrated energy of the great lake into its magnificent lungs, excites the water into a frenzy of tossing and roiling, and then turns towards the folded shoreline in a great shout that shivers the core of every living thing. The flat, grey stones of the shingle bar clatter and tumble over each other, are thrown up in a hump against the stubborn roots and trunks of the cottonwoods and the balsam poplars and the crack willows whose thousand leafed branches flail in the wind. The tangle of chokecherry, bindweed, and cocklebur snag errant bits of shingle. There is no meanness in this turmoil; there is nothing malignant or malicious in the crash of water and wind and earth. This is passion without fury. The shingle bar is the child of time and of the storm; the marsh is its innocence.

In the relief of aftermath the sun heats the flat stones, glazes the marshwater, speckles the ground beneath the trees. Killdeer lay their stone coloured eggs in the pebbly fringes of the shingle and trust the hard cobble to protect the delicate shelled embryos. The undergrowth is veined with red osier dogwood and silverweed.

Sometimes a thin channel insists itself through a depression in the shingle bar where lakewater and marshwater can taste each other and sense "this is what it is like to be great" or "this is what it is like to be still and shallow."

Spring — Winter 1854

Chapter 1

IT WAS GOD'S FIRE. Sparked from heaven like a sudden thought about beauty, for no reason.

I could smell storms before they came. Baketigweyaa taught me how to do that. He said it was nothing more than being aware of where you are. Of letting your heart beat with the pulse of the earth and the sky. He said that the earth and the sky spoke to each other, and how could we help but listen. How else could we be human.

So I could smell the storm coming. It was to be a dry storm, a storm with much lightning, and already if I pressed my eyes closed very tightly I could hear the slow waves of thunder seeping out of the horizon.

From our farm on Merigold's Point near Slade's Marsh it was two miles along the shore of the lake to the marshes by the Credit River. The shoreline described a long, sweeping arc that pressed the rising green woods away from the lake so that on a clear day I could stand by the water at the edge of our farm and see the mouth of the river, like a dimple in the far end of the arc. But that day the dark sky of the storm was sneaking into the fading grey light, and I began to walk quickly towards the river, trying not to run. I liked to live inside anticipation, knowing that something was coming, but wishing at the same time that it would never arrive. There was no time to explain to Father or Mother what I was doing, as if any explanation could serve their needs and mine, anyway. I knew, or at least I hoped, that when I got to the marshes I would be a witness.

The stony parts of the shoreline kept my feet, but not my passion, in check. My feet made a hollow sound as I moved over the shingle, as if either there was nothing but air underneath, or as if I, myself, had nothing inside me. Smooth and flat, the stones are perfect for skipping across the water, but now it was I who was skipping across them. When I got to the sandy stretches I could break out into a full run. I kept close to the water where the sand was still hard and wet from the weight of the receding tide. My feet felt so fast and light; I weighed nothing at all. I felt a wild exhilaration running at full speed, knowing that there were no obstacles before me except my own want of breath. The smell of new lightning was getting stronger and thicker, and the roll of thunder began to break up into jagged shards of sound. And then, there it was way up off to my left. A shock of silver-white veins cracking out of the fleshy grey sky, and I knew it had happened. Time was stretching and collapsing in on itself all at once. I felt as if I had been running forever or for no time at all. I was close to the river and the marshes now, and just over the tops of the trees I could see a dim orange light rising.

When I reached the river I rushed up to the wooden bridge that crossed it not more than a stone's throw from where the river emptied into the lake. I leaned on the railing, trying to catch my breath, but immediately my eyes were drawn to the magnificence of the flames. Like earthbound lightning full of blood and purpose, they consumed great swaths of dry marsh grass and then leapt wildly at the sky.

I felt something wild and leaping inside of me, too. A sound from somewhere primitively deep inside me. I felt my body expanding, preparing itself to speak with the thunder. I felt as if I was becoming a witness to myself, to my own body. Lightning slivered the sky. The thunder crashed, and crashed again, and again. The marsh crackled and gasped. And I was vibrating with sound. My own sound. It terrified me and excited me at the same time because I had no control over it. I was so absolutely alive; as big as the sky, as loud as the world. I could not hear the thunder above my own voice. I was disappearing into the world of the storm.

The next morning, I woke up in my bed, my room filled with the smell of storm-damp clothes.

"She's only fourteen for God's sake!"

"John . . ."

"Lydia, I will not have my daughter . . . we cannot allow our child to run off to God knows where without our permission and stay out half the night in a storm that could . . . she could catch pneumonia . . . she could . . ."

"I'll speak to her, John."

I had witnessed scenes like this before, sitting on the landing of the stairs, peering through the railings down into the parlour.

"I'll speak to her, John."

And then Father would stand stiff and straight and resignedly silent, his arms rigid by his side, clenching and unclenching his hands until he could control his emotions enough to turn and walk with deliberate calmness out of the room.

I survived episodes like last night because I stood between Mother and Father in that space where they dared not go; that space they stepped into when Mother was fifteen. It was all there in her eyes; she needed add no words to what I could see there.

The first marsh fire was in 1848 when I was not yet nine years old. I saw it from my bedroom window in the upstairs of our house. Mother was just about to tuck me into bed when we heard Father calling out as he ran around the edge of the house from the orchard.

"Look at the eastern sky, Lydia! Quick!"

He never called me by name, always regarding me as part of his wife, as if I had never left her womb.

Mother hastened to the window, pulled the curtain aside, and looked out. I could hear her stop in mid-breath as her hands stopped in mid-rush from her waist to her open mouth.

"Gretchen, come see!"

I remember at that moment understanding for the first time that Mother had been as young as me once. It was her young self that had called me to the window before her older self could censor the action. I did not wait for her to realize this lapse, and jumped out of bed almost before the words were out of her mouth. Just north of the lake's edge the horizon glowed, as I thought the aurora borealis might. Miss Jenkins explained to us how far, far up north, beyond where there were any settlements, there were sometimes lights that would shimmer in the night sky right from the ground all the way up to the top of the heavens. Like coloured mosquito netting fluttering in the breeze, is how she tried to describe it. But this light I was looking at was more attached to the ground than to the sky, although it was trying hard to escape upwards. And it wasn't shimmering or fluttering; it seemed to be pulsing like the heartbeat of something that was afraid.

"Did the lightning do that, Mother?"

"I hope so, dear."

I didn't understand until years later that she had not been hoping for the divinity of the occurrence but for the absence of man's hand in it. That way, if there could not be thanks offered for the brilliant, fiery halo hovering over the marsh, at least there could be resignation in the face of God's will rather than blame and castigation placed on the head of some poor soul who may have lost control of his small, human fire. For this was, indeed, God's fire.

Ever since that night I had waited for such an ignition to come again. Every storm that brought lightning filled me with a glorious anticipation, and I promised myself that I would not stand and watch from so far away the next time. But I did not mention this to Mother. Not to anyone. Except Baketigweyaa.

"Baketigweyaa! I got there in time! I smelled it coming just like you showed me how to do!"

He was standing by the river, staring into it. He often did that. I didn't know if it was because he was very old and didn't want to move around any more, or if there was something he was looking at in the water. Maybe he was just remembering being a boy.

I had first met him a couple of months before. I was skipping stones across the lake at the bottom of our property when I noticed an old Indian man standing a little ways down the shore from me. I was startled for a moment, not simply because he was an Indian, but because he seemed oddly out of place. Of course I had often seen Indians before, but only when they came into Port Credit to sell the moccasins and gloves and baskets they had made. I had certainly not, though, ever spoken to one, nor had one ever spoken to me. It seemed to me that they moved among us like ghosts of ourselves, but I had often heard Mother, in conversation with friends, use words like guilt and indigence in whispered tones when referring to the Indians, and Father mutter words like salvation and responsibility while making clucking sounds with his tongue and shaking his head.

Mr. Donnerton, my first teacher, would, in his lessons on history, refer to Indians as if they were as mysterious and awful and remote in time as the explorers, like Cartier and Champlain. He seemed to ignore the fact of them just a few miles away. Miss Jenkins, who is our teacher now, says simply that their wisdom is different from ours, though I'm not sure exactly what that means. I did know, though, that they were Mississauga Indians and that they were part of the Ojibwa tribe, which was part of the Algonkian tribe.

As I stood there on the shore, having paused from skipping stones and wondering at the old Indian, I remember thinking that he looked like a shepherd's hook with a blanket hanging from it.

"You do that very well," he said.

I didn't know quite what to say in response, but after thinking about it for a few seconds, I decided it was best for me not to say anything, and kept skipping stones. Except that now I couldn't make any of them skip, even once.

"Now you are not doing it so well."

Still, I didn't say anything. What was I going to say? Just agree with him? I didn't want to sound stupid.

"You must show me how to do that."

He bent down and picked up a stone.

"Is this a good one?"

I walked over to him with an outward confidence that did not reflect what I felt inside. He handed me the stone. I turned it over, then bounced it in my hand a couple of times. I handed it back to him.

"Sure. That's a good one."

"How do I hold it? Like this?"

I realized all of a sudden that no one had ever taught me how to skip stones; it was something that everybody just knew how to do. And then I was pretty sure that he already knew how to do this, too.

"Are you sure you don't know how to do this?"

"Not the way you do it."

"What's so special about the way I do it? Everybody does it the same."

"If your mother was walking across the floor of your house and you were in another room would you know it was your mother?"

"Yes."

"How would you know?"

"Because she walks differently than Father."

"Do you have brothers and sisters?"

"Two sisters. They're younger than me."

"Do they walk like your mother?"

"No."

"Well, then."

He turned the stone over two or three times. Then he bounced it in his hand.

"This does feel like a good stone, doesn't it? Here, you throw it. I'll watch."

I took the stone, walked up to the water, and threw it as carefully as I could. No skips at all. So I picked up another one and threw it. Same thing.

"Turn around. Don't look at me. I can't skip them if I know you're watching me."

Without speaking he turned and faced away from the water and from me. I picked up another stone and threw it. I knew right away from the angle of my throw and from the first skip that it was good for at least six or seven skips.

"Turn around quick! Look! It's skipping!"

As I turned to look at him he was still facing away from the water.

"You didn't look. It was a really good one."

"How many times did it skip?"

"I don't know. I was looking to see if you were looking."

"Seven times. That was a good one."

"How do you know it skipped seven times?"

"I heard it."

I looked at him, then I looked at the water. Then I looked back at him. He was smiling, either because he really could hear every single skip a stone made across the water or because he had just fooled me and knew that I wasn't sure if he had fooled me or not.

"I must go now. I must get back to my family before the storm comes. I don't enjoy walking in the strong rain as much as I used to. Especially with so much thunder and lightning."

"How do you know there's going to be a storm?"

"I can smell it. Can't you?"

After that first meeting, I began to search for him whenever I was in Port Credit, and of course, I would keep sniffing the air whenever it clouded over, to see if I could somehow recognize the difference between how the air smelled normally and how it smelled just before a storm came, to see if I could be aware of the sky speaking to the earth.

The next time I saw him was a week later when Mother and I were in the village to get supplies. He was standing down by the marshes near the bridge, and just as I was about to call out to him, I realized two things. The first was that I didn't know his name; the second was that I wouldn't know how to explain to Mother how I knew this old Indian man. So I asked Mother if she wouldn't mind if I wandered around in the sunshine while she ordered the supplies we needed, and then I would help her load them on to the wagon. I promised to stay within sight of the General Store.

As soon as Mother walked into the store, I turned and ran down to where I had seen the old Indian man. He hadn't moved from where he had been standing before. It occurred to me that he hardly ever seemed to move. When I reached him, I walked around in front of him so he could see me and so I wouldn't rudely surprise him.

"My friend who skips stones," he said, nodding his head.

"Yes. My name is Gretchen."

"I am Baketigweyaa."

"Ba . . ."

"You may use my name in your language — Where The River Forks."

"I would rather learn your real name. Please say it once more . . . but slowly." I listened very carefully, and said it back to him as best I could. "Bah-kay-tig-way-uh?"

"Very good. Almost as good as you skip stones." Then he paused and looked away from me to the river, as if the conversation was over for now. But I didn't want it to be.

"How does the air smell just before a storm?"

"It smells like the thunder. Like lightning."

"But what do they smell like?"

"Too many questions for something that is very simple."

"I'm sorry."

He smiled at me, and then he turned to go.

"*Gigawabamin Menawah*, Gretchen." When I looked at him in utter confusion, he said, "See you again."

And so I did see him, as often as I could find him.

"She's been off to see that Indian again, I can tell."

Now, whenever I returned after having been away from the house unexpectedly or for a longer time than he thought was appropriate, this was what I overheard Father say to Mother. I thought that in some way it allowed Father a kind of comfort in his displeasure with me because he now had a clear target at which he could aim his frustration. These words were meant as a scolding not only for me, but indirectly for Mother, too.

The third or fourth time I saw Baketigweyaa, Mother saw me speaking to him. I didn't know that until, as I was standing next to him down by the marshes, I heard her voice, as calm as it could be, right behind me.

"Are you ready to go now, Gretchen?"

I felt as if I was caught between two worlds that I could in no way reconcile. It was not so much standing there between Mother and Baketigweyaa as it was the absence of any heightened emotion in Mother's voice. Why was she so calm? I decided that there was nothing else I could do but introduce them.

"Mother, this is Baketigweyaa. Baketigweyaa, this is my mother, Mrs. Williamson."

"How do you do?" Mother said as she reached out her hand to him. I wondered how much courage she had to summon up to do this.

"It is an honour," he replied, bowing his head slightly, taking her hand and shaking it with great courtesy.

I was flabbergasted. Mother was behaving as if Baketigweyaa was just another man in the village whose acquaintance she was making, but I was sure that she had never spoken to an Indian before. I think I expected her to shun him with silence or to simply ignore his presence; I expected her to behave as I believed Father would. When we turned to leave, I said over my shoulder, "*Gigawabamin Menawah.*"

"What does that mean?" Mother asked.

"It means 'See you again.'"

"Is he a nice man, Gretchen?"

"Yes, Mother, he is."

And then she spoke no more of the meeting, and as the rest of the ride home and then the rest of that day and then the next few days passed, I wondered if it had really happened at all. I suspect that Mother may have told Father about this incident, because next time we went to Port Credit, a couple of weeks later, Father came with us, which he hardly ever did. If he was hoping to catch Mother and I out with Baketigweyaa, he was disappointed, for we didn't see him. I had to live for some weeks with a gnawing in my stomach, because I did not want to forego my friendship with Baketigweyaa, yet I did not want to invite Father to release his temper on me. The problem was that I did not feel I could be honest with Father because his love for me was conditional upon my being the daughter he thought I should be, which was not always the girl I wanted to be.

So, when Father said in his most stentorian voice, "I suppose she's been off to see that Indian again," I wasn't sure if he was speaking from knowledge or from apprehension, but even though he seemed to be addressing himself to Mother, his eyes were focused on me. And so it was that I talked back to him without even thinking what I was doing. It was his tone of voice more than what he actually said that sounded like an attack.

"What's wrong with Indians?"

"I beg your pardon, young lady?"

"What's wrong with Indians?"

"Lydia, you must be more firm with the children. I shall not be talked back to."

Mother hesitated for a minute. I knew she felt she had to choose sides, and I knew that she would not do that.

"John, I think the child only wants to know if you are scolding her."

Before he could answer I jumped in again. It was as if I was trying to keep up with my own voice.

"Reverend Ryerson likes the Indians. One of them was even the first minister in Port Credit, and he and Reverend Ryerson built a school for the Indians, and they were all Methodists. The Indians even gave the Reverend an Indian name, Cheehock, because they liked and respected him so much. So why don't you like Indians if Reverend Ryerson does?"

"We are Episcopal, not Wesleyan! And even John Wesley himself did not think highly of the Indians. When he . . . "

"John," Mother said as she put her hand gently on his arm. Her voice soothed like honey on a scratchy throat, and none of us, including Father, could hold our anger against it.

Father did not like it when I used facts. It was not becoming for a young girl. His anger now had nowhere to be released, for Father was an honest and fair man as much as he was able to be, and he was never so foolish as to take his anger out on a fact or a person citing a fact. He had tried once before to put as much blame as he could for my knowing facts on Miss Jenkins, partly because she was not Methodist — neither Episcopal nor Wesleyan. That was the only time I can remember Mother looking at him as if he had just taken the Lord's name in vain. I often wondered, though, where Father's anger went, and I was afraid that if he never let it out, it would somehow break him apart inside. So he turned as calmly as he could and walked out of the kitchen, onto the back porch, and out to the orchard.

I think it is the orchard that he loved most. The field of buckwheat, and the several rows each of beans, corn, peas, turnips, carrots, and potatoes were mostly Mother's domain, but the orchard was Father's. He loved his family, of course, but it seemed to me to be a love born of obligation and Methodist principle. There was certainly a principle and a method involved in the raising of trees, but they were not only Methodist in nature. Father also trusted completely in *A View of the Cultivation of Fruit Trees and the Management of Orchards and Cider* by William Coxe. It was a book his father had given him along with the land before he moved up to Streetsville once grandmother had died and he felt too tired to take care of the orchard and the animals. That was in 1837, two years before I was born. My grandparents on both sides came here from Kingsclear Parish in New Brunswick with the Merigolds, the Jarvises, the Bradleys, and the Mongers. It was they who cleared the land, built our houses, and planted the orchards. Great grandfather Williamson was born and raised in Somerset, England and brought his wife and children to New Brunswick in the last century. Grandfather Talbot, on Mother's side, was born in Concord, Massachusetts a few years before the American Revolution. His father, my great grandfather, descended from the Earl of Shrewsbury, was a Loyalist, and decided to move his family up to Nova Scotia. I thought great grandfather's brother chose to stay in the new United States, because Father sometimes talked of "distant relatives down New England way."

So he was walking in his orchard after having left all his words unsaid in the kitchen, where Mother and I would each begin the process of building meaning into his absence.

We had two kinds of apples, Snows and Ribstone Pippins. The Snows were sweeter than the Pippins, and juicier, too. Though they were not usually fully ripe until just after the first day of fall, we started picking them as early as late July or early August, and Mother made pies with them. The Snow apple orchard was already established when we got the farm. Father chose the Ribstone Pippins because they were unusual and because they were mentioned in Coxe's book. There was only one other orchard, somewhere east of Port Credit, that had them, so he arranged with the farmer of that orchard to purchase a few dozen scions, which he carefully grafted on to one section of the Snow apple trees. Though Father did not often speak to me, he did let me help him sometimes. He let me help him mix the paste for covering the scions; it was my job to measure the tallow, beeswax, and resin and then spread them on strips of linen six inches by two inches, exactly as Mr. Coxe instructed. Father would then do the wrapping. Sometimes he would even smile at me when I handed him the next strip. "Have faith in the method," he would say to me, "and the method will make strong your faith. These apples," and he would wave his arms towards the trees as if he were presenting a great show to an audience, "will return your faith if you have faith in them." I think he said that especially because of last summer. We had no rain for almost two months, and the temperature stayed around 100 degrees for that whole time. Everything just dried up, and we lost our whole crop. But so did everyone else, and so we had to put up with the same hardship all together. Sometimes the only way to feel that you can survive a great trouble is to know that many others are trying to survive that same trouble. I remembered last summer that there was nowhere you could get cool except to walk into the lake until the water was up to your neck. There would often be a dozen people at a time bobbing in the water, and from the shore they would look like strangely painted pumpkins or cabbages floating in from some mysterious shipwreck.

    My favourite apples were Butter apples and Summer Queens. The Summer Queens are ready and ripe at the beginning of August, when the weather gets really hot. The Butters are later, sometimes not until October. There's a Butter apple orchard up by Clarkson's Corners, north of our farm, and I went there sometimes with my little sisters and just sat under the trees in the sun and ate as many apples as I could before I started to feel sick. They were big, fat apples, so I could only eat maybe three if I was really hungry. And then Mother knew what I had done, but she didn't say anything. If I thought about it, Mother didn't speak to me all that much more than Father did, but we had a kind of understanding. I didn't know exactly how we did it, I just knew that Father and I didn't seem to have the same way of not having to talk. I thought he was disappointed that he had three daughters and no sons. I was fourteen and spoke too forthrightly for my age, Sally was eleven and spoke not at all, Victoria was six and spoke in the curiosity and riddles of a precocious child. In between Sally and Victoria was Jackie, who died the day he was born. I thought Father had given up trying for a son.

Our village had a marsh, too. It was four properties to the east of us, just the other side of Slade's farm. The part of it nearest the lake was a cranberry marsh; the rest was just marsh. There was a shallow creek that flowed into it from the northwest, and I liked to walk in it all the way from the marsh right up to where it ran between Russell Bush's Inn and the Church on the Lakeshore Road. Some stretches of the creek were as still as ponds, and the deepest parts were only just past my waist. Nowhere did the water flow really quickly, as in rapids that the coureurs de bois had to go over in their canoes. I liked this creek because it was too small for anyone else to pay attention to. It was not like the Credit River, whose mouth was the centre of a village. Baketigweyaa told me that he and his family and part of his tribe lived on the river when he was a child. They would catch many different kinds of fish, but especially salmon. And then the government and the Methodists decided the Indians should stay in one place and have their own village, instead of moving around all the time, so they built houses for them and tried to make them be farmers instead of hunters and fishermen. They also tried to make them into Christians, like us. Baketigweyaa did not like this and so he and his wife and a few other elders kept walking up the river until they found a place where they could live in their own wigwams and hunt and fish as they had always done. Eventually, most of the Indians of the Credit Band of Mississaugas, including Baketigweyaa's own children, who were now grown, moved to Brant County, but Baketigweyaa stayed.

These days, though, because of all the mills and dams up river the salmon have all but disappeared. They couldn't jump the dams and so couldn't make it to their spawning grounds. Baketigweyaa was very sad about that.

Father did not like fish very much. For him water was a boundary line, and sometimes you could swim in it, but he trusted in the land for food — the plants and trees that grew in it, and the animals that grazed on it. And even then he trusted only animals like the cows and pigs we kept inside fences on our property. He was not a hunter, and many times at the dinner table he let some of the anger that he often did not know what to do with be heaped on the heads of deer hunters. "These men . . . these hunters" — Father almost spit this word out rather than speaking it — "they have no respect for the dignity of living creatures. It is one thing to shoot a deer; it is another thing altogether to chase that animal into the lake, to frighten it beyond what is necessary, to watch that poor animal swim out into the lake until it drowns from fright and exhaustion or until they fire their guns into it." We never ate wild game in our house.

I remembered once when I was playing in the woods just above the marsh I saw a fox. It was the first one I had ever seen and I had not yet been taught to be afraid of wild animals, so I tried to walk up to him. He trotted away from me for a little ways and then stopped, so I tried to go up to him again. Then he started to run, and I ran after him, until it looked as if he fell into a long, deep hole in the ground. I couldn't believe what I saw. I stopped as if I had all of a sudden been frozen stiff. So many thoughts were racing through my head, and before I could try to sort them out I was crying. Crying so hard. I was waiting for God to do something bad to me because of what I had done to the fox. But I wasn't even sure what it was I had done. It just felt like something wrong. All I wanted was to touch his soft, red fur. And now I had pushed him into hell, because I knew that's what was down inside the earth where the fox had fallen. I didn't want to get close to the hole, because I didn't want to fall into hell, too.

I remembered a sermon Reverend Swinerton had given just a few Sundays before this when he came through on his circuit. It was about sin and hell and damnation and fasting. The parts I remembered most were the awful parts, and this is something that has always troubled my mind, this ability I have to remember everything I see and hear, especially those things that trouble me, as if the words were printed in the air before my eyes. What I remembered was, "When men are overcome with sin, and understand damnation to be the result of it and see before their eyes the horrors of hell they will want more than anything to be delivered from this hell and damnation. And so they will give up all desire of meat and drink, will loathe all pleasure of worldly things. They will weep and lament and show in everything they do and say that they are weary of this life."

So when I got home I refused to eat dinner and I refused to be happy. And I wept strongly, even though I couldn't make the tears come. And I walked up the stairs to my bedroom as if I had no energy left in my body and would surely expire before I reached the landing. But when I got up the next morning I had dressed and eaten breakfast before I remembered how damned I was. I tried hard to carry damnation and weariness with me for the whole day, but could not. Eventually, I came back to myself, though a certain fear lurked inside me and would come out every now and then to remind me that I was a sinner, no matter how happy I thought I felt.

Once I learned about foxes in school, I changed my ideas about hell and weariness. It was like a revelation, though not one that Father or Reverend Swinerton would appreciate as such. It was also at about that time — I was eleven years old — that I began to grow and grow and grow. Now I am taller than Father, and I have a ways to go yet, if my sore bones are any indication. I am becoming used to being stared at, but I am not frightened, because now I know where foxes live.

When I told Baketigweyaa that I had smelled the storm coming and that I had made it to the marshes by the river in time to see God's fire, he just smiled at me and didn't say anything. He had the kind of smile that wrapped you up like a thick, warm blanket, and you didn't even want him to say anything because it would ruin the whole peacefulness of the feeling. He just put his hand on my shoulder to point me in the direction he wanted to walk, and then we began to move along the river's edge away from his wigwam.

When he first invited me to walk with him to his wigwam my curiosity was tempered with apprehension. Would I be safe? What would Mother say or do if she found out? I was certain of Father's reaction, but as always, I let my curiosity have the upper hand.

It was about as far from the mouth of the river to his wigwam as it was from the river to my house, but there was something less wild about the long, gently winding shore of the river than there was about the lakeshore.

There was a kind of comfort, too, in being able to always see the other side of the river, as if I was held more securely to the ground than I felt I was by the lake.

When I saw the wigwams — there were four of them in a huddle — I felt for a moment as if I had stepped out of my familiar world into one to which I did not and could not belong. The wigwams looked like covered wagons without the wheels, and it occurred to me how the one was for traveling and the other was for staying put. They were constructed of large sheets of birch bark on a frame of saplings which were bent over to form an arch. Baketigweyaa did not invite me to go into his wigwam, and I dared not ask. I already felt like an intruder, though it was not he who made me feel that way.

After we walked along the river for a while, he said, "So you think it was God's fire. Who told you that?"

"Nobody."

"Hmm. Yes. There are some things you just know."

We walked some more without saying anything.

"Do you know where thunder comes from?" he asked.

"No."

We walked along some more. I had learned to figure out his pauses. He was waiting for me to ask him to tell me the story about thunder. Sometimes he would just tell me stories, and other times he wanted me to say out loud that I was curious. I'm still not sure what the difference is; I'm not sure why sometimes I have to ask. But I knew this time I did.

By this time we had turned back towards his wigwam. The sky was getting dark. When we reached his camp his wife had already started a nice, welcoming fire. We walked up to it and sat down on the ground. He had a way of folding his legs before he sat down. Then he would just sink into a cross-legged sitting position without moving any other part of his body. I tried to do it, too, but fell over sideways and had to break my fall with my hand.

There was some kind of bird stuck on a stick hanging over the fire. The fat was dripping into the flames.

"So, where does the thunder come from?"

"You hear that fire crackling? That is the heart of young thunder." He paused for a long while, and we listened to the fire. "A long time ago, before the fighting between my people and your people, even before there was any fighting between the tribes of my own people there was no fear of things unknown. Except for the Ahnemekeeg — these were the great birds who covered almost all the sky when they spread their wings to fly. We could never see them land, and we did not know where their nests were. This was because we would only see them at night when the moon was fat and there were no clouds to cover it up. We did not so much fear them if they flew only at night. But sometimes we would see them during the day, and when we did we knew some great misfortune would befall us.

"Fear is like your father calling you to him when you have done something wrong. You are afraid to go to him because of the punishment you might receive, but you are also drawn to him because he is your father and you dare not disobey. It was in this way that one of our ancient people learned about the Ahnemekeeg. One day in the middle of winter in that time long ago, there was a young warrior who lived with his tribe on the shores of Kechegumme, a lake to the north and west of this lake, but much bigger. He had been hunting and killed a beaver, which he was carrying back to his family. It was night and there was a big, bright moon showing him where to walk, when suddenly, the light of the moon was covered by the wings of a great bird, an Ahnemekeeg. The bird picked him up in his strong talons and carried him for a long time up to the far end of the lake where he had never been. Then the young warrior felt the talons open up and release him. He fell to the ground among some younger birds, but as the great bird flew away he could hear its voice of thunder echo across the water. He realized then that he was to be food for the young thunder birds. They came towards him, their eyes shooting out flashes of lightning every time they blinked. The warrior still had his spear with him and he killed the birds. He skinned one of them and wrapped himself in the thunder skin. Then he jumped off the high rock where he had been put down and flew back to his people and told them his story. It has been told through more moons than even I can count. It was told to me, and now I have told it to you."

༄

Some of my life I kept in my book journal, some of it I stored in my memory, but some of it I wrote in my sand journal. These bits of my life were the ones that I gave away to the world of wind and tides and rain and snow. These were the bits I didn't need to remember if I didn't want to. But I always seemed to.

The pages of my sand journal were anywhere there was a wide stretch of sand that would take the large, looping scrawl of a stick long enough so that I didn't have to bend over too far when I was writing. Some of these pages were on the stretch of beach just before Slade's marsh; the others were up along the creek, past Garter Snake Hill. The script of my beach journal entries was fat and not very deep, because the sand was so dry that when I ran my stick through it, it filled itself up again, almost like the surface of the lake smoothes out the ripples of boats passing across its surface. When I wrote in the wet sand of the receding tide, the letters were darkly furrowed against the deep brown and glistening page. My creek journal pages stayed much the same in any weather and season. They were in the shade of the black oaks and willows in the summer and in the shade of the hill in the winter, when the sun couldn't quite rise above it to shine on the creek.

Today was a beach journal day. Summer was hiding somewhere behind the low blanket of grey cloud, and I was standing on the wet sand with a stick in my hand. Here was where I have written about the silence of Father and the fuzziness I sometimes feel just before I go to sleep, not being able to figure out what kind of a day I have had and wondering if I have squandered a gift that may never be offered to me again. But today I wrote about Baketigweyaa and Father — the one who talks to me and teaches me, and the other who tries to love me through Mother, who translated me into the world for him. One who found me, and one who keeps me. The sun and the moon.

"Do you have a boyfriend, Gretchen?"

I was lying in my bed waiting for sleep to come, listening to the last few sparks from the woodstove down in the parlour as they bounced their way up the stovepipe that ran up through the corner of my room. I had my own room; Sally and Victoria shared a bedroom next to mine.

Often Victoria would wander into my room after Mother had tucked us all in. It was not that she felt she was doing something adventurous by sneaking out of bed and coming to my room, nor did she feel any sense of doing something out of the ordinary. Even though Victoria was the youngest she was the most curious, out loud, of us all. Sally never spoke, and I often got the sense that even though her body was there with us, her spirit was off somewhere else. Wherever it went she did not share its travels with me and Victoria.

So Victoria walked nonchalantly into my room and sat on the corner of my bed, as if I was expecting her.

"Why would I want a boyfriend, Victoria?"

"I didn't ask why you would have one, I just asked if you did have one."

"You would know if I had one; you would see us together at school. Do you ever see me with a boyfriend at lunchtime?"

"No, you always have lunch with me and Sally."

"Well, then?"

"Do you ever think about having one?"

"Would you like me to have one?"

"Well, it would be interesting to have a boy to talk to sometimes."

"There are boys at school; don't you talk to them?"

"That's not the same. I mean a boy who would come here and would be sweet on you and then I could ask him questions."

"You could get your own boyfriend."

"I'm too young to have a boyfriend. Besides, you're the oldest; you have to have one first. And then Sally. And then me."

"All right then, if I did have a boyfriend, what would you want to talk to him about?"

"When he grows up and marries you and if you have only baby girls but no baby boys if he would still love the baby girls even though they weren't boys."

"And why would you ask him that?"

"So I could understand why Father hardly ever talks to us."

"I think most fathers are like our father, Victoria."

"Why?"

"Because they have a lot of responsibilities. They have to work the land, they have to provide for their families, they have to know how to solve problems . . ."

"What kind of problems?"

"Well, for instance, if we do something bad, he has to know how to punish us properly."

"What if we do something good?"

"Then that's its own reward. God knows when we do good things, and then He remembers all the good things we do, and if we do enough of them we get to go to heaven."

"But how do we know if we've done something good? I always know when I've done something bad — at least when I get caught."

I think I realized then that I would probably learn more about my own life and who I was in the world from Victoria than I would from Miss Jenkins. I just wished that I knew if any of the answers I was giving were the correct ones.

"But, Victoria, don't you know when you've done something good and when you've done something bad?

Don't you know the difference between the two? Can't you feel the difference somewhere inside you?"

"Inside me where?"

"In your soul."

"Is it something like my stomach or my lungs? Miss Jenkins said that we couldn't live if we didn't have lungs. Look, I can make my lungs puff out really big." She took as deep a breath as she could and held it for a few seconds before the air burst out of her.

"No, your soul is invisible."

"But I can still feel it?"

"Yes, you can."

"What does it feel like?"

"Victoria, it's time for you to go to bed now. We'll finish this up later."

"I did it again, didn't I?"

"Did what again?"

"I made you try to think something that's older than you."

"Yes, you did Victoria."

Though I had not successfully managed to describe to Victoria how a soul feels, I did avoid talking about boyfriends. There was a boy I was sweet on. But I did not meet him at school; it was during the summer after the marsh fire.

About once every week during the summer break from school I would walk the water's edge by myself all the way to the Credit River and sometimes into the heart of the village. A week or so after the fire, I was standing on the bridge watching the Ann Brown move out of the harbour into the lake. It was a wonderful two-masted schooner with huge, flappy sails, but they hardly ever put the sails up when it was stonehooking. That day it was just easing slowly out along the shoreline, towing a scow behind it. I watched for a long time as two men stood on the flat scow and raked stones from the bottom of the lake. They were the same kind of smooth, flat stones I used for skipping, only bigger. Big enough to make into sidewalks and even to make stone walls. Miss Jenkins explained to us that this is called Dundas shale. There was also a road to the north of the village called Dundas. I didn't know if these two things were the same kind of Dundas or not.

The men on the scow moved slowly and surely, like the schooner itself, rocking easily on the small, even waves of the lake. They each had a long pole with two hooks on the end. The poles would be lowered into the water and get shorter and shorter until the men were holding the very ends of them. Then they would carefully pull the poles back up, with stones caught in the hooks. It reminded me of fishing; you had to be patient and precise.

As I was standing there on the bridge, a tall boy came walking along from the other side and stopped beside me. For a while he didn't say anything; he just watched the stonehooking the same way I did. But his presence started to make me uncomfortable; I felt that two of us standing so close together and watching the same thing was too crowded. I couldn't take deep breaths. So, I looked away from the schooner and the scow, out onto the wide space of the lake and tried again, as I always did, to find words to fit the changing colours of the water. I had a habit of staring out at the lake to see what colour it was, depending on the weather or the time of day or the season of the year. First, I tried counting all the different colours — grey, green, blue, black. Soon I realized, however, that the lake didn't so much change colour as it did shades of each colour. So then I tried counting all the different shades of grey, green, blue, black — although there is really only one shade of black. The greys were the hardest to tell apart, but I think this may have been as much a problem with words as with my ability to see, for I'm sure I could see several different shades of grey; it was just that I didn't have enough words to fit them all. I tried light grey and dark grey, or medium grey and strong grey, but these terms weren't at all satisfactory. I wondered then if it was just that I didn't yet have a grown-up's vocabulary, like Milton's "Now glow'd the firmament with living sapphires," or if the words I needed simply didn't exist. After talking to Mother I realized the problem was with the words. There weren't enough of them. Which is why I couldn't tell Victoria what a soul felt like. This failure of language to describe such things as the soul and water was something, I was sure, that would frustrate me for the rest of my life.

"What do you see out there?" asked the tall, young boy.

Just like Baketigweyaa, he didn't believe in introductions to conversation.

"Just water. The colour of the water. The different shades of colour in the water." I said much more than I wanted to. I should have stopped with "just water."

It was then that Patrick explained to me about the colour of water. Actually, I didn't know his name until after we had talked for quite a while. His name was Patrick Monaghan and he lived in Cork Town. It wasn't really a town; it was just a couple of streets in the Port Credit village, where all the Irishmen who came to work on the new rail line lived. He seemed to be about sixteen, but what was more important was that he was taller than me — the first boy I knew who was taller than me. That and his thick Irish accent made him appeal to me in a way I hadn't been appealed to before.

"If you think about it, water doesn't really have any colour at all. It only reflects the colour of things above it . . . " and here he let his eyes drift upwards and away from where we were standing, " . . . the sky, the clouds, the sun, the trees. Or," and here he pointed his eyes at the river below the bridge, "what's underneath it — sand, seaweed, rocks."

This did not resolve my problem, however. There was still the problem of naming the colours. It didn't matter where they came from; it just mattered that they were visible. Patrick said that water was so pure it didn't have any colour of its own. It was beyond colour. He said that pure things were like that; we could only see them by what was reflected in them.

"What if there were nothing in the world but water? How would there be any colours then?" I asked him.

"There can never only be one thing in the world. It wouldn't make any sense."

I thought about this for awhile, and then I turned to him and asked, "Are you Catholic?"

He looked back at me with a wonderfully confused look. I was sure that Patrick must be Catholic because he was Irish. Mother had told me that most Irish people were Catholic, the same as most French people. And Father said that Catholics were "mired in the mysteries of the Latin language," so that none of the other religions could understand them, but he was convinced that they couldn't understand it either. I knew they had to do something called confession, where they would tell all their sins to a priest who was hidden behind a curtain, and the priest would tell them prayers to say and they would be all cleaned up and ready to go to heaven if they died right then.

"Yes, I suppose I am."

"Don't all Catholics, like all Christians, believe there is only one God. Isn't that like only one thing in the world?"

"Just because people believe in only one thing doesn't mean that other things don't exist."

"So, do you believe in only one God, or do you believe that other gods exist?"

"I believe that you're trying to tie me up in knots." He sort of chuckled, nodded his head a couple of times, looked out at the lake, and then looked back at me.

"I'm just Patrick Monaghan."

That's when he told me who he was and where he lived and where he came from. He told me about the sickness in the potatoes in Ireland—"the potato rot" he called it — and how people had nothing to eat. I thought of last summer and how all the apples shrivelled and died in the incessant heat, but I knew that what had happened in Ireland must have been far worse than I could imagine. And then he told me how the Sassenachs — that was what his people called the English who owned the land in Ireland — forced them off their land, even as they were starving and sick and dying.

"There were families that died, huddled all together in their cabins and we just pulled the cabins down on top of them. Such were their graves."

He looked out across the lake, squinting his eyes as if he were trying to see the images he had just described more clearly. Then he relaxed his eyes and focused them on his hands, which were knotted together by the interlacing of his fingers.

"My parents and my sister and I sailed for Canada soon after that. I think we just needed to be able to hope again. But the passage across the ocean, in the bottom of the ship . . . well, we were crowded together like too many sheep in too small a pen, barely enough room to take a deep breath without pushing into someone else or breathing in the sickness and the coughing almost directly from their mouths." He paused. "Anyway, my mother and father died of the cholera soon after we docked in Quebec. The authorities put us in fever sheds that were no better than the ship we had just stepped off — worse, even. I watched my mother's and father's skin turn blue from the sickness. Have you ever seen blue skin?" Without pausing for an answer, he continued, "You don't ever want to see that."

He turned and leaned his back on the rail and looked across at the harbour, at the boats bobbing in the breeze.

"The last thing I saw before my sister and I left that Godforsaken place was a bundle being hoisted from the deck of the ship. As it rose higher and higher into the air, I could see it was a rope tied around the bodies of a man and his wife and two children. Their arms and legs hung from that awful bundle like branches from an uprooted tree. And the long, red hair of the girl was blowing so beautifully in the breeze."

He and his sister, now orphaned, were brought to Port Credit by a childless couple who had taken care of his parents while they were dying. I tried to picture in my mind Mother and Father and Sally and Victoria dying in wretchedness before my very eyes, with nothing I could do to save them. I forced myself to look at the lake and the stores and the people around me to prove that I was here and safe, to remove myself from the wrenching misery of Patrick's story, but the collision of these two worlds was like a physical weight on my chest. I grabbed hard onto the rail of the bridge so I wouldn't collapse. Patrick looked at me and almost put his hand out to steady me, so obvious was my distress, but then he turned and looked back out across the lake, as if to separate us both from the strain of the moment.

After some silence, he turned back to me, seemingly fully returned from where his story had taken us, and asked me, "And who would you be?"

I could not speak.

"Perhaps you don't give your name to strangers on first meeting." He could see where my thoughts had taken me, but refused to let me stay there or to keep him there with me.

"I'm Gretchen Williamson," I said, with effort. "I live at Merigold's Point."

"And are you here in the village today with your family?"

"No, I'm just by myself."

I knew that he was about to ask me if my parents would allow me to come all this way by myself. But he didn't, and

I liked him for that. I think it was the first time I realized that I liked someone who refrained from speaking, not because he didn't know what to say, but because he knew what not to say.

"So, Patrick, do you go to the school here in Port Credit?"

"No. I do that," and he pointed at the stonehookers.

My name is Sally, and a heron took my voice, except that I didn't know it was a heron yet. It happened in a dream when I was as young as I can remember ever being. In the dream, I was sitting in the bulrushes by the marsh, the one that is close to our house, and a big, grey bird with long legs and a long neck and a long, pointed beak was standing in the water close to me. It stood very still and did not move, looking down at the water. I wanted to know what it was looking at, so I crawled out of the bulrushes and into the water and I crawled under the water along the bottom of the marsh until I was right underneath the heron. I wondered how it was I could breathe under the water, but it seemed quite a natural thing to do. I looked up into the heron's eyes. We stared at each other for a very long time. And then I thought I should ask the heron what he was looking for, and it was just at that moment when I opened my mouth to speak that everything happened at once. I could feel myself being shaken up and down, I could hear a voice shouting at me, and the heron's beak shot into my mouth like a spear. I started gasping for breath and then Father's hands were gripping my shoulders and he was shouting at me to wake up. Mother was right next to him with her hands covering her mouth.

"She's breathing, John! She's breathing! Oh, thank God!"

When I was awake enough to look into Father's eyes, they got really big and afraid and then he let go of my shoulders as if his hands were suddenly burnt. Mother grabbed on to me and held me close to her breast and stroked my hair as if she was trying to dry me off. My mouth was still open to speak, but nothing came out. But I wasn't scared like Mother and Father were.

It's a secret between me and the heron about why I don't speak. I'm not sure that Mother understands about it, but Father has never stopped being afraid.

When Uncle Silas gave me my fiddle two years ago he said, "Here's a voice for you, Sally." He didn't know about the heron, but there was something he knew. I could tell that. He is Mother's brother and I think she knows now, too. I think maybe she always knew. I think Gretchen wants more than anything to know. She trusts me, and she will wait until she understands me.

For the rest of the summer whenever I walked to the Credit River and the marshes I would hope to meet either Baketigweyaa or Patrick. But sometimes it was fine enough to stand on the bridge or walk along the river mouth just to be alone in the midst of men preparing their boats and gutting the fish they had caught. Once when I was lazily clacking my way over the shingle by the edge of the harbour I heard my name come sailing through the air. I looked around me, but could see no one who might have been attached to that voice. Then I heard it again and realized it was coming from out on the water. I put my hand up to my forehead to lessen the glare from the sun and looked out at the lake. There was a scow close to shore and a man on it waving to me. It was Patrick. And I thought he was a man.

For the next few days I thought about that word, *man*, that had drifted into my senses as if for the first time in my life when Patrick waved to me from across the water. It was the sudden coincidence of Patrick and water and sunlit silence that seemed to speak it to me. Man. Of course, there were men in my life already — there always had been. There was Father, Reverend Swinerton, my uncles, grandfather, Baketigweyaa, and Mr. Donnerton, my first teacher. Some of them I knew and some of them I just knew about. And now there was Patrick.

Maybe what surprised me about this was that Patrick had so suddenly shifted from boy to man in my mind. How could that be? What exactly had he done to accomplish such a thing? Maybe he had done nothing at all, and it was just some odd turn my own mind had taken. But it was not my mind that was at work here. I wasn't sure what exactly it was instead; I just felt it as something physical rather than mental.

I met Patrick again a week later in the Port Credit village. Mother had decided to take me and Victoria with her when she went to Mr. Cotton's General Store to buy some sewing materials and kitchen goods. We had no stores or businesses at Merigold's Point or Clarkson's

Corners. I took the time while Mother and Victoria were exploring the store to do my own exploring, making my way to the harbour and MacDonald's Dock, where the stone hookers clunked against the wharves and each other. There was a soft breeze off the lake, and the sun coated everything with a warm layer of light. I took off my shoes and felt the heat of the boards press into my feet, careful all the while to watch out for slivers. My feet felt oddly naked out there on the long wharves amongst the weathered, wooden boats. I never felt this way when I walked barefoot along the lakeshore or through the thick grass of the orchards. The dock was a place that wasn't "mine." It was an unfamiliar geography; it was a man's geography. My girl's soft feet were seeking a gentleness in these rough boards that knew only the hard-soled boots of men in their wave- and sweat-soaked clothes, with bits of pipe tobacco stuck in their rough beards.

Patrick did not smoke a pipe that I knew of, and he had no beard, but I suddenly remembered his sweat. I hadn't really thought about it or noticed it when we were talking on the bridge, but pausing there on the dock it came to me. It was the sweat of the sun on skin, the sweat of a body that moved with energy in whatever it did. Strange to think of sweat like that — that's what I was thinking when his voice came up behind me, and my reverie dissolved like milk into a cup of tea.

"Are you looking for a ride somewhere?"

I spun around, almost losing my balance, so flustered was I by his unexpected appearance and by the question to which I could think of no intelligent or witty answer. He stood there with his arms lazily crossed, his strong body seeming almost to slouch into the ground, and his smile disarmed me as much as his voice did.

"I could take you out on the water if you like."

I looked around at the stone hookers and scows and wondered if he meant for just the two of us to manoeuvre one of them out of the harbour and into the lake. He must have noticed my confusion.

"Not one of these. There's a rowboat just up at the mouth of the river. We could row to the island up around the bend. If you have time and you'd like to."

"I'm just in the village with my mother and sister Victoria. I'd have to ask her — she's in Cotton's looking for some things."

"Well, here's my proposition then. There's room enough for three people to be comfortable in the boat. Why don't you bring your sister along, if your mother is willing to trust the two of you to me."

"Yes, thank you. I'll go and ask."

"I'll wait here for you then."

I had to walk past Patrick to get to the landing. He stood in the middle of the wharf, waiting for me to pass him, and leaving only enough room on either side that I would not be able to get by without brushing against him. Just as I moved past him he said over his shoulder, "Is your sister as fair as you are?"

His question caught me quite unawares and flustered me. I hesitated for just a moment, wondering if I should reply to his comment somehow, but I could feel my cheeks turning bright red, so I simply kept walking.

When I explained Patrick's offer to Mother I knew full well that she would at the very least be hesitant about letting me go off into a confined space, like a boat, with a boy — I did not use the word *man*. It was the fact of Victoria being invited along which made her a little less uneasy. I wondered if Patrick knew everything rested on Victoria's presence. I was given an hour's grace, which meant that Victoria and I ran all the way back to the dock.

"Are we going courting?" Victoria gasped as we ran with great intent, my one hand holding tightly to hers, the other keeping my dress from getting tangled in my feet.

"Two women don't go together to court one man, Victoria."

"Does he think that we're women, then?"

"Now is not the time, Victoria."

In the boat, Victoria and I sat on a cross-bench together at the back facing Patrick, who worked the oars from the bench near the middle. I was sure there were proper words such as stern and bow for various ends of the boat, but I didn't know how to apply them. For the first few minutes as he steered the boat away from the shore and out into the middle of the river there was no sound, save the oars rubbing in their locks and their wide blades dipping into the water. The river sounded cool and happy to have us on it. I could see the dark green weeds on the bottom in a slow motion sway, and sometimes the dull flash of a fish, like a silver muscle of the river itself.

"So, you're Victoria, then?" Patrick began once he had set us on a straight course.

"Yes. And you're Patrick."

Victoria was ready to take him on sentence for sentence. Before I could pinch her arm for being too precocious Patrick responded.

"You've got your own style. I like that in a woman."

"See," Victoria whispered loudly into my ear, "he does think we're women."

With Patrick's eyes on us I could only push my elbow into her side instead of pinch her. How could I be comfortable in his presence with Victoria simply being who she was?

"Maybe you can explain something to me," Patrick said as he shifted his eyes from us to the water. "Why is it that everyone calls the west side of the river the American side, and the east side the Canadian side?"

I had often wondered about this myself, but I had no answer for him. Rather than simply saying I didn't know, however, I thought I should attempt some sort of explanation.

"I'm not sure. It might have something to do with the war of 1812, although we're not anywhere near the American border here, so then it might . . ."

At this point, Patrick saved me from making a silly fool of myself, as he jumped into the middle of my tortured attempt at reasoning.

"Wars . . . I'd rather not talk about those on such a lovely day as this." He paused for a bit and then turned the conversation in a new direction.

"So tell me, Gretchen, what is it you do with your days?"

"Now that school is out for the summer I mostly help Mother with keeping the house and Father with keeping the orchard and the animals . . ."

"And sometimes," Victoria leaped in, "we go up to the orchard at Clarkson's Corners and just sit in the grass and eat apples and talk about things . . ."

"Victoria!" I tried to scold her and smile at Patrick all at the same time.

"And what do you talk about?" asked Patrick, either unaware of my flustered state or consciously teasing it. I could not read him well, yet.

"Well," continued Victoria, quite pleased with herself, "we talk about whether there are spirits in the apple trees and whether we should have boyfriends or not. And sometimes we don't say anything at all; we just sit in the sun and chew our apples. The other day, though, we were talking about how Gretchen wants to be a teacher when she grows up. I think she'd be a very good teacher. She helps me a lot with my exercises and she knows lots of things, but not as much as real grown-ups, but she will when she's a grown-up."

"And just how do you tell when someone becomes a grown-up?" Patrick pressed her.

"Well, I'm not sure. I can tell who the grown-ups are, but I've never seen anybody change into one before."

"You keep a close eye on your sister, then. I think she's not far off from changing right before your eyes."

"She has to finish school first, I think," replied Victoria quite seriously.

Since I had been overtaken by Victoria in the area of conversation I focused on the easy rhythm of Patrick's body as he pulled the boat up river. He was lean, like the oars themselves. But fluid, too. Like the river. And then I got that feeling again — a feeling I all of a sudden remembered from when I was a very young child. It was so very familiar, even though I'm sure I had not experienced it for years and years. It was a feeling of not being separated from anything around me. Me, the boat, Victoria, Patrick, the oars, the river, the trees, the sky — we were all part of one great breathing, pulsing thing. Something more alive and more real than any one of us could be on our own. When Patrick dipped the oars into the water I could feel them dipping into some soft and yielding part of my body, though I could not say exactly which part of my body it was. And when Patrick leaned back, pulling the oars and the boat forward, I could feel the trees and the shoreline sliding against me like my own tongue over my lips when I tasted something good.

When Patrick spoke to me—"And where have you drifted off to?"—I came crashing to the ground like a kite whose string had been cut. I tried frantically to get my bearings, to release myself from my daydream, to think of something to say. But he just smiled that easy smile of his and said, "The colour rises to your face in quite a lovely way."

And then we were around the island and on our way back to the docks. And then I was bumping along on the hard seat of the buckboard beside Mother and Victoria, the tails of the horses waving like weeds in a river. And then I was lying in my bed wondering if I was about to go to sleep or about to wake up.

In the beach sand that was almost too hot to stand in with my bare feet I wrote a column of words: *man, boy, water, stone, boat, girl, woman.*

I heard their voices just as I was about to walk into the kitchen for dinner. Father was already seated at his end of the long table, while Mother was going back and forth between the stove and the table.

"She's too young."

"Oh, John, it was all very innocent. And besides, Victoria was with her."

"And that is your defence? It only doubles the sin."

"There's no reason to be upset."

"There is a reason. She is too young to be with a man."

"Do you forget that when I was only a year older than Gretchen you met and married me?"

"Do not try to trick me, Lydia. I will not be tricked."

"It is not a trick, John; it is simply our history."

"And this is Gretchen's history. She has a father. You had none at her age. She is my daughter and she is too young. It is not her time."

"And when will her time be, John?"

"It is not yet her time."

"John, we can't change what time does with us. You thought me a woman when you courted and married me, father or no father. Can you not recognize that Gretchen is now a young woman?"

"Please, Lydia . . ."

That single word, "please," was a plea and a command at the same time, and I knew from the tone of his voice that it was a signal to the end of the conversation. Though I was not standing in the same room, I could see Mother's shoulders droop and her hands begin to worry each other. And I could see Father's body stiffen into that rigid pose that meant he could no longer hear. The sound of his heart closing echoed through the house, like a lamp dropped and bouncing down the stairs.

Chapter 2

AUTUMN WAS THE BEGINNING OF THE NEW YEAR FOR ME. I understood about January 1, of course, but it did not seem to be attached to anything new, except for the calendar. There was nothing reborn about it. But autumn meant going back to school; it meant the leaves would soon change colour and then I could think about the shades of leaves instead of the shades of water for a while. This was my favourite season because everything changed. There would be that one day when I would walk out of the house and feel the sudden crispness in the air, like the snap of biting into a perfectly ripe apple. I would feel that I had somehow been cleansed, that everything inside me was fresh and pure. My breathing would become bigger and I could look out at the world as if I had never seen it before, but knew that it could only be beautiful. Spring, of course, was the other season of change, and I knew that it was supposed to be the season of rebirth and resurrection, but it was not a crisp season. It was a soggy season.

And September was the month of my birthday. September 17. That was today, and I was fifteen years old. I was not sure yet whether I was pretty. Mother thought I was, and so did Sally and Victoria — Sally in the way she looked at me when she thought I didn't notice her, Victoria in her less than subtle bursts of compliments — but their judgement was meant more to please me than to enlighten others. Besides, there was what a family called pretty, what other girls my age called pretty, and what boys and young men called pretty. The girls from school thought, or feared, that I was too tall, as did many of the boys. As for young men, say Patrick, for instance, I didn't know yet. No matter. Today I was fifteen, Mother had prepared apples in syrup for my special treat, and Father gave me a book of John Donne's *Holy Sonnets*. They were not "holy" as in Methodist holy, but that was because John Donne lived before John Wesley. Donne was Catholic first, and then Anglican, and Wesley was Anglican. He even said that Methodism was just a different part of the Church of England. Anyway, Father obviously thought a lot about this gift. He knew I liked to read and that I liked poetry, and he managed to not betray his own sense of morality while giving me something that was important to me. All in all, he was a good man and he loved me, although I often had to work hard to remind myself of this fact as I grew older and he resisted it. Where he relied on method and discipline I too often gave in to serendipity — my favourite word that Miss Jenkins had taught us.

Still, the sonnets, at first glance, seemed to be quite intensely remorseful. Like this one,

> *O might those sighes and teares returne againe*
> *Into my breast and eyes, which I have spent,*
> *That I might in this holy discontent*
> *Mourne with some fruit, as I have mourn'd in vaine;*

In mine Idolatry what showres of raine
Mine eyes did waste?

 I was not sure I had lived enough of my life to be that remorseful. Indeed, I hoped not to live to be in such a state as that. Perhaps these sonnets would be helpful in impressing upon me the dire consequences of taking good things too much for granted.

 Victoria made a cross-stitch of my name in fall colours, and Sally created a special concert for me with her fiddle. Although she had had it for only two years she was quite proficient and could play slow airs, jigs, reels, set dances, and even some pieces she had composed herself. The fiddle had been a gift for her ninth birthday from our uncle Silas Burke, Mother's older brother, who had never married and who still lived in New Brunswick. He came to visit us the summer of Sally's birthday and stayed until we went back to school. Sally was a quick study and had a whole handful of tunes under her fingers in no time at all. I thought that maybe these tunes were her voice and that she had been waiting all these years for someone to give it to her as a gift, or just as a recognition. I especially liked Southwind and Planxty Eleanor Plunkett, so she played each of those twice during the evening.

 Mother made me a new flannel dress, dyed a deep burgundy, my favourite colour for fabric. She also bought me some ribbons for my hair, as I often tied it back because of its length. There was another gift which Mother was continually giving me, and that did not rely on birthdays or Christmas. That was bound books of clear pages for my journals. The first one I received for my eighth birthday, but after that she would make sure that as each book was filled, another was ready. I think this made up for all the words we do not say out loud to each other. But there was something else. I felt that as I opened each new, fresh book I was opening pages of Mother's life which she had never taken the time to inscribe. So much of her life seemed to me to be still waiting for acknowledgement of some kind. Perhaps part of my duty to her as her daughter was to speak to the world the words she could not. Or would not. Sometimes she made me afraid to want to be a mother.

In my creek journal my stick traced out the words: A *birth day, a day of birth.* The moon and the sun and all the stars were there in that stick, in my hand. My hand moving on the end of my arm, the leaves moving on the end of the branches. The leaves falling from the tree to colour the ground with autumn, my hand moving the stick in the sand where the leaves would rest and look up at the moon and the sun and wait for the snow. I was waiting.

I played for Gretchen today because it's her birthday. Mother and Father and Victoria were there, too, but I played especially for Gretchen. Mostly I close my eyes when I play, but today I opened them ever so slightly so that my top eyelashes and my bottom eyelashes were just barely touching each other, like sparkly rainbow lace curtains. This way everybody was shaped like stories telling themselves to me. Gretchen was tall like a cedar tree in a garden, like a soft angel not wanting to be in anyone's way but wanting to give them something, as if rain was falling off her beautiful laced branches and everybody was thirsty but didn't know it. Victoria was like a star glittering in the sky, and even though we are taught to draw stars with five points, when you look at a star you can never tell how many points it has because it is always glittering quicker than your eye can stay still. Mother didn't have any edges and it was hard to tell where she stopped and Father, who was standing next to her, began. Father is stiff as a preacher's starched collar. He is the shape of crying that never cries.

As I played, I sewed all these stories together with the tip of my bow. I think God must have played the fiddle.

"You never speak of your sister, Patrick."

We were walking down Front Street towards Bay Street and the Wilcox Inn, where there was a large ballroom for dancing. I wondered what it would be like to go into such a place and to be squired by a handsome young man who would take my hand and ask me to dance. Of course, Father was very much against dancing and such "frivolities as weaken the soul and cloud the good and clear mind that God gave us." Patrick had his hands in his pockets and was staring more at the ground than at where we were walking. I wondered if he danced.

"What is your sister like?"

Patrick said nothing for a long while, and then, "She's my twin; not identical, though. She's much fairer of face than I. Her hair is near as long as your own. She's had a beautiful singing voice ever since she was a young lass barely as high as a stone wall. On the ship from Ireland she would entertain us all — make the elders cry for the memory of the land they had left only days before and would probably never see again. Do you sing, Gretchen?"

"Not for anyone to hear. But my sister Sally plays the fiddle. I think you and your sister would enjoy her playing. What is your sister's name?"

"Rosaleen."

"Rosaleen — I've never heard such a pretty name."

"She was named after Róisín Dubh."

"What is that?"

"I'm sorry, it's an Irish name — Row-sheen Duv — it means the Dark Rosaleen."

"And who was she?"

"Some say she was just a legend and some say she was a real flesh and blood woman. In any case, she was the most beautiful woman in all of Ireland; she played the harp — or at least, she had a harp. Some say the harp is silent — will always be silent until the Sassenachs are gone forever from Ireland. My father had an old book — I can't remember what it was, for I could barely read at the time, but on the inside of the cover was a picture of a woman looking off into the distance. There was a large hound sitting beside her, and the ocean in the background. She had a harp at her knee. It was a picture of the Dark Rosaleen. I have always remembered it, and I think of it when I think of my sister."

"Does your sister play the harp?"

"I wish that she could have. I remember saying to her when we were just young that one day I would build her a harp and she would be the Dark Rosaleen and save all of Ireland. It was my plan to be a carpenter like my father. But then . . ."

From Bay Street we turned on to Joseph Street and made our way back to the Lakeshore Road. More than anything, I wanted to meet Rosaleen, and I said so to Patrick. But when he went to answer me it was as if he had not heard what I said, and was just continuing on from where he had left off.

"There are some things we plan to do and strive as hard as we can to do them, knowing that it might take our whole lives in the accomplishment of them. And there are other things we plan and it makes no matter at all. Rosaleen would have made a fine harper. She would have."

And then I understood.

To describe the grey shades of water: like a wind tinged with thunder; like a white dress hanging in the rain; like the cold ash of a fire; like a cut potato left all afternoon on the table; like a ridged and weathered barn board.

To describe the blue shades of water: like an unwashed blueberry; like a vein in a baby's temple; like a resolution seen through tears.

To describe the green shades of water: like a fluttering poplar leaf in the moonlight; like skin stained by a copper bracelet.

∾

Our school was located on the southern tip of the Merigold's farm, very near to the edge of the lake. Much of their land was heavily treed — oak, pine, maple, and beech — and Mr. Merigold was, therefore, first in the business of supplying timber for masts. When I looked at those strong, tall trees I tried to imagine them as the masts of ships that would sail the world; I tried to imagine what it must be like to have been rooted in one place in the ground for a hundred years and more and then to be cut down and put in a magnificent ship with the responsibility of holding all the sails and propelling explorers around the globe. If there was a sadness anywhere in this it was that the trees themselves, even if they were somehow sentient when alive, could have no idea, once harvested and trimmed, of the adventures they were bound for.

The school building itself was quite a stable structure consisting of one large room with a proper woodstove in the middle. It was painted red, and so everyone called it The Red School House. On one of the side walls was a large, coloured map of the world; on the other were drawings by the younger students and examples of penmanship by the older students. Among these latter was a passage I copied from "Dialogues. Section III. Locke and Bayle. Christianity defended against the cavils of skepticism" in our *English Reader*. I chose a sentence by Bayle: "The more profound our searches are into the nature of things, the more uncertainty we shall find; and the most subtle minds see objections and difficulties in every system, which are overlooked or undiscoverable by ordinary understandings." I think that when I copied out that passage I had but an "ordinary understanding," and still do, though my pride tries to convince me otherwise. The front wall had all the individual letters of the alphabet, each on its own card, some Bible sayings, and a reproduction of a portrait of Queen Victoria up high in the tip of the triangle where the roof goes to a peak.

The only problem was in the coldest parts of winter — it was too hot to sit close to the stove, and too cold to sit around the edges of the room. When Mr. Donnerton was here he liked to keep his desk midway between the stove and the front wall, which meant that all that particular space behind him could not be used for student tables. He would in no way permit anyone to sit behind him; everyone had to be in his view at the same time. As a consequence of that, and the problem with the uneven distribution of heat, all of us students ended up crowded together in a kind of jagged and layered horseshoe around Mr. Donnerton's desk. With the arrival of Miss Jenkins more space was opened up for our tables because she moved her desk almost against the wall. This was not a problem for her because she spent most of her time walking between our tables when she taught and even when we were doing our exercises.

Last school year was Miss Jenkins' first at our school. She replaced Mr. Donnerton, who was asked to leave after two years because of his lifestyle, which was considered inappropriate by Reverend Swinerton and most of the parents. Although I never saw him actually take a drink, I could see the consequences in his bleary eyes and large, red-textured nose. Indeed, his nose was the only large thing about him. All the rest of him was long and thin — very many bones and very little flesh. For all that, though, he was not a bad teacher. I suppose that if he had tried to be a stricter disciplinarian than he was, he would have been relieved of his position even sooner. But he was more bluff and bluster than executioner. Although he did have a menacing-looking birch switch, he spent more time waving it in the air than whacking our hands with it. It was likely for this reason that the boys felt they could play the tricks on him that they did. Mr. Donnerton was prone to drowsing off now and then while we were doing our exercises in class. Once, during his last year, when he was in a particularly drowsy state — his head falling back on his neck and his mouth wide open and snoring loudly — four of the boys decided to fill the pockets of his frieze overcoat, which he wore at all times, with stones they had brought up from the beach for just this purpose. When they ran back to their seats they all shouted together to wake Mr. Donnerton. He came to with quite a start, and his first reaction was to jump up and see what all the noise was about. Of course, he couldn't lift himself off the chair because of the weight of stones in his pockets. The combination of being startled awake and being more or less pinned to his chair caused him great confusion, so he reached for his switch and began madly carving the air with it, which only caused all of us girls to giggle and the boys to guffaw. When finally he realized what the situation was, he set to, with great and painstaking effort, to pick the mounds of stones out of his pockets, by which time he had spent all the energy he may have wished to use in meting out whatever punishment he could think of. Then he just fell back in his chair and presently fell back to sleep.

I liked Miss Jenkins very much. I thought she was not much more than twenty years old, and she was quite pretty, though not in the way that most men might think. There were as many shades of pretty as there were of colours of water — that's what I had come to think after looking at myself for these past few months in the mirror. Her prettiness came from inside her, as I was hoping that mine did. At least that was how I was trying to wear beauty — as something that rose out of me like birches rise out of an early morning fog. She stayed with us for just over two weeks during the last school year. Such were the lodging arrangements for the teacher that she stayed two to three weeks with each of the families who sent children to the school. That was another reason, I was sure, that Mr. Donnerton was asked to leave — no family looked forward to their turn with him. The two times that he stayed with us, Father was in a constant state of discomfort because Mr. Donnerton would never cease talking — even through meals when Father hoped to have some guarantee of peace. But it was either that or the drink. I thought Mr. Donnerton tried to talk himself out of temptation, and so this required much toleration and listening on the part of those he lodged with. No one seemed to know for sure where exactly he got his drink from, but get it he did. The same was true for where exactly he did his imbibing — no one knew for sure.

With Miss Jenkins, however, we were sad to see her go on to her next lodging. At least the females of our family felt so. Whether Miss Jenkins felt the same, I wasn't sure. In the summer she returned to her family in Sherbrooke in the Eastern Townships of Quebec. Once she received a letter at our house. It was addressed to Cecilia Jenkins. I remembered thinking how odd it was for her to have a first name — if Mr. Donnerton had one, none of us ever knew it. But Cecilia — what a beautiful name. It was a shame that no one ever used it here. I thought that if I would ever her call her Cecilia I would feel completely different about her. Cecilia would laugh and maybe even skip along the road. But also she would sing and write poetry. If she did those things now she did not share them with any of us here. It must have been difficult for her — she must keep a certain distance from her students in order to maintain authority; and with our parents she must again remain at a distance so as not to show favouritism. How sad to always have to be on one's guard — to always be Miss Jenkins and never Cecilia.

Some of the children are used to me, and some of them aren't. "Why doesn't she say anything?" "Hey, you there, Sally Williamson, where'd you leave your tongue?" But I'm used to it. And Gretchen has always protected me from the meaner boys. The girls aren't so bad. And there is one boy who is not so bad, either. Tommy Lamer. He's almost as quiet as I am, but he chooses to speak when he wants to. He hardly ever speaks to me, though. At first I didn't know if it was because he liked me or didn't like me. Now I think it's because he likes me. He will sometimes come and stand by me at recess and he won't say anything because he thinks that's what I would like. Sometimes we will lean against the side of the school house with the sun in our faces and he will point at a bird that has just landed in the willow tree, or he will point at something funny or ridiculous that some of the other girls and boys are doing. Every now and then he will say something like, "The kildeer is my favourite bird," or "I had trouble doing my sums last night." He doesn't seem to have any friends that he is with all the time. Maybe he likes me because I seem to be alone most of the time, too, except when I am with Gretchen or Victoria, but that doesn't really count because they're my sisters. But I am not lonesome, and I don't think he is either. Or maybe he is.

One day he asked me when my birthday was. I held up seven fingers.

"Let me see," he said, "that's January, February, March, April, May, June . . . is it in July?"

I nodded my head.

"Which day?"

I held up all ten of my fingers, then I held up just two.

"Ten . . . eleven, twelve. July the twelfth. Mine's in October. The twenty-seventh. That's a lot of fingers."

And then he got caught somewhere between a smile and a laugh.

I felt like we had really become friends that day. Sometimes after that day he would even walk home from school with me and Gretchen and Victoria, even though he lives on the other side of the school from us.

Autumn and the new school year arrived together, and I treasured even more my time to walk along the creek, the marsh, and the shingle bar. They were three different worlds that held onto each other like three old and wise women who had seen every change the world had to offer and yet remained constant in their mysterious silence. They spoke in the shishing of small stones that roll over each other with a receding wave, in the mournful creak of high trees rubbing against each other in the wind, in the spluff of snow falling from a pine branch in the afternoon sun of winter, in the crinkle of creek water over miniature rapids, in the silence of herons standing like statues of themselves along the edges of the marsh. John Donne would not have been so melancholy if he could have been here with me when the maples flamed with colour in October. Surely he would have seen that there was no room for disparity between heaven and earth and that both were alive within each of us. I sat there in the high, brown rushes and I read,

I am a little world made cunningly
Of Elements, and an Angelike spright,
But black sinne hath betraid to endlesse night
My worlds both parts, and (oh) both parts must die,

and I was sad for him. Sad that he could see only the dark side of all that is bright. I certainly felt that I was a little world like the one of which he wrote, but both parts in me were gloriously alive because the world around me was gloriously alive. But perhaps that is what happens when one gets older — like John Donne. Or like Father. Perhaps our lives are a sliding from glory into bitterness and fear. Or into a kind of silent standoff, like Mother. Is it because one has children that one loses glory? John Donne had children. Will Miss Jenkins have children some day and forever lose the possibilities that lie with Cecilia?

All I knew was that it was autumn and the trees were crisp and fiery, and so was my heart.

Patrick and I were walking along the water away from the mouth of the river. The sun was falling to the horizon in front of us, and there was a slight breeze at our backs as if the sun were sucking the heat of the day into itself to keep it warm during the night. The shingle still held the heat of the day, like an echo.

"Are you looking forward to Halloween, Patrick?"

"You mean bobbing for apples and jumping over the fire and all that?"

"I'm sorry. You probably prefer All Souls Day."

"Why do you say that?"

"Because you're Catholic."

"So, we're on about that again, are we? People are larger than you give them credit for."

I had never seen Patrick impatient before, but I think that he was sitting on the far edge of comfort just then.

"I didn't mean to poke at you, I was just curious about Halloween, that's all."

"Well, that's okay. Sometimes living here makes me feel too Irish, too Catholic, too sorry a being altogether."

"Do I make you feel that way?"

"No, it's not you, Gretchen, though I can see that I've dropped some of my trouble in your lap without you asking for the privilege. It's just this torn feeling that I get sometimes — a feeling I've been carrying about with me for too many years, given how young I am."

"How do you mean, 'torn'?"

"Torn between the Church and the fairies. Do you know what fairies are?"

"I know fairy stories."

"Ah, those are something else altogether. No, Gretchen, the fairies are the life of the land. At least they are where I grew up."

"Tell me about them."

"Well, now, I'm not the best person to be telling you those kinds of stories. If you're truly interested, I'll introduce you to The Red."

"Is that a person?"

"Oh, she's a person, sure enough. Sometimes more than a person."

"What's her real name?"

"I'm not sure that anyone knows. I'm not sure that even she knows. We've always known her as The Red, and that's the only way she's ever referred to herself. But she knows everything about the old ways. It doesn't make much sense for her to have come over here with us. Taking her away from Ireland is like trying to plant a cut flower into a slice of dry rock."

"She must be very unhappy then."

"Unhappy's not exactly the right word to describe The Red anymore. She may have been that for a time, but now it's more like she's detached from a part of herself. The hills and the bogs of Connemara birthed her, and it's that land that's as much a part of her as the green of your eyes is a part of you. Still, she's worth listening to if you ask her the right questions."

"And you think I should ask her a question about Halloween?"

"Oh, yes. That I certainly do. If you're not afraid."

And, of course, I had no sense of fear at all until he opened up the possibility. But I knew myself well enough to know that I was starting down a road that I would not, nor could not, turn away from.

"When can we see her?"

"Do you have some time right now?"

I had expected that I would have some time to prepare myself, but then I thought that having any more time to think about it would only lead to a difficult hesitancy.

"Yes, now would be fine."

I wasn't sure if I truly believed it would be fine at all. The day was nearing its close, and I knew that soon Mother would begin to fret if I didn't return; Father would simply let my tardiness seep into him and slowly mix with his blood until it produced a quiet but steamy anger, which he would not be sure where to direct, and so would keep inside himself until it came out of its own accord.

We walked back across the bridge into the village along Toronto Street, turning left on Helene Street. From there and up towards Park Street was Cork Town. I had never been that far into the village before and so felt somewhat adventurous, but a little nervous, too. Voices knotted with thick, Irish brogue hung in the evening air like wild, brown chestnuts. Several greetings came at Patrick from both sides of the street, but we just kept walking like royalty through adoring crowds. I knew that I was glorifying the moment beyond its own needs, but I sensed that I was walking into a place in my life I had never been before and might not ever be again. It was very difficult to revel in anticipation when the sheer presence of arriving was so clearly upon me.

"It's just around the corner here."

I had fallen a step or two behind Patrick , so he had to turn around to make sure I was still with him. He put his hand, for just a second, on my elbow to point me in the right direction. It was the first time he had ever touched me. Maybe it was the unexpectedness of the movement or maybe it was the sudden shift into this new and curious world. Whatever it was, I experienced a sensation I had never known before. There was not enough time to try to understand it before Patrick had knocked on the weathered door of a rude wooden structure that was not quite a house and not quite a hut. The knocking of his hand against the thick wood of the door seemed like exclamation points emphasizing the strangeness of this night. I had lost all sense of time and so I don't know how long it was before the woman answered Patrick's knock. The door opened on a rectangle of yellow light that flickered and glowed dully, like an aura on the edges of a woman's body. She was almost a full foot shorter than me, and at first I couldn't distinguish her long, wild hair from the shawl and dress she was wearing. As my eyes adjusted to the light from the inside of the dwelling hitting the darkness we were standing in I could see that her eyes were fixed on mine. It was not a stare, but rather an intense curiosity, part friendly, part defensive. Finally, she turned herself sideways as a signal for us to enter. Again, Patrick put his hand on my arm; again that sensation.

"This is Gretchen. She lives at Merigold's Point down the lake from here."

The Red eased herself into a rocking chair without seeming to move at all. She began to rock in a soft, measured rhythm that somehow harmonized with the shifting of our shadows on the wall opposite the fireplace. Still, she had not spoken a word. Patrick seated himself on a pile of blankets near the wall, leaving the only other chair in the room for me.

"Gretchen here is looking forward to Halloween."

Now that I could see The Red more clearly by the light of the fire I was captivated by her presence. I don't know how else to say it. She was intensely and beautifully present. I don't know whether she was physically beautiful, because in a strange way she didn't seem quite physical at all. As for her age, at one moment she looked no older than me, and at the next she could have been a grandmother. Her hair was everywhere about her — it radiated from her face. It was obvious to me now why she was called The Red.

And then I noticed it. The one eye that did not move. Her left eye followed us as we spoke or moved about in her space, but the right eye always stared straight ahead as if it could see in every direction without needing to shift perspective. It was this eye that the whole world was subject to, that nothing in heaven or earth could trick.

"Halloween, is it."

She spoke it as an observation rather than a question. I did not know how to reply, or if I was supposed to reply at all. So I waited for the situation to resolve itself without me.

"All Hallows Eve. All Souls Eve. Samhain. You won't have heard it called that last one, I'd be sure of that my young willow. Now Patrick, here, he's heard many things, but he's not one for admitting what he's not sure of. He keeps everything in his head and denies passage to his heart, but he's young yet. But you," and she moved her head so that her magic eye was fixed on me along with the one that moved, "you pretend to be afraid of what you might not know, but you're not afraid. You wouldn't let yourself grow so tall if you were. Curiosity turns fear into life. There can be no other way to have it."

And then she paused, and the sudden silence held me in stillness until she spoke again.

"Do you know the two worlds?"

Immediately, my mind began to stumble over itself, as if I had been posed a question and I had to get the right answer, or at least not display my ignorance. There was no help for it, though. I may have known how many worlds there were before Patrick and I stepped into The Red's dwelling. Right then, however, I had no idea whether there were two or twenty worlds.

"What kinds of worlds are we talking about?"

It was not the answer I wanted to give, but it was the only one my voice could speak. The Red leaned her head back as if she would let out a great laugh, but there was no sound. Only a smile that gathered in the whole room.

"Patrick, you can leave now. It's just the two women that need be here for the next while."

I looked at Patrick to see if this made sense to him or if he would show any concern at leaving me alone with this extraordinary woman. He just got up as naturally as could be, smiled quickly at me, and turned to leave the room. The Red could sense my confusion.

"Don't be looking so confused when you know you aren't. Move your chair over here by the fire. You'll be hearing me better there."

I took my chair and placed it so that the fire was between us. Its glow lit up the half of her face with the magic eye, and for the briefest of moments I think I had an understanding of the two worlds.

"There's this world where we're sitting here by fire. That's the one of the two. The other one — now, that's the one that you've come here to know about. Well, I can't tell you much about it. But I can tell you how to find out for yourself. You see, Samhain is the night of the year where the space between the worlds opens up, and you can move from the one to the other and back again without harm. You'll see what you're meant to see on the other side; I can't be telling you what it is. This much I will tell you, my young willow: you find yourself a stone where you think the best stones are, and you carry it with you on your All Hallows Eve. You go to a place where you know you're safe, and build yourself a fire. Look into that fire with all your might and then place your stone in the flames and leave it there til the fire dies away. The next day you bring that stone to me. You'll tell me what you've seen, and I'll tell you the rest."

I could not tell exactly where she stopped talking and the silence began, nor could I tell how long the silence lasted until I understood that she would say no more and that it was time for me to leave. And so I did.

It was five days before Halloween and I felt as if I was looking forward to it as I never had before. No longer as a child would.

The pumpkin crop was good for everyone in the village this year. I loved to see the bright orange globes lying amongst the green and browning remains of the surrounding gardens. They were like soft, thick lamps that swelled out of the earth to light our way into the early darkness of autumn evenings. Pumpkins were full of that kind of magic. Magic. That was a word that I must not use around Father. For him it meant the same thing as evil or abomination. I remembered the first time he used that word, *abomination* — I think it was when Victoria asked him if there were spirits that lived in the apple trees — I looked it up in the dictionary. It meant "a disgusting thing." It was my fault that poor Victoria received such a scolding reply. I had been sitting in the Butter apple orchard at Clarkson's Corners all day, just feeling the heat of the summer's day speckle all over me through the leaves of the trees and smelling the soft yellow of the apples, and I got to thinking that if the presence of God was in each one of us, as Reverend Swinerton said, then why couldn't it also be in the trees. I mused about this to Sally and Victoria, forgetting that Victoria heard everything with such innocence and would repeat what she heard in the same way. I still didn't think she understood that others, especially grown-ups, did not speak about the world in the same way that she saw it. In a way, I hoped she would never lose that special connection to the living creatures — human, animal, and vegetable — around her.

But now I was thinking about magic again because of my evening with The Red. Before, when I got such ideas in my head as the one I told to Sally and Victoria, I would feel as if I were trying to cross a deep river, walking on a narrow and twisted log. I wasn't sure if it was better to make it to the other side or to fall in the water. Was the water the holy water of Christ or was it some sort of abyss of sin? Was the other side the gate to religious knowledge or was it the entrance to hell? And what about the log? Why was it even there, and who put it there? Was it temptation or salvation? Now I wondered if the log might not be the passage between the two worlds The Red had spoken of, and I was anxious now more than ever to know what that other world was at the far end of the log. As for the water — well, I would have to wait until I took my stone out of the fire.

Gretchen thinks that God might be in the trees instead of somewhere way up in the sky where no one can see him. I think sometimes He is and sometimes He isn't. He moves around a lot, though. He just about always comes to our church on Sundays. But sometimes Reverend Swinerton talks as if he isn't sure what he wants to say, and that's when I think God is probably somewhere else on that day. He must get tired of going to church every single Sunday, just as we don't always want to go either. And on beautiful sunny days why wouldn't He want to sit in the orchard with us and be happy like us because the apples smell so good in the sun?

Father doesn't think like this. I think he is afraid of God. When he prays in church he gets all stiff as if someone is about to hit him with a birch switch like the one Mr. Donnerton had. Sometimes I feel like walking up to him and putting my arm around him so that he doesn't feel so all alone, but when he sees me coming he gets all stiff again, and I know I can't make him soft enough to hug.

Miss Jenkins says that the Indians' God is not like our God, and once when I heard Gretchen and Baketigweyaa talking about smelling storms, I thought this was interesting because maybe it meant that Baketigweyaa had learned how to listen really closely to God so that when God decided to make a storm He would tell certain people, and Baketigweyaa was one of those people. And He wanted Gretchen to be one of those people, too. So I didn't know if I should listen to Baketigweyaa talking to Gretchen or not. How many people were supposed to know how to do this? I decided not to listen. Instead, I moved away from them just far enough so that I could still see them but not hear them. And then I made my eyelashes into rainbow curtains and looked at Gretchen and Baketigweyaa to see if I could see the shape of God somewhere near them.

Today in school Miss Jenkins taught us about the Battle of the Plains of Abraham. This was when the British defeated the French to capture Lower Canada. It was a famous battle also because both leaders died in the fight — Wolfe for the British and Montcalm for the French. But surely many other soldiers must have died on both sides. Who were they? I wondered about this because Miss Jenkins had told us how just before Wolfe's troops scaled the bluffs during the night before the battle, he recited to his men lines from Gray's "Elegy Written In A Country Churchyard." When he finished he said to them, "Gentlemen, I would sooner have written that poem than beat the French tomorrow." This was curious because the poem talks about how so many people die without anyone ever really knowing who they were. They work hard in the fields of their farms and raise families, but they never do anything famous, and so when they die no one remembers them. Just like all the soldiers that died on the Plains of Abraham. Was Wolfe thinking of these soldiers when he read that poem to them? Did the soldiers understand that they were going to die and that no one would ever remember their names? So many of them were young men, hardly into their twenties. What could they have become if they didn't die in that battle?

> *Perhaps in this neglected spot is laid*
> *Some heart once pregnant with celestial fire;*
> *Hands that the rod of empire might have sway'd,*
> *Or wak'd to ecstasy the living lyre.*

What if I were to die tomorrow? Would anyone say of me that my heart was once pregnant with celestial fire? I liked to read poetry, but I didn't think that counted. I had tried writing poetry, but I didn't think it was good enough to spark a flame, either. I liked history and the stories of famous people, but could I ever be someone like Joan of Arc? She was pregnant with celestial fire. She was barely older than I am now when she led the French troops against the British in Orleans. If she were alive in 1759 would the French have let her lead them against Wolfe on the Plains of Abraham? Her fire was God's fire that burned inside her and spoke to her in the voices of saints and angels. Even when she was captured and was put on trial and she was offered to be sent to the Pope to discuss her situation, she said that she was more loyal to her voices than to the Pope. That's what got her burned at the stake. Whose fire was that?

But really, she came from a small village of Domremy where everyone believed in spirits and talked to them. They must have seen spirits in all living things, just as I was thinking in the orchard. How many of them were burned at the stake, even though they weren't famous? I believed in the spirits. Could I be burned at the stake? Only if I told everybody that I believed in them. But did I really see them or hear them or talk to them? I didn't think so. It was more that I felt them — I felt their presence. Did that count as believing in them? Maybe on Halloween I would be able to do more than just feel them.

Creek journal entry: *Things that burn — wood, marsh grass, human bodies. My skin when I think of fire. When I think of Patrick's hand. This stick.*

∾

Baketigweyaa did not understand Halloween in the way that The Red had begun to explain it to me.

"Do you really believe that you can walk from the Land of Living into the Land of Souls and back again in the same body? Who would let you do that?" As we stood in the cool green of tall grass by the river's edge I could see through the clear water to the silky brown bed of the river. It seemed as if it were rippling like a soft blanket shivering in the breeze, but it was just the reflection of the surface of the water. As on the top, so on the bottom.

"I hadn't thought about that. Who else's body would I change into?"

I watched a silvery speckled fish move through the invisible water as if it were weaving the river into the land.

"It is not a matter of changing bodies; it is whether or not you can take the body and the spirit you have here in the Land of Living and keep them both in the Land of Souls and then return with them both to the Land of Living."

"Are spirit and soul the same thing?"

"Sometimes people collect words the way they collect feathers. Sometimes they know what kind of bird the feathers come from and sometimes they don't, but they keep the feathers just the same. They wear them in their hair and in their clothes and these feathers are sacred because they remind them of the moment when they first found them. Soon the feathers become something that exist without the bird. Those who keep the feathers tell stories about them so that every feather has its own story."

I liked when Baketigweyaa explained things to me in this way. I liked it because I couldn't completely understand it but I knew that some day I probably would. It was as if he was planting seeds of experience in me. I just didn't know when they would sprout or what kinds of flowers they would have.

Baketigweyaa looked at me to see if I was understanding him. Then he looked back at the water. We seemed to talk to the river rather than to each other. Then the river would speak the words back to us. He could always tell when he had to say something over again in a different way.

"My people believe that while we live here in this world we have soul-spirits attached to our bodies. When we sleep, when we dream, our soul-spirits can leave our bodies and travel to the other world and return before we wake up. The only other way to go to the Land of Souls is to separate your soul-spirit from your body outside of dream. When you do this you must leave your body forever and stay in the Land of Souls forever. So you see, your body can never go to the Land of Souls. That is what we believe."

I realized suddenly that what Baketigweyaa and The Red had been talking about was death. And that's what Thomas Gray's poem was about. And the Battle of the Plains of Abraham. Death. I realized that I had been thinking a lot about it, but that I didn't really understand the clear reality of it. Death was when somebody was living one moment and not living the next. Not living ever again. I had never known anybody who died. Of course, I knew that my grandparents had died and that relatives of some of my friends had died, but I had not been a witness to those passings. Death was not a part of my life; it was not truly a part of my understanding of it. It was the opposite of what I was, the opposite of everybody I knew or ever knew. If we each had a soul-spirit, did that mean that we all carried our own deaths around with us? Was it a living thing inside of us, waiting to be released?

The Saturday morning before Halloween I walked along the lake to the marsh and then tramped my way through the dry rattle of cattails to where the creek emptied itself into the mucky water of the marsh. I liked the thick, dark smell of the muck. It changed with the seasons and even with weather and the time of day. Sometimes I could carry the smell inside my nose for hours after I was home and even up until I went to bed. Then I fell asleep with the marsh inside me and I felt myself as blessed as it was possible for a fifteen-year-old girl to be.

As I made my way along the bank of the creek everything around me seemed to give off its own light. The water of the creek glowed like transparent silver, the birch trees were hung with thousands of leaf-shaped lanterns shining a muted yellow light against the brightness of the sun. The trunks of trees mixed brown and grey together and pressed their rough textures into the clear air. I was lost in this reverie for I don't know how long until I noticed the bittersweet lines of a fiddle tune weaving itself through the branches that hung over the water. For just a moment I felt confused about where I was. It was the overlapping of two worlds that set me off balance. I realized then that it could only be Sally's fiddle I was hearing. I never did know what Sally did with all those hours when we weren't together either at school or at home; I didn't know where she went or what her favourite places were, other than the Butter apple orchard.

So there she was. For just a second or two I thought I felt that she had invaded my private world, my place to be, where no one else should be. But then how would she know that I was there?

I crept as quietly as possible towards Sally and her fiddle, moving when the music did, pausing when it paused. Just when I got to where I could see her I stopped and folded myself against the bottom of a willow tree near the bank of the creek and listened. The more I listened, the more I realized that these were no tunes I'd heard her play before. They weren't the jigs and reels I had come to recognize either by name or by simple familiarity with their rhythms. With each phrase she played, the boundaries between Sally and the fiddle and me and the creek and the trees began to shimmer and then sift into each other until I couldn't tell where the one ended and the next began. But it was not an uncomfortable feeling; it was more like a sweet letting go of something we try too hard to hold onto without really knowing why or even what exactly it is we're holding on to.

Time passed. And the tears ran down my cheeks like the glory of rain after a drought. I cried joy. I cried sadness. I cried longing. For the first time in my life I longed for something. But it was not for something in the past — I hardly had a past. No, it was for something in the future.

Anticipation had changed its shape, had transformed itself into something so strange, so beautiful. This future I would step into whenever Sally decided to let the fiddle fall from under her chin was waiting for me, and it was quite clear to me that that's where I truly wanted to go.

Today is Tommy's birthday, so I made him a present. I drew a picture of my fiddle on a nice piece of white cardboard and coloured it golden brown with black pegs, just like it really is. I have permission to go to Tommy's house right after school because he is having a birthday cake. Tommy promised to walk me home later. I'm bringing the card and my fiddle, but I'm carrying my fiddle in a cloth bag so he won't know that I have it with me.

When we get to his house his mother is at the door waiting for us, and she gives me a big, smiling welcome. I realize then that I'm the only guest, which is what I thought, but I wasn't sure.

"It's so very nice to have you come over, Sally. Come in and take off your shawl — I've got everything ready. Maybe while Thomas is bringing in some wood for the stove you can help me get the cake ready in the kitchen."

She leans over and whispers the last few words to me as if she is sharing a secret with me that Tommy can't know. But he knows. By the time Tommy has unloaded the wood and taken off his coat, his mother and I are in the parlour, and a small side table is set with the cake, three plates and forks, a pot of tea, and three cups and saucers. Mr. Lamer is in Oakville "doing some important business," so he won't be back until after I'm gone home. Mr. Lamer is a cobbler. Sometimes he works in a shed he built specially for doing his work in, and sometimes he goes to people's homes or to Oakville to buy leather hides and tools.

Mrs. Lamer pours the tea, just as if we were ladies come over after church service — everything is just so. She lets Tommy cut the cake; it is a dark chocolatey brown. Tommy is very polite to his mother; he thanks her for the tea and for making the cake — his favourite. I watch the two of them together; he doesn't look much like his mother. She is quite short, not much taller than me, and her face is round at the top like a moon, but then pointed at the bottom like the bottom part of a heart. Tommy is thin and dark with eyes like coals, and his face is more bone than flesh.

When we have finished our cake but are still drinking our tea, his mother brings out his birthday present. It is a wonderful large bow, almost as tall as he is, and a leather quiver of arrows with fine, even feathers on the ends. Tommy smiles widely at this and winks at his mother. I have never seen anyone wink at his parents before — it seems so unexpected but so natural at the same time. So I smile, too.

Then it is my turn. I take the card out of the paper I have wrapped it in and I hand it to Tommy. I let him look at it for a moment or two, and then, before he can say anything, I put my finger to my lips, telling him to be quiet and be still. Then I reach my hand up to his face, with my fingers spread out, and touching his eyelids, I close them. When I am sure he understands that he is not to move or to open his eyes, I take his hand with the card in it and I put it up to his ear so that he is holding the picture of the fiddle against his ear. Then, quickly as I can, I take my fiddle case out of the cloth bag, take the fiddle out of its case — I have already resined and tightened my bow — and I begin to play. It is a slow air I made up myself especially for him, though he will probably not know that, and I don't know if I will tell him or not. For now, all that matters is that I can read his face, and it is saying that he doesn't know what to say.

The night before Halloween Victoria came to my room and took up her place on the end of my bed.

"Guess what, Gretchen."

"Aren't you going to give my any clues? I can't properly begin to guess unless I have some idea what it is I'm guessing about."

"Okay, then. Guess what's happening next week."

"Well, let me see. Does it have anything to do with apples?"

Victoria giggled. "No, Gretchen. Why would it have anything to do with apples? We weren't talking about apples."

"We weren't talking about anything, silly. All right, does it have anything to do with you?"

"Yes."

"Does it have anything to do with me?"

"Yes."

"Is it about something that's going to happen or is it about somebody other than you or me?"

She giggled again. "It's about all those things you just said. You already know, don't you?"

"Maybe I do and maybe I don't. It depends what you're trying to get me to guess."

"What do you think I'm trying to get you to guess?"

"That Miss Jenkins is coming to stay with us."

"Aw, Gretchen! That's no fair. You knew all along, didn't you."

"Well, I didn't know at the beginning that that was what you wanted me to guess, but yes, I've known for a while now that Miss Jenkins is coming."

"Are you excited?"

"The part of me that is just me is excited; the part of me that is her pupil feels a little awkward, I guess."

"I'm not in parts; I'm the same wherever I go. It would be too hard to be in parts."

"It's not like I try to be different parts at different times. It's not like that at all. It just happens."

I thought about asking Victoria if she didn't feel different, depending on whether she was talking to Father or talking to me or to Miss Jenkins, but I didn't bother because I knew full well that she was the same for all the world to see. It didn't occur to her that she could be somehow split as I felt I was. And then I got to thinking harder about the whole idea. Was I really different people with Patrick, Baketigweyaa, Mother, Father, Sally, Victoria, Miss Jenkins? I was the same for Sally and Victoria because I was a sister in each case. And I was a daughter to both Mother and Father, although it was much easier to be Mother's daughter than Father's. Baketigweyaa and Miss Jenkins were probably both the same because they were both my teachers — one adopted and the other "official."

And Patrick. What about Patrick? What about Patrick's hand on my arm? And was I really different with all these people? Did each of them see me as a different person, or was it just me who felt like a different person? At which point Victoria, as was her wont, voiced my dilemma.

"Well, if you don't try to be different parts, then who makes you be different parts?"

I paused for a bit, and then Victoria summed it all up. "It's time for me to go to bed now, isn't it?"

He's looking at the water as if he's trying to remember me. I remember him. I wonder why, if he took my voice, he doesn't use it. I've only ever heard him squawk when he's flying, as if he has a sore throat. But I like to watch him. I like to think we're friends, even though he doesn't ever seem to notice me when I see him.

He just caught a fish. I wonder if he's disappointed because it's not me. I wonder if he misses me.

Sneaking out of the house after everyone had gone to bed was difficult, but not impossible. My room was on the second floor with all the other bedrooms. Mother and Father's bedroom was across the hall from mine and faced west; mine, and Sally's and Victoria's faced east towards Port Credit. Running up the east side of the house was a vast trellis against which grew an ancient rose at the south end towards the lake and a wisteria at the north end. Mother did not particularly like the combination of red roses with purple wisteria, but she loved each plant well enough in itself to refrain from moving or tearing out the one or the other. There had always been enough space between these two plants for me to climb down the trellis to the ground without injuring myself or the plants. I had been doing this since I was five years old, especially on full moon nights or summer nights that were just so gentle I could not resist easing myself into their soft lap. Now that I was older and taller I was more careful about how I placed my weight on the cross pieces. The trellis was well enough built to still support me, but I thought my secret nighttime wanderings would necessarily have to be abandoned soon.

The sun had been down for hours, and a three-quarter moon showed itself every few minutes through slow moving streaks of clouds that shifted between dark grey and wispy white. When my feet touched the ground at the bottom of the trellis I could feel the squishy softness of the grass already heavy with dew. With my wool cape snug around my shoulders I moved, half way between running and walking, towards the shoreline. I felt a shiver of excitement run the length of my body as I followed the faint glimmer of the shoreline towards the shingle bar and the marsh.

When I got there the marsh stretched like a thick, black blanket away from the alders and poplars on the edge of the shingle. I dropped into a crouch and felt around me for a stone whose shape would fit comfortably into my hand. Then I left the dull glow of the lake behind me and moved into the deeper darkness, keeping the marsh to my left and the rise of Garter Snake Hill to my right until I reached the creek, whose dark rippling line I followed almost as much by sound as by sight through the woods.

The farther I felt my way along the creek the more my eyes adjusted to the night. And my body, too, which felt as if it were shifting on its axis, as if it were entering into the night through a passageway that I had never before been aware of.

And then, it seemed as if the night and the creek and I were held, suspended in time, and at that moment I knew to choose the spot where I was standing. A single birch spired its thin, white light into the darkness. I gathered up all the dry sticks, twigs, and branches I could find immediately around me and piled them carefully in a mound over some pieces of paper I had brought with me from home. As I was kneeling and adding my own breath to the newly birthed flames, I felt as if I were both inside my body and outside it at the same time. I watched the fire for a long time without thinking of anything beyond the soft circle of light that seeped into the trunk of the birch tree on one side of me and slid across the silver surface of the creek water on the other.

And then, as if in a dream, I remembered the stone I had picked from the shingle bar on my way to this spot. I took it carefully from my pocket and placed it in the fire. I watched and waited, moving in and out of myself like the shadows shifting in and out of the trees and bushes around me. Suddenly, I recalled to myself exactly why I was here on All Hallows Eve, on Samhaim, watching a stone in the fire, and time came rushing back, almost pushing me over where I knelt. Had I been approaching the other world? Had I been on its borders or even in it? I looked down at the fire and it was a feathery mound of grey ash that seemed to have oozed out of a single stone at its edge. I put my finger to the stone to test its heat. It was barely warm. I jumped up quickly and looked at the sky, afraid that it might no longer be night, but the blackness was as it had been when I first began following the creek away from the marsh. How long had I been here? I leaned down, picked up my stone and stumbled my way back home.

⁓

I woke up the next morning feeling as if I had been away from home for a long time. First, I looked around at the walls of my room to make sure that I really was home; then I looked out the window to convince myself there was daylight on the other side of it. Finally, I reached over to my night table to feel my stone. It was the stone that focused my reflections on what had been during the night, what was now, and what would be when I went to see The Red.

My knuckles felt so soft against the hard wood of her door, and once inside sitting by the fire two things occurred to me at the same time: One was that it seemed to be perpetual night there in the old chairs by the fire; the other was that the space between my first visit and this one seemed to disappear altogether. The fire was a forever fire, and The Red was a timeless presence.

I handed her the stone before any words were exchanged between us. She took it into her hands softly, like a bird's egg and turned it carefully, studying it from every angle. And then her face lifted from the stone and aimed itself at mine. Although both her eyes were fixed on me, it was the right eye, the one that did not move, that held me.

"What have you seen, my young willow?"

I had been fearing this question because from the time I had placed my stone in the fire until I reached my hand into the night cooled ashes to retrieve it I could remember nothing. But the silky lilt of The Red's voice suddenly opened that lost time to me, and I could see into it. I listened to my own voice as I spoke.

"The night air became thick and smooth like water. I pushed myself from the ground with my hands and feet and could feel myself rise into the water. I was suspended there like a strand of seaweed, and the flames from the fire began to leak into the water like hundreds of streaming rainbows. They began to flow through the tree branches like blood, and I looked at my arms drifting beside me to see if the rainbows were flowing through me, too. And they were. I felt just then that I wanted to let myself float as far into the watery heavens as I could, as if there were a rocky shoreline somewhere as high as the moon. I wanted to keep floating up until the moon gathered up my whole horizon. But I looked down to see my stone in the fire — it was the only thing that the rainbow blood did not wash through. The stone became like an anchor that would not let me drift away. I kept looking at the stone, and then the fire was gone. The water and the rainbows were gone and all that was left was the stone in the grey ashes of the dead fire. And me reaching in to lift it out and put it in my pocket."

As soon as I finished talking I felt a great sadness wrap its arms around me as if trying to comfort me. I looked back at The Red and her eyes had not moved from me.

"You are haunted by colours. Colours will always trap you. They will keep one part of you for themselves and release the other part to the winds that are swirled by the moon and the sun. The spark of the world holds every colour inside it. That spark flies through your veins; it sends fire into your brain, and smoke into your heart. That is why you must always breathe from your heart."

Then she held the stone between us, as if she were both offering it and receiving it as a gift at the same time.

"The stone is grey. The fire has drawn blue lines like veins from deep inside it. But there is no blood in these veins. The blood is somewhere else. These colours, the grey, the blue, and the red are waiting for you. You will find them without searching." She did not move for many minutes, her eyes locked on mine, the stone between us like some ancient egg whose embryo was slowly shaping itself into my future.

I was very quiet for the next couple of days. I felt that speaking was almost too violent an action, as if I would bruise the air with my words. And what would my words be? To whom would I speak them? The whole world seemed so delicate. Even as I walked across the grass and down to the water I placed my feet so carefully on the ground so as not to injure it. When I walked to school with Sally and Victoria I could tell that they were perplexed by my paucity of words, speaking only when spoken to, and even then not offering my usual observations and comments. Victoria kept looking up at me in anticipation, kept squeezing my hand in short spasms as if to remind me that I was still at least physically connected to her. Sally looked at me only once or twice as if in recognition. And indeed for these last couple of days I had felt some indefinable urge to be with Sally, to spend time alone with her. There was nothing in particular I wanted to say to her, but I knew that would be fine. I knew that somehow she would understand something about me that I, myself, might not yet understand.

If I was soil and marsh muck and shingle stones, Sally was air and cloud. Where Victoria sat on my bed each evening and challenged me to untangle my thoughts with words, Sally seeped into me like a cool wind rising off the lake. I have never felt that I needed to explain myself or the world to her; I have never felt that I needed to consciously be her big sister. I just knew that I was. In the same way that the world inhabited me, Sally inhabited me. There was something natural and awesome about it — something comfortable, yet almost dangerous.

One Saturday evening when Sally was six and I was nine, I went out in the yard to call her in for dinner. It was late summer and the sun was just beginning to slide into the branches of the pines and maples by the edge of our property. I looked everywhere for her, but couldn't find her. As I was about to go back into the house, frustrated and concerned, I turned to look up at the sun through the high branches of the maples — I loved the way the floppy, jagged leaves shone so brilliantly green in the intense evening light — when I was struck by a colour that didn't belong to the scene. Near the very top of the tree fluttered a soft, white shape, like a fluffy flag. I shaded my eyes with my hand and stared intently at the spot, walking slowly back towards the tree. I took a few steps one way and then the other, trying to find the best position from which to get a good view of whatever was up there in the tree.

It was Sally. Curiosity quickly turned into fear and almost panic. And then just as quickly into wonder — almost a peaceful sense of wonder. She was so easy and serene sitting on that high branch amongst the leaves and sunlight that I could not be afraid for her. She was no longer just my sister up in that tree; she was my blood. I didn't know why I thought of it that way. Where did the idea of blood come from? I could only say that it seemed obvious at the time. And still does, I guess. How else can I describe my attachment to Sally, my understanding of her, her understanding of me?

So there I was, going to school and trying to listen to Miss Jenkins explain long division to the class — it was new material for the younger children, review for us older students. But I couldn't get my mind to focus on something so stripped bare of imagination as numbers. How could I count or measure what had happened to me on Halloween night and what The Red had told me about my stone? I was sure Miss Jenkins could sense I was not quite present; I was just thankful that she did not try to reel me back to earth.

After school was over for the day, and Victoria, Sally, and I had walked back home I asked Sally if she would like to go for a wander through the marsh. We walked down to the water and then along the shoreline, I matching her silence with my own. When we got to the shingle bar we curved around the bottom of Garter Snake Hill and followed the creek away from the marsh and into the woods. I didn't know if I would be able to find where

I had built my fire, but that was not my mission. I just wanted to be deeply surrounded by trees.

"I heard you playing your fiddle out here last week. I didn't mean to — I was just walking by the creek and I heard you."

I didn't look at Sally as I said this because I felt that I would be taking away her privacy somehow. And then I decided not to say anything for a few minutes. Sally looked up at the trees, as if counting the few brown leaves that were still clinging to the spidery, grey branches above us. I swished a stick in and out of the water of the creek. I wanted to give Sally time to respond in her own way if she wanted to. I wasn't quite sure how long I should wait before I seemed to be forcing an answer from her.

"I like your playing, Sally. It makes my bones feel like willow branches."

She just kept looking up into the trees as if I had said nothing. But that had always been Sally's way. It made Mother almost frantic until she realized that Sally was listening to her, that she was paying attention. For some reason we've come to believe that people can only be paying attention to us if they're looking directly at us. We consider it rude to not be looked at when we're speaking to someone. We had all come to accept Sally for the way that she was. Except for Father, which had always puzzled me somewhat. For some reason he seemed to fear Sally's silence, and sometimes that fear festered into anger, and it was the anger that I didn't understand.

"Sally, I think something is going to change drastically in my life. Something soon."

Finally, she looked at me, but her expression remained the same. Then she reached out her hand and put it on my arm, the one that was holding the branch and swishing it in the water. I stopped swishing. She held my eyes firmly but softly, as she might catch a feather falling from a nest. Then she stood up, sliding her hand into mine and started walking me back towards the marsh and the lake.

When we got home she took me into her room and played Southwind for me.

In the cloud coloured sand of the moist beach: *Tell me everything you know and I will tell you everything I don't know. Tell my stick to say something to my hand. This sand is real. This stick is real. The sand and the stick are imagining me.*

Finally it was the day of Miss Jenkins' arrival at our house to stay for two weeks. We had our first snowfall of the year that morning during church service. It was such a wonderful, uplifting feeling to walk out the broad doors of the church into a landscape completely changed from the one we had walked through just a short hour ago. Everything that was bleached grey and brown was now reborn in white. The world was a child once again, and it invited our souls to be new and clean and hopeful. I paused on the step of the church to look at the perfect, white road before it was etched with boot prints, wheel tracks, and the crescents of horseshoes. I wanted to look out at the world as God must have looked out at it before He created all of us.

As we walked home Victoria kept running ahead of us to be the first one to sign herself into the new winter. Her bootmanship was almost as free and neat as her penmanship — that's what Father said to her as he followed the large letters of her name in the direction of home. Even Father could not resist the urge to step out of himself on such a day as this. And I thought that a good part of him was as excited as we children were that Miss Jenkins was to arrive that evening. Most of the rest of the day was spent preparing for her arrival. It was decided that she would have my room and I would move in with Sally and Victoria. I felt honoured that Miss Jenkins would be living in my room for two weeks, but I was not as enthused about sharing my bedtimes with my sisters, much as I loved them. Of course, Victoria was pleased beyond words that I would be so close by — she could have her nightly conversations with me without having to leave her room; indeed, without even having to leave her bed. Sally, being Sally, would take it all in silent stride.

I often wondered how Sally and Victoria managed to sleep in the same bed for all these years. Whatever closeness there was between them was not obvious in their behaviour around each other. Perhaps Victoria got what she needed from each of us — a patient ear from me, and a calm silence from Sally.

I spent the couple of hours after arriving home from church in arranging my room for Miss Jenkins. I wanted her to walk into my room, look around, and be somehow impressed. I wanted my space to speak for me, to tell her about me in a way that I could never dare to do person to person. My books of poetry and history would tell her that I was a young woman of refined taste and curiosity about the world. My hymnal and book of prayers would show my attention to moral living. My brushes and combs, I hoped, would attest to my respect for my person rather than an inappropriate concern for my vanity. But was I vain? To be sure, I did love to brush my hair before going to bed. Each long stroke of the brush pulled my head to one side and then to the other, as if I were a boat sliding back and forth between two gentle waves. Often I would look out the window while I was brushing; with the lamp extinguished I would let the stars speckle my window with their tiny pricks of light, or I would look out to the lake beyond the trees and try to hear what my eyes could barely see. My hair was as long as my arm could reach, and I felt that I was stretching myself away from the earth, and sometimes I imagined that my feet lifted from the ground, just a little. Was this how a person who was just about to die would feel, I wondered. If so, then I was not afraid to die; I was not afraid to pass into the next world.

What if I spoke these feelings to Miss Jenkins? What if I went into her room — my room — and sat on the end of her bed and spoke with her the way Victoria spoke with me? Could I do it? I had no time to think this any further because just then Victoria burst into my room, shouting, "She's here, Gretchen! She's here!" As Victoria pulled me by the hand down the stairs I could hear Mother and Father greeting Miss Jenkins at the front door. By the time we reached the bottom of the stairs I could hear Father saying, "Now girls, please behave in a manner befitting the charming presence of our guest," and then turning back to Miss Jenkins, "I believe you know all too well the rest of the family." I couldn't see his face when he said this, but I hoped there was a twinkle in his eye. I took Miss Jenkins up to my room and showed her in.

"It's very gracious of you to give up your room to me, Gretchen. I will do my best not to disturb your things."

She looked around while still standing in the doorway, respectful of the space she was about to enter. Her eyes paused for a moment on the small shelves of books.

"Although I may peruse your poetry collection if you would allow me."

"Of course I would!"

I knew I answered too quickly and too enthusiastically, so I tried my best to maintain whatever dignity I could have in this situation.

"I mean, do you like poetry very much, Miss Jenkins?"

What a silly question, I thought as soon as the words had left my mouth. I tried to decide to leave before I made myself seem any sillier than I already had, but Miss Jenkins either did not think I was being silly, or she gracefully passed it over to save me embarrassment.

"Yes, Gretchen, I do like poetry very much. I find that it will usually speak to me no matter my condition, though I enjoy it most when I can bring it out of doors. I love to go for a long walk, stopping now and then whenever I feel like it to take out my book and read a poem. It is like showing the world to the poem and the poem to the world. I suspect that you may do the same from time to time."

Though I had decided not to run and hide, I did decide that the less I spoke, the better. So I simply smiled back at her.

"And what is your favourite poem, Gretchen?"

"Well, Father just gave me a collection of Donne's *Holy Sonnets* for my birthday, but I prefer the sonnets of Wordsworth. My especial favourite is 'The World is Too Much With Us'."

"Ah yes," Miss Jenkins said as she dropped her leather case to the floor,

"Great God! I'd rather be
A Pagan suckled in a creed outworn;
So might I . . ."

at which point she broke off as if suddenly obeying an unseen and unheard reprimand. "Oh, I hope your father didn't hear that!" And then she giggled into her gloved hands, just like a beautiful and innocent child. I loved Miss Jenkins more in that moment than I could ever have imagined.

In the days that followed I was in a state of bliss mixed with confusion. Bliss because Miss Jenkins had become a heroine in my life, and confusion because I was feeling that as each day of this late autumn passed I was moving more and more quickly towards some momentous event in my life, though I could not imagine what it might be. Thus it was that on the Thursday evening after Miss Jenkins' arrival I was lying in my bed staring at the window and thinking as the slow, even breaths of Sally and Victoria wove around each other and softened into the darkness of the room. I was drifting uneasily on the edge of sleep, so I got up quietly and walked to the window to look out at the lake.

The three-quarter full moon shone a cool, silvery white ribbon across the barely rippling water, and right where it fluttered against the shore was the tall shadow of someone standing at the water's edge, a long shadow that reached across the pale snow towards the house. I remained standing at the window, watching, not moving, so that I might notice any change in the shadow's shape. And then it defined itself as Baketigweyaa.

My first impulse was to go out to see him, but as I looked down from the window I could not see the trellis, and realized that I was not in my own room. I would have to go down the stairs and out the kitchen door. As noiselessly as I could I dressed myself and then tiptoed out of the bedroom with my boots in my hand. Even when I was out of the house and making my way across the snowy yard to the lake I kept moving as silently as I could. Once at the shore I wasn't sure how to let Baketigweyaa know I was there; I didn't want to frighten him. But as I hesitated a few steps away from him, he turned to look at me.

"I've been thinking about this railroad your people are building," he said as he turned to face the lake again.

And then he said nothing for a long while. I looked at Baketigweyaa. I looked out at the lake with its long, thin scar of moonlight. I looked back at the house, black against the innocence of snow. I watched the white puffs of my breathing, so hopeful and delicate, like small packages of spirit going home to the wide, invisible air of the world.

"Do you think you could walk on that path of light across the water and up to the moon to stand there and look back at this world?" He asked me this with his eyes focussed on the water, the moon, the ribbon of light. And before I could answer him he said, "Try to imagine that."

So I did. I tried to imagine walking on nothing but light and water all the way to the moon. I imagined the farther I walked, the more alone I would be — not necessarily lonely, but simply alone. Would that be simple? It would take forever. I would have to understand eternity;

I would have to believe in eternity to do it. And would I turn back now and then to see how far behind I had left my world? What would it look like from eternity? I kept walking and walking. Since I was being reeled in by the moon, it would always be dark around me. Freedom would swirl around me like the air become visible, and my skin would want to speak its joy into the star-speckled universe. Stars, like the leaves of autumn, always on fire but never falling from the trees.

I wanted to tell Baketigweyaa what it was like to walk that path, but I didn't want to break the spell of my imagining — I didn't want to give it up. So I began to turn my head as slowly and smoothly as I could, hoping to remain in both worlds at the same time. When finally I had turned far enough to see Baketigweyaa where he was standing, he was no longer there. My imagining self sped away from me like an arrow from a bow, and I spun full circle to find where Baketigweyaa was. He was nowhere to be seen.

And what was he wondering about the railroad?

I heard Gretchen stirring in the cot beside my bed. Then I heard her get up and go down the stairs. I knew she sometimes climbed out her own bedroom window and down the trellis. I like when she does things like that because it makes her mysterious and I love things that are mysterious. So when I heard her going down the stairs I got up and went to the window to see if I could see where she was going. There was a beautiful not quite round moon over the lake. I followed its light down onto the water and then along the water to the shore. Then I saw the shape of Baketigweyaa, just as Gretchen's shape was walking up behind him.

They stood beside each other, but didn't look at each other. They both looked out at the lake and at the moonlight on the water. At least that's what it looked like. That's what I would do if I was down there. The more I watched them the more I felt that I wanted to take out my fiddle and play it, but I knew I couldn't do that, so I just kept watching and thinking about fiddle tunes in my head. I tried to match the shape of the tunes to Gretchen and Baketigweyaa and the moonlight and the lake and the snow. Everything was either white or shadows; that's how it seemed. The two tunes that came into my head were "Johnny Faa" and "I Saw Three Ships," but they played themselves much slower than usual — like slow airs with just enough sadness in them to not make you really sad, just thoughtful. I said to myself that I should remember to try to play these tunes this way tomorrow.

At the same time that I could hear the tunes playing in my head I could also hear how quiet it was. It seemed to be the same quiet inside the house as outside the house, except for the soft crinkle of my fiddle tunes as they got cold in the night air and fell to rest on the perfect white of snow on the ground.

And then Gretchen's footsteps coming up the stairs and Baketigweyaa gone back into the night. And then more footsteps, and then Father's voice like a piece of lost thunder looking for its storm.

I walked slowly back to the house, not yet fully returned to this world as I followed the moonlight ribbon across the snow and wondered where Baketigweyaa went and why. I stopped in front of the door and waited a moment for the world to resolve itself into firmer lines before going back in. Something made me turn back to face the lake — something in the air that seemed familiar. I sniffed the night like some cautious animal, but could not make visible to my mind what it was I sensed.

I opened and closed the door as softly as I could and then paused to let my eyes adjust to the darkness before moving towards the stairs. I had just put my foot on the first stair when the night was cracked open with such violence that I cowered against the wall.

"Gretchen Williamson!"

There was barely a space between Father's shouting of my name and the chaos of doors opening. Then feet punching the floor from many directions as if defending themselves against the cold floorboards. Frightened gasps of breath as everyone bunched up behind Father, fearing to get too close. And Father, risen like the fury of God at the top of the stairs. Looking down at me from a great height.

"Gretchen Williamson!"

This time his voice was choking out my name as if it had bitten him and he was trying to rid himself of its venom. Mother separated from the crowd of bodies behind him and lurched to a point halfway between them and him.

"John?"

She was not sure what to say or how to say it. She just wanted to say something to protect me, to protect us all from a force she was desperately afraid of.

"Lydia!"

He did not turn to look at her; he just kept staring down at me. And then he began to spit words in spasms.

"This child has been with that Indian . . . in the middle of the night . . . with that Indian . . . this child . . . the devil . . . this is not . . . she . . . I am not . . . you must . . . we cannot . . . "

And then he fell to his knees, great sobs shaking his body which was still straight and stiff from the knees up. Mother still dared not come any closer to him. At that moment Miss Jenkins went to Mother and gathered her into her arms. Sally and Victoria looked at one another and held each other's hands. I had sunk to a half sitting position against the wall and I could not move. I had never been so terrified in all my life. The awful and crushing realization that our lives could never be the same again and that it was my fault kept me weighted to the floor. I knew that as soon as I moved, this horrible new life would begin. If I could just stay still, we could all somehow float away from this moment, from this house, from these damaged lives.

The next thing I knew Miss Jenkins and Sally and Victoria were huddled around me, and Mother was on her knees next to Father trying to hold him and not hold him at the same time. The odd thing was that there were no words being spoken by anyone. It was as if Father had scared all the words back into the things they represented. The stairs were no longer the word, stairs; they were just stairs. The walls were nameless. And so were we all. There was nothing anyone could say. We could only move our bodies in ways we thought might mean something to those around us. As I was lifted to my feet by several arms I wondered what it now meant to stand up, to walk. If I breathed too loudly, what would that mean? If I closed my fingers on someone else's hand would that mean comfort or fear or love or need? What could anything mean anymore?

Miss Jenkins walked me and Sally and Victoria back to our room and sat us down on the bed like a row of oversized dolls. Then she pulled a chair to the side of the bed and sat and looked at us. Still no words. I was hoping she would be able to speak. She was the only one who might still be able to do it, who might still be able to bring some of the words back that we needed to use. I didn't know what they were, but I trusted in Miss Jenkins. I prayed towards Miss Jenkins. Whatever words she decided to use first, they had to be perfect words. She was the only one who could save me, who could save us, now. I wondered if Mother could save Father. I wondered if she was waiting for Miss Jenkins, too.

She looked us each in the eyes, one at a time, down the row, and then back again.

"Do you love your sisters?"

This question was asked into each pair of eyes. We instinctively grabbed onto each other's hands and nodded our heads.

"Do you love your mother and your father?"

We nodded.

"Do you love your father?"

And she looked at me a little longer than at Sally and Victoria. They looked over at me, waiting for me to answer first. I looked at them. Sally focussed her eyes on mine and nodded her head as if showing me how to do it.

"Yes," I said. It was time to put an end to this night.

"Then let's all go to bed. I can bring my blankets in here and sleep on the floor next to you."

∾

As the muted daylight seeped through the curtains I opened my eyes and immediately felt how painfully exhausted I was. Sally and Victoria lay in their bed, spooned against one another, like a pair of snakes in their winter torpor. Miss Jenkins must have risen early, for she was not in the room. But she had left a note lying on the top of my blanket, "You and Sally and Victoria may be excused from school today."

Bit by bit the events of last night rose into my memory, and I felt myself sinking even further into exhaustion. I wondered if this was the drastic change in my life that I was awaiting. I tried to picture it as that, but I couldn't do it. I wasn't sure that this was it. But what could be more drastic than this? And then everything gave way to the tortured sound of Father's voice pounding my name into the darkness of the house. My name in his voice was now a permanent part of the belongings of this house, like the beds and the wallpaper and the kitchen table and the rag rugs in the sitting room. Everyone who came into our house from this day forward would be able to hear that sound. I had shattered my father.

I tried to sit up, but fell back down. Were Mother and Father up? What would they be thinking, what would they be doing? Could we ever speak to each other again? All these questions assaulted me; I could feel them almost as physical forces battering against me, and I could not stop them. Even if I could get up and beat them back, what would I do then? Could I walk out of this room? Where would I go? What if I saw Father on the landing or on the stairs or in the kitchen? Questions, questions, questions — fists with hard and sharp knuckles. I was afraid to lift my gown and look at my body for fear of finding great blue and yellow bruises.

But Miss Jenkins was not here, and it was up to me as the oldest to resolve this situation somehow, though I had no idea how. I decided to see if I could make it as far as Sally's and Victoria's bed. If I could do that, then I could rest there for awhile and try to figure out what to do next. With all my might I rose, pushed off my blankets, and staggered to the bed. I sat heavily on the end of it, trying not to disturb my sisters and whatever sleep they were managing to have. Everything was silence. This is what it must be like to be under the ground with a tombstone on your head. The silence of death, of something having ended forever. And now I had need of nothing less than the miracle of resurrection. I thought about praying, but it did not feel right. Had I lost my faith, too? Did I ever really have it? I thought of Baketigweyaa and of The Red, but I could not think of Reverend Swinerton or of God. It was all too much.

Next thing I remembered was reaching back to my cot to gather my blankets and then lying down next to Sally and Victoria, covering myself against them, trying to coax their heat into my body. Sleeping a sleep that made my blood hurt.

The week after that night passed in minutes and hours rather than in days. And for every one of those minutes

I was trying to find a way to pray, and something or someone to pray to. But I could no longer direct my will; it became limp and lifeless, like a bucket with a hole in it, lying in the corner of the yard, waiting only for the grass to start growing through its broken bottom.

When Miss Jenkins asked me that night if I loved Father, I said yes. But did I? Certainly, I feared him. And because of the shock I felt at the severity of his reaction to my connection with Baketigweyaa, I feared for him. I was bewildered, too — what was there in Father that was so beyond my understanding, that did not allow me to feel guilt for what I had done, even though my responsibility was inescapable?

And I felt pity for him; pity tempered with compassion. But love — love was too complicated and tangled. I tried to remember back to before that night. Did I love Father before that? The question was too hard; it made me dizzy. So I tried to remember if I loved Mother or my sisters. It was no use; I could not do it. I could not remember love, but I had a distinct feeling that it would be the only thing that could get me through all this.

None of us had been to school all week, but in spite of the extreme unordinariness of the life in our house, Miss Jenkins stayed. I don't think it occurred to any of us that she might leave, or even that we should ask her if she would prefer to leave. Maybe we all — Miss Jenkins included — understood that she was the only one who could keep us in some sort of motion that resembled a normal ordering of days. We were like planets around her sun, though I could feel no heat from her. It wasn't that she wasn't giving off heat by the very sensitivity of her presence; it was just that the planet that was me had a thick and invisible atmosphere, which no kind of heat could penetrate. Neither Sally nor Victoria nor I wandered farther than the confines of our property, and even though it was winter and cold we tried to spend as much time as possible outside the house. Father never set foot outside. The inside of the house felt like a ghost ship that had been drifting on the sea for a long time and no one knew what had happened to all the sailors. I could feel the ghosts all around me; I could feel them move out of the way as I walked down the stairs and across the floor to the kitchen.

We gathered once a day for meals. Either I or Miss Jenkins took care of breakfast for me and my sisters. Mother and Father did not come down to the kitchen while we were there. As for the mid-day meal it was everyone for herself. It was supper when we would all be together in the same room, eating in the silence that had become our new language. We would all steal glances at Father and at Mother when we thought they were not looking back at us. They never looked back at us. Mother would look at Father. Father would look out the window at the apple trees. Sometimes he would say "apple trees" to no one in particular, and his voice was sore, like a fresh wound. The thin and wobbling sound of the words was as unsettling in its own way as his thundering of my name those few nights ago.

At night, lying in bed, I tried to imagine the people who still lived in the world beyond our house. Baketigweyaa. Patrick. The Red. My schoolmates. My mind was strong enough to wonder about them, but my body did not have the strength to carry my spirit out of this house to seek them out. Did they wonder where I was?

Did the rest of Merigold's Point know what had happened to our lives?

Our absence ran through the village like the toll of a bell through the still air of evening. That Sunday afternoon, Reverend Swinerton came to our door.

Perhaps it was Miss Jenkins who asked him to come. If so, it could be a good thing. If not, what good could he do? We children would not know that day if anything had been shifted by Reverend Swinerton's visit. As soon as I heard his voice follow his knock into the house, Mother sent us upstairs, out of sight and out of hearing. I would have preferred to have been sent outside — it would have been less claustrophobic. But Miss Jenkins came up with us, so I tried to feel some measure of comfort in that.

And then there we were again, seated on the bed in a row, with Miss Jenkins facing us. For just a moment I was thrown back to that night. The room suddenly went dark, and I had to shake my head and blink my eyes to save myself from falling into that deep, lightless pit. Miss Jenkins must have noticed my near faint, and when I felt her hand on my shoulder I was shocked back to the present, though I wasn't sure that it was any safer a place to be. Then Victoria spoke.

"Miss Jenkins, I'm afraid."

I had felt up to this point that the weight of sadness could get no heavier, but Victoria's perfect, childlike voice knocked the breath out of me. So much truth and so much hurt. I could feel the innocence being ripped out of her. Too soon; this was happening too soon in her life. All the pain I felt for myself was that moment transferred to my dear baby sister. I jumped over to her and gathered her up in my arms as if trying to squeeze time back into the past before all this had happened. I wanted to hold her long enough to make this a dream from which she would awaken, but the harder I held on to her the more I could feel hopelessness rushing through every vein of my body. Desperate sobs began to fill the room like a clutch of birds frightened from a tree by some horrible presence they could not see, but could sense in every other part of their beings. The sounds were coming out of my throat, out of my body. And then it was Victoria holding me, trying to keep me from falling to the floor.

"I love you so much, Victoria . . . I love you so much . . . so much . . . I'm sorry I did this to you . . . but you'll be all right, Victoria. I promise. I promise to take care of you."

I remembered nothing else until I awoke in the middle of the night in the perfect stillness. The perfect darkness. And yet, there was enough light to see the form of Miss Jenkins sitting on the floor by my cot. Whether it was actually Miss Jenkins or some angel in her guise was not important; there were certain distinctions I could no longer make and that were no longer significant.

"How are you, Gretchen?"

It seemed like such a simple question, but I did not know how to answer it.

"I'm not sure how I am." And then I paused. "Do you know how I am, Miss Jenkins?"

"I think you are fragile right now, but I think you are strong enough to be all right if you decide to be."

"Is it such a simple matter to decide?"

"It's the only thing that is left to you to decide. Nothing else is under your control. But that's nothing to be afraid of."

"Am I afraid?"

And then I thought of Victoria and instinctively looked over to the bed to see if she was there; to see if she was sleeping; to see, if I could, if she was stronger than her hurt.

"I'm not sure that you are, Gretchen. I think you are trying to find your ground in the midst of this upheaval."

As my eyes grew more accustomed to the darkness Miss Jenkins' face became clearer. I could see faint shadows defining the curve of her cheeks and her jaw. And her eyes which did not leave me.

"Is God in this house?"

"Of course He is, Gretchen."

"How do you know?"

"Faith."

"Is that all?"

"That's everything, Gretchen."

That morning I woke up to the cold, hesitant light of day hovering in the room like a stranger who had lost his way.

I walked to the snowy beach to stand in the blank pages. I wanted the snow and sand to write me away, to make me blank. I walked up the creek. More blank pages. To be as blank as a birch tree, as a sheet of water, as the sky with no sun and no moon and no stars and no clouds. To come back to earth as if I had never been here before. There were no sticks today that reached out for my hand.

Miss Jenkins is still staying with us, even though it is now longer than two weeks. She is trying to take care of us, especially Gretchen. We have gone back to school now. The first day back, the day after Reverend Swinerton came to see us, was very difficult. All the other school children stared at us as if they had never seen us before. But Gretchen is very brave; she holds her head up and does not look at the ground. She keeps reminding me and Victoria that we shouldn't look at the ground either. We should look into everyone's eyes, even if it seems like the hardest thing in the world to do.

Miss Jenkins does not treat us as if she is staying at our house; she does not treat us as if our father has become a crazy man. Crazy man — that's what we can hear the other children whispering. She treats us just like all the other pupils. After a couple of days this begins to work. It makes the others begin to treat us as if we were normal. But we aren't normal anymore.

Winter is normal. Snow is normal. Sometimes it is still beautiful. Today in school Miss Jenkins was teaching my part of the class about constellations. Orion. Cassiopeia. Pleiades. Big Dipper. Little Dipper. And at the very same time it was snowing outside, so I pointed my eyes out the window to look at it through my rainbow curtains while I kept my ears listening to Miss Jenkins' voice. The snowflakes were like dried and frozen stars that were falling from the sky because they weren't attached anymore. Or maybe because there were new stars being born and it was time for the old ones to fall away to make room, like baby teeth being pushed out by grown-up teeth. Were these baby stars coming back to earth? Maybe they were some kind of heaven seeds and they became flowers in the spring time when all the snow melted.

This made me feel better, and I wished that school could be over for the day so I could hold Gretchen's hand and let her know that some things in the world were still all right. As soon as my free time came up, though, when Miss Jenkins taught the oldest pupils their lessons, I made a snowflake from a piece of paper and drew stars on it and gave it to Victoria who sat just across from me. It made her smile.

It was not so much a tension in the air anymore as it was a limpness of spirit. Life could not be like it had been, but neither could it remain the way it was if we were to survive ourselves into the future. There should have been excitement in the air with the approach of Christmas, but there was only resignation. I had decided, however, that Sally and Victoria and I must seek out what joy there was available to us. So, after supper one evening I asked Sally to take out her fiddle and play for us all. She had not done so since that night.

We decided to have the music in our room upstairs because Mother and Father were still in the kitchen, she staring at him, he staring at the apple trees in the falling darkness, dully tinged with the white of snow. When Sally began to play it was not the jigs and reels we were used to, but the wistful music of the woods and the creek — the music whose notes were flecked with summer sunlight through the fine lace of branches and leaves. Only now those flecks of sunlight were more like the slow ooze of sap bleeding amber and gold from the split bark of maple trees in the spring. Sadness and sorrow there certainly were in those strains and melodies, but persistence and hope, too. For the first time since that night I felt confident enough to write in my journal.

I made three lists. The first was a list of the things I thought I knew for certain:

in winter it snows, in spring it thaws

in summer there are apples

in fall the leaves bleed red and orange and gold

the sun is always warm, even on the coldest day of winter.

The second was a list of the things I thought I knew for sure but that I was now no longer certain of:

Father will always protect me;

I will always be charmed by the smell of apples;

I will know God;

I will be as strong as Mother.

The third was a list of things I promised to do:

I will learn all the colours of water;

I will always keep a journal;

I will always live near the water;

I wanted to write something about Miss Jenkins, but my relationship with her, and her relationship with our household was outside the bounds of things I knew and didn't know. I did know, though, that Miss Jenkins could not stay with us forever, and so I feared that when she left, all order would fall away into chaos, and there would be no centre ever again to our lives. At the very latest she would leave at Christmas time to go back to her family in the Eastern Townships. The birth of Christ; the death of our world.

It occurred to me then that I could not remain passive in the face of my life; if I did I would die. But still I felt that I was being dragged along by some force which tolerated my existence only if I did not try to resist it. This was not something that I knew; it was something that I felt.

Chapter 3

SINCE THAT NIGHT I have not left the confines of our property except to go to school and back. We have not been to church because we cannot bring Father, and it would be too awkward to go without him. By now everyone in the village knows that there is a strangeness that has settled over our house, over our lives. But there are two strangenesses — the one we have brought upon ourselves, and the one the village people have woven around us.

When I realized that the prison I had made for myself was now one to which others had the key, I decided I had to escape, if only for a few hours, even though I might be stared and wondered at. To avoid this as much as possible I decided to walk the shore of the lake to Port Credit on Saturday morning. Maybe I would meet Baketigweyaa along the way, or maybe I would see Patrick by the wharves at the river.

Just as I was about to set out, dressed in boots and sweaters and my long coat, Victoria came up to me and pulled softly on my sleeve.

"Can I go with you, Gretchen?"

"You don't know where I'm going."

"It doesn't matter. I just want to go with you."

"Well, I was planning to walk the whole way to Port Credit along the lakeshore. Do you think you could make it that far? It's pretty cold out."

"I can make it. You won't go too fast for me, will you?"

"No, Victoria. I won't go too fast for you."

I wondered if somehow Victoria was feeling left behind by the world these past few weeks. And left behind especially by me. Each of us seemed to have been wandering around in glass bubbles, afraid that if we got too close to one another we would shatter our protective casings and be choked by the onrush of cold and foreign air. I put my hand on Victoria's head, and for a brief moment I felt what it must be like to be a mother. And inside that moment I also had the sense that I would never feel this again.

I made sure that Victoria was dressed warmly, and then we stepped out into the wintry air. As we crunched across the yard to the water's edge and then began to make our way along the shore, I felt an odd sense of adventure. There was an apprehension and an excitement, but I was detached from them; it was as if those emotions were walking along beside us.

"I like that Miss Jenkins is staying with us, even though you don't get your own room. But I like that, too, that you stay in our room with us. I like being all together at night. Do you like it, Gretchen?"

I had to think about my answer, for it wasn't clear and immediate. Victoria's question confused me because staying with her and Sally didn't seem to have anything to do with whether I liked it or not. Liking it or not liking it was irrelevant. But I realized that if I tried to explain this to Victoria she would not be able to understand it.

"It's good that we get to stay together for a little while."

We walked on in silence. The flat, grey stones of the shingle bar rose out of the white snow, like freckles on a cheek. We had to be careful with our footing because of the slipperiness, and when we reached the sandy part of the shoreline the relief of walking on level ground was almost exhilarating. How curious that such a simple shift — one that I had experienced every time I made this walk — should seem so profound, so comforting.

"Are we going to see Patrick?"

"Not particularly. We're just walking, and Port Credit is where we happen to be walking to."

"Sometimes I just go walking without wanting to go anywhere, too. I walk through the orchards like that sometimes. I probably wouldn't want to walk somewhere just to see a boy, though. But you can, Gretchen, because you're older and that's what older girls do, isn't it."

"Where do you get these ideas, Victoria? How often have I ever walked somewhere just to see a boy?"

"I don't know."

Again, we walked on in silence.

"What's the difference between a boy and a man?"

I sometimes wondered how such questions came into Victoria's head. I don't remember having such questions occur to me at her age. But then, I didn't have an older sister. Whether that made any difference I wasn't sure.

"Well, Father is a man, Reverend Swinerton is a man, Baketigweyaa is a man. All the boys in our school are boys. So what do you think the difference is?"

"Is Patrick a boy or a man?"

"What do you think?"

"That's not fair, Gretchen. You're supposed to make the answers."

"All right, then. A man is someone who is old enough to be married or to have a profession."

"How old does a man have to be to be married?"

"That depends."

"On what?"

"Well, it depends on how much schooling he'd had or if he had to support his family . . ."

"But I thought you said he couldn't be married unless he was a man, and he can't have a family unless he's married."

"I mean if his family — his parents and brothers and sisters — are poor and need him to work to help with food and things like that."

"Then if I was a boy and our family was poor and I decided to help them then I'd be a man, wouldn't I?"

"No, Victoria, I still think you'd be too young."

"Why would you be the one to get to decide?"

"Well, it wouldn't be up to me to decide, really. But seven years old is too young to be a man. You'd have to be at least fifteen."

"That's how old you are."

"Yes, it is."

"So you can be a woman, then. I think you'd make a really good woman."

"I don't feel like a woman."

I was, however, a woman in certain inescapable ways. Last year I became a woman in that way that one does not talk about, but which has forever rendered my childhood something that can now only be a part of my past. Still, when Father shouted my name into the darkness that night I felt like a very little girl, even a baby — or hardly human at all.

We walked all the way to the river and the wharves and back again and didn't see anyone we knew. No Patrick, no Baketigweyaa. Once we didn't see them I understood how much I really wanted to see them and talk to them, though I was not sure what it was I wanted to say. I just wanted to ask somebody who it really was they saw when they talked to me.

I could feel it the first time I took it out of its case and put it under my chin and moved the bow across its strings. I could feel the sound buzz my skin, not just on my fingers, but up my arms and all over my whole body, and I was afraid and excited all at the same time. If the bow across one string did that to my body, what would a whole tune do? So I put the fiddle down because I thought I should think about this. Father has always told us that nothing done in haste could ever bring a good result. He told us about eating green apples, but I remember learning that lesson for myself. But as soon as I laid it back in its case I knew I had to find out. I picked it up again, this time feeling the wood and the strings just as they were, before putting the bow on the strings. I held the fiddle under my chin and hoped for it not to scare me away. It was like when I picked up the sparrow after it had flown into the window. I could feel it being warm in my hands and I could feel its heart shivering. And then all of a sudden it woke up and we were both scared because I had never held a bird in my hands before and because it had never been held before. But then it calmed down, and then I could let it go and it flew away.

So I held the fiddle against my chin like that and then I touched the bow on its strings, first on one string and then another one and then another one. The buzzing on my skin went all over me again and it made me think about the sparrow flying away into the sky. I still like that feeling.

I woke up because the sun kept going in and out of the clouds. One moment the room was so bright I could almost remember true joy; the next moment it became like the house has been since that night. I got dressed and went out into the yard.

The colours of snow: white like the moon seems it should be, but never is; white like a bone that lies in a field years after its flesh has disappeared into the ground and into the bellies of scavenger birds; white like milk in a pail in the corner of the barn; white like a handkerchief a mother pulls from her sleeve when she is about to cry; white like the sky when it is not grey or blue or dark with the night; white like an eye that is wide with surprise; white like the skin of my thighs; white like a mirror that only God can look into.

"What should I do? I don't know what to do."

This is what I said to Miss Jenkins after school on the last Friday before Christmas holidays. On the last Friday before she left to go to her own home back in the Eastern Townships of Quebec. What I was really trying to ask her was what we would do without her. Could she understand that? That she was holding us all together? Perhaps I was the only one who thought that. What was everyone else thinking? Were we all looking to someone else to guide us through this black time? Victoria and Sally were looking to me, but I did not want that responsibility. I wanted Miss Jenkins to have it. I wanted her to stay until we were all better.

"What do you think you should do, Gretchen?"

"Please, Miss Jenkins, don't turn the question around on me. I can't answer any more questions. I can't do it anymore."

"And you want me to do it for you?"

And there it was. The words I most feared to hear. Those few words fell on me, like a great weight of snow sliding off a roof and burying me in its pure white coldness. Miss Jenkins was leaving us; she was leaving me. She would not save us.

"I am not much older than you are, Gretchen. You must not look at me as if I had all the strength in the world that you do not have. You do have it."

"No, I don't."

I sobbed the words into her dress. I didn't care anymore about being strong. I wasn't strong, and I didn't want to be. All those thoughts I had had about facing up to my life deserted me, and this made me even more desperate.

"I'm sorry, Miss Jenkins. I'm so sorry."

I pulled myself up to my feet again and wiped my eyes with my sleeves.

"Sit with me, Gretchen."

She put her hand under my elbow and led me the few steps to the edge of the bed where we sat next to each other, our faces turned to the window where the light of a mottled day was leaking away into the night.

"Though you have been painfully sad, you have survived these few weeks well enough to still get up and go to school and spend time with your sisters, haven't you?"

"Yes," I answered grudgingly.

"And what exactly is it that I have said to you that has helped you to do all this?"

"It's not what you've said . . ."

"Is it something someone else has said?"

"I've hardly spoken to anyone else except who lives in this house."

"Have you spoken with Baketigweyaa?"

"I wasn't able to find him the one time I looked, and he doesn't seem to be looking for me."

"Then it isn't speaking with someone that helps you through this."

"It's being with people . . . it's being with people that helps. Knowing that there are other living beings in this darkened world with me."

"I am only one person, Gretchen. There are so many others . . . even here in this house. Don't they count?"

"Sally and Victoria are younger than me. They count, but I feel that they need to be looking to me for strength because I'm the oldest. Mother seems to be caught between us and Father. I know she wants to care for us, but she has to care for Father more. And Father . . . he seems to have gone away, even though his body is still here. I'm afraid he won't ever come back . . . I'm afraid he can't ever come back. And if you leave, too . . . "

"What are you doing to help bring your father back?"

I had never thought of being able to bring him back. I had never thought that it might be up to me to do it. That was Mother's responsibility. I was the child.

So I thought about what bringing him back might involve, but as soon as I tried to think on it I felt myself standing before a great wall which I could neither see the top nor the ends of. I was not connected to Father. He was my father, I was his daughter, but these now were only words that tried to define some attachment that I had never understood. I put Mother in Father's place and tried to see what I would do in that situation. I would go to her, I would talk to her, I might even take her in my arms.

And in that moment of realization I prayed as hard as I could that I actually loved Father. I had to love him. How could I not love him?

"I can't bring him back."

And then it was all right. It was all right that Miss Jenkins would leave on Sunday, after church. After school term. After being in our house like a witness and a saint.

After all.

In the dream I was a kite. There were a thousand kites in the blue air, and I was one of those kites. I was longer and more tapered than the rest; my colours were more muted, and I was thinking to my kite-self that in this way I did not fight the brightness of sky and sun and grass and tree leaves around me. I did not fight for glory with the other kites. I fluttered in the high wind, no arms and legs to worry about. Just the long, fine string that tugged at me from somewhere down there on the earth.

They passed me from hand to hand, their heads bent back on their shoulders, their eyes following me this way and that way, across and up and down. I wondered what it was like to be them, to have all those human parts that made them run and jump and speak and cry. I was sure I was like that, if I could only remember. But I didn't try to remember.

Still, there was a dearness about all those hands and faces. Victoria was taller down there than Sally, than even me when I was down there . . . I was sure I was down there. And Patrick was fuller and heavier. Even Baketigweyaa took a turn, but he hardly looked up, though I knew he sensed up. Miss Jenkins was not part of the knot of bodies. She was walking away and waving up to me.

First they were passing the string back and forth a few minutes at a time, and then more quickly. And then too quickly. Their hands and arms were getting tangled up, but they were still smiling peacefully, as they had been before. Before . . . That meant there was an after, but I could not remember that, either, because I was still trying not to remember. The only thing I could remember was that to be a kite one must not remember.

They were tangling up their bodies and I couldn't tell them apart. I shouted down from my sky voice, "Let go of the string! Let go of the string!" And they did, but not because they wanted to. I felt the sudden release of pressure. Suddenly, I was afraid that I didn't have arms and legs, that I couldn't grab on to anything. I kept looking down to see where everyone was. All the other kites were being reeled in. And then I saw her running along the shore of the lake. Mother was running to the house, to the orchard. Where was Father?

I was being sucked into the sky. Where was Father? It was snowing, and the apples were falling from as high as the stars. They passed through me like fish through water. Mother was running; everyone else was tangled up. Where was Father?

And then Mother's voice, thicker than the kite string ever was. John! That was the word she was shouting. I remembered it; it was Father's name. She was trying to attach Father's name to his body; she was trying to reel him in, but she couldn't hold on. John! John!

I was suddenly frightened out of my dream. I could hear the fretful voices of Sally and Victoria through the wall just before the sound of their bare feet got louder as they got closer to my bed. At first the separation from them in my dream seemed to have become too real until I remembered that I was back in my own room, now that Miss Jenkins had left. I realized then that they were reacting to Mother's voice, the voice from my dream shouting Father's name. I felt so cold. I thought it must have been from the strangeness of my dream and I did not yet notice that there was only a sheet covering me. The blankets were gone.

And then the eerie silence — eerie because Mother's voice had suddenly disappeared. And just as her voice disappeared, Sally's and Victoria's footsteps stopped. For a moment I could not move. I felt as if the world had ended and an awful kind of eternity had begun. The idea of movement was foreign, as if suddenly unlearned. I listened for anything. Any sound that would recreate the world, any world. There was no wind; the lake was still.

So I tried to breathe. If only I could breathe I could prove myself still somehow alive. And then . . . I could hear my breathing. I could hear the sound of my breathing. I was alive! God, I was alive! I threw off my sheet and ran into the hall. Sally and Victoria were standing just outside the door of their room, stiff as statues. I ran past them and down the stairs; it was up to them if they wanted to remember how to move again. My mind did not know where I was running to; it was following my body. My body the kite.

When I got to the kitchen I noticed that the door was open, and through its frame like the frame around a picture of another world, I saw the painting, its colours not yet set because still being shifted by some invisible brush. The first four apple trees of a longer row, each tree slightly smaller the farther away it was. Each tree dark grey against the dull white of the snow. Blankets neatly swathed around the base of each tree. At the fourth tree the slumping black shape of Father kneeling in front of it, Mother standing behind him with her hands on his shoulders.

They had stopped moving. Father was out of blankets, and there were so many trees left. It was Christmas morning.

Spring — Summer 1855

Chapter 1

PORT CREDIT, APRIL 3 1855 — *This past Easter Sunday, March 31, saw the destruction by a great fire of the entire business block of Front Street along the west bank of the Credit River, including most notably the MacDonald's Dock warehouses, Murray and Cotton's General Store, and Henry Neeson's Hotel, where the fire is said to have started in the tavern.*

The fire was first noticed by Abram Block, his son Abram, Jr., and Charles Hare, who were sitting enjoying the morning sunshine on the pier on the east side of the river. By the time a volunteer brigade had been formed and was passing buckets of water from the river to the burning structures it was clear to Mr. Cotton that none of them could be saved.

Attention was then turned to the several stone hookers at winter anchor in the harbour. By much hard work and good fortune all the boats were saved, either by moving them out towards the lake or by soaking their decks. Among the boats saved were Abram Block's Ann Brown, *Charles Hare's* Hunter, *Robert*

Collins' Barque Swallow, William Naish's Mary Ann, and Thomas Blower's Catherine Hays.

The grain schooner Raleigh, which had just entered the harbour, had managed to come about and avert both the fire and the escaping schooners, thus saving itself from any damage.

No lives were lost, nor were there any injuries suffered. The loss of the dock and businesses, including the post office in the General Store, will be a great strain to the community for some time to come.

This was how I, Gretchen Williamson, anonymous reporter, reported the great harbour fire for the *Port Credit Bulletin*. What I, Gretchen Williamson, just myself, saw on Easter Sunday morning was far more awful and wondrous.

I had made a habit on Sunday mornings, when weather permitted, of walking the shoreline towards the Credit River. Since Christmas and Father's collapse we no longer attended church services. It was mostly Mother's decision not to go, and Sally, Victoria, and I were not pressured to go without her. Indeed, I think it was Mother's wish, without her saying so, that we not go unless we went as a family; and that was not possible.

Spring was early this year, and Easter Sunday dawned sunny and warm. The walk along the lake was so pleasant that I had forgotten where I was, until I found myself at the mouth of the river. From there I made my way along the short knob of land between the canal and the basin, and found a comfortable rock to sit on. Leaning back so that my face was full in the sun, I took deep breaths through my nose, smelling the vegetable moistness of spring steaming its way through the melting snow. If I could just keep filling my body with this smell I could believe the world was perfect.

And then the first subtle wisp of smoke. At first I kept my eyes closed and did not move my head away from the sun. Probably someone's hearth fire releasing its smoke through a chimney. Or an outdoor fire of brush and stumps. But I soon realized that I did not recognize this smoke. I opened my eyes and looked over my shoulder towards the docks on either side of the river. And then I could hear a couple of young boys shouting. I followed the sound of their voices to the pier on the east side of the river, and then I followed the line of their arms pointing back across to MacDonald's Dock on the other side of the river. Their excitement was in complete contrast to the calm, ragged grey and black cloud of smoke that rose so naturally into the sky blue air. It did not occur to me to move or to respond in any way to what I was seeing, other than to simply observe, as if I were watching a candle lamp projection show.

And then the calm of the morning was stirred as if with some hot, demon breath, and the still landscape of water and masts was infected with a confused running about of figures, shouting out of fright and purpose mixed together. Some of the figures strung themselves into a chain, along which were passed buckets of water; some flitted in and around the masts, and soon, the masts began to take on the confused movement of the figures. Boats knocked against each other as they moved in frenzied motion away from the dock and into the river. And always the shouting, as if somehow the louder the voices the more optimistic would be the outcome.

Once the boats were safe in their element the commotion began to subside. Although just as much toil and near manic effort had been devoted to saving the buildings on shore, it was soon clear that they could not be saved. From where I watched it seemed as if a decision had been made, without need for discussion or consideration of any kind, that the boats were more important than the buildings, that the hotel and store and post office were limbs which could be sacrificed to save the body, and the heart of that body was in the boats. A fire on land is to be expected, even to be accepted in some sort of religious way, whereas fire on the water is unnatural and to be fought against with the wild energy of instinct.

Eventually, everyone stood away from the fire and watched it gorge itself to death. They watched it all together; I watched alone. No one paid any attention to me sitting out on my rock; no one knew I was there.

Mr. Standemyre let me have the job both because he was tired of doing all the setting and printing and writing himself, and because he was a good friend of Father's. Mostly because he was a good friend of Father's. "This is not woman's work, much less a young girl's work," is what he said to me, "and don't you be broadcasting to the world 'round about that you're the one writing the odd story for my newspaper. I can't be having that." And then he would stop shaking his head at me, and he would look off just above my head as if he were speaking to someone standing behind me, "But your father's a good man, no matter what anybody says, you hear me?" And then with his eyes back on me, "And you're as fine a girl as your father is a fine man. You have your wits about you, and you know how to turn a phrase when you want to." Of course, he would not let me be lyrical in the *Bulletin* because "newspapers are for news and not for making the world into some poetic thing that it isn't and never was."

I had decided after Christmas that I would not go back to school. I was a girl, after all, and I'd had more schooling already than most girls my age. Besides, with Father no longer himself, Mother needed the extra help at home. Sally became Victoria's "guardian" now at school and I became . . . I suppose I just became more Gretchen. That's how it felt to me. So, as well as helping to keep the house orderly I thought I might like to earn some money for us all. We didn't know how we would fare with the orchard, since we weren't sure what Father would be capable of doing. If he could at least tend to the trees we could keep accounts and look after the animals and gardens. It was while Mother and I were shopping in Port Credit one day in February that Mr. Standemyre saw me loading provisions onto our wagon and took me aside. I found out later that Miss Jenkins had spoken to Reverend Swinerton who had spoken to Mr. Cotton who had spoken to Mrs. Standemyre who had spoken to her husband about my "very great talent in writing, composition, and grammar."

The *Port Credit Bulletin* was not a weekly newspaper like the *Streetsville Review* or the *Oakville Weekly Sun*; it was a simple broadsheet that Mr. Standemyre printed single-handedly. I was his first and only employee, though only he was privileged to have that information. His name was the only one to appear on the broadsheet. What I liked about the job, though, was not just the writing and reporting of a story here and there; it was helping Mr.

Standemyre with the actual printing of the paper. Mr. Standemyre would do the typesetting, placing the individual letters in the composing stick as quickly and easily as if he were flicking marbles into a pit, and then placing the full stick of type onto the galley. Then he would tie a string around the type to keep it snugly together before carrying it to the old but reliable wooden screw press and laying it on the stone bed. I would then ink the balls and roll them over the type, while he placed a sheet of paper on the tympan. This way he wouldn't have to worry about getting ink on the clean paper before it was to be pressed. Mother was not pleased the first day that I came home with ink stains on my fingers—"You look like a common labourer!" But my smile was so big she had to smile, too. It was the first time she had smiled since that night. Then Mr. Standemyre would fold the frisket, a frame which kept the sheet of paper properly in place, and the tympan, a second, sturdier frame which kept even pressure across the entire sheet of paper, over the stone and wind it under the platen. Two strong pulls to press frisket and tympan against the platen, unwind the stone, carefully take out the broadsheet, hang it on the line beside the press, and wait for it to dry before proofing it. When Mr. Standemyre first named all these parts of the press as he was explaining the printing process to me, I was as excited by the musical sound of the words as I was by the sounds of the mechanism itself. It seemed to me that this was a most perfect conjunction of language and the process which it described. I was allowed to do the proofing a couple of times, with Mr. Standemyre showing me the various proofing symbols; then he would proof my proof. Now he trusts me to do the proofing, saving him another step and more time. I think we make a good team.

When I was first taught to print and then to do script with an ink pen I understood it as something to be learned, as history and multiplication tables and religion were to be learned. These were simply the things that children did when they went to school. I didn't really think much about the reason for learning these things; I did them simply because I was required to. But then I realized that I could write words down, not because Mr. Donnerton or Miss Jenkins instructed me to do so, but because there were thoughts I had in my head that didn't want to just stay in my head. Nor did they want to be spoken out loud to others. They just wanted some air, some space to breathe. At first I would write these thoughts on spare bits of paper, some of which I would save by folding and putting in my pocket and thence into a drawer, others which I would soon throw into the fire or bury in the ground somewhere in the orchard. And then I decided to keep some in a proper journal and write the rest in my sand journal, so that they were all saved in one way or another.

Especially in the years and months and then days before that night, I believed that writing somehow kept me walking through the landscape of my life without being pushed off the road and into a gully or ravine, where I might twist my ankle or bruise my soul. I believed that I would always be able to make sense of the world if I could first think about it and then write it down if I needed to. But after that night I would try to write my thoughts, and it would seem as if I could not control my own hand, as if some great and dark force were pushing my hand across the page or across the sand because it fed on the sheer movement, but did not want any of the sense. What I once thought would always preserve my sanity was now seemingly trying to keep it out of my reach. It was then that an awful kind of panic seized me — what if I could not let my thoughts out? What if they could not get out and roiled around inside me until they consumed me? And then I wondered if that was what happened to Father. So I decided to seek out the two people who might still be able to understand me.

Just before Miss Jenkins left to go home at Christmas I presented her with my problem and my fear about what to do with my thoughts.

"What is it exactly that you write, Gretchen? What are these thoughts that you feel you must provide an escape for?"

We were walking through the orchard, the snow just wet enough to sound like tired hinges being opened with every step that we took.

"They are just thoughts — I don't know how to describe them."

"Well, are they about people, about things, about you? What is the subject of your thoughts? Can you tell me that?"

The last question was a challenge, a scolding. And yet it was also a comforting hand on my arm.

"They're about all those things."

"Are they about how you see them? What I mean to say is, are you always a part of them? If you picture the thoughts in your head, do you see just the other people and other things, or do you see yourself looking at them?"

I had never considered my thoughts in this way before. As I tried to make the pictures in my head I suddenly realized that there were always pictures, and that I was always in them. It was as if I were looking over my own shoulder to see what I was seeing.

"Yes, I'm always there."

There was a note of hope in my voice, which I could not hide. Perhaps Miss Jenkins would be able to save me after all.

"Could you write about something without making your presence a part of it? Could you write about this orchard, for instance; about the snow and the sky? Write it so that someone else reading it would not know you were present?"

"But I am not writing for anyone else to read — I am just writing for myself."

"I'm not suggesting that you write for someone else; I'm suggesting that you see yourself as a part of the world rather than the world as a part of yourself. There can be landscapes that don't have you separate from them. That doesn't mean that you can't see them or can't understand them."

We walked on in silence for a few minutes as I tried to make sense of what Miss Jenkins was saying. I was thinking that she was too much older than me right at this moment, that she was too wise a woman, and I was too simple a girl. We walked for a few more minutes; and then silence became a space we were comfortable in. Our legs were cloudy, and we drifted effortlessly across the snow, through the rows of apple trees. We were soft, cloudy sticks writing words beyond all script, beyond all colour, beyond all texture or definition, guided by two great invisible hands — hands that could both write at the same time, writing thoughts that were similar and different at the same time. Miss Jenkins and I reached our hands out to each other, and we held onto each other as we kept moving across the snow, through the rows of apple trees. We had been here before; we had never been here before; we had always been here.

We never spoke of what happened in the orchard that day. That day that we were God's breath. All I knew was that I could still write. I could write anything.

"I'm sorry to hear that your father has lost his way."

That's how Baketigweyaa responded to my explanation of Father's condition. I did not tell him all the details of that night, nor did I tell him that the horrible events of that night were precipitated by his midnight visit to me. I could not tell him that, because it would seem as if he should carry a measure of guilt for the consequences, and I in no way wanted to believe that.

"Let me tell you about my father, Kineubenae — Golden Eagle."

We had been walking along the river by the marshes, with no other intention than to move through this world of water and snow and bulrushes and boats and bridges as if all this creation, both of God and of men, was there to stir our thoughts with equal measures of gentleness and purpose.

"It was more than forty years ago, during the war between your country and the Americans, a time when the balance between what was and what might be, caused great confusion in the minds of those who carried too much power on their shoulders. The Americans wanted your land, just as they wanted our land. Just as the Canadians wanted our land. All this trouble to take something that belonged to none of us. The fish were dying, the deer were dying. My people were dying. All of this became a great burden for my father. The people looked to him to use his warrior's medicine, to save them from what he knew they could not be saved."

Baketigweyaa stopped for a moment and looked around him, as if to make sure that he had not transported himself too far out of the present. He squinted his eyes, and then relaxed them. And then he nodded his head as if answering some question that I could not hear. I waited, still and silent, until he started walking again.

"So my father went on a fast to make himself ready to receive the warrior's medicine. When he had finished the fast he gathered his warriors around him and told them that he had received a great gift. It was a protection against any weapon that could be used against him, even against bullets. To prove to his warriors the power of this gift he picked up a tin kettle and then handed a rifle to the warrior he knew could fire it with better aim than any of the others. Then he walked slowly away from the circle of warriors. He stopped and turned back to face the warrior. 'Shoot the rifle at me and I will catch the bullet in this kettle.' My father, Kineubenae, was a great chief, and all the people honoured his medicine. Their trust in him was as great as his medicine. So the warrior raised the rifle to his shoulder and fired at my father. He was a good shot. The bullet passed through the kettle and into my father's forehead. He fell to the ground, dead."

Baketigweyaa stopped again. He turned to look at me.

"The warriors now had to choose whether to believe in the medicine they had never questioned before. But sometimes the power to choose can overwhelm us so that we believe we have no choice at all."

By this time we had left the marshes, crossed the bridge, and were standing by the river bank that would eventually lead to his wigwam.

"I still have that kettle. Sometimes, when I believe that if I stay here long enough," and he swept his arm in a slow arc that took in the river and its reaches, "the white men will go away and leave us alone again, I pick up that kettle and look at the bullet hole in it." He brought his arm back to his side. He looked at me and then away again. "And sometimes when I think I should take down my wigwam and move into the houses, I pick up the kettle again."

Baketigweyaa put his hand on my shoulder and started walking.

"Come. I will make you some tea."

That first day in March that Mr. Standemyre let me ink the type on the press, that first time that I left his small shop with ink stains on my fingers, I felt older and even somehow wiser than I had ever been. I walked down Toronto Street towards the bridge, swinging my arms like wings that might fly me up into the glorious sky. Everything was glorious that day. Then, just by the docks before the bridge I saw him standing there. Patrick. I had not seen him since before Christmas, since that awful night when I had lost the connection to Father. All of a sudden time broke into a hundred little pieces, and I could not put them back together before he spoke to me;

I could not re-order my history so that I might be sensible if I were to open my mouth and try to speak.

"Patrick . . ."

The syllables of his name stumbled out of my mouth, and I hoped that the sound would prove to me that I was actually there, and that the world had not collapsed into confusion around me. I hoped that he would not see me as the jumbled up girl that I was at that moment. But as he spoke I realized that he was as unsteady as I was.

"Hello, Gretchen."

And then a pause during which neither of us knew where to look.

"I've heard about your trouble and I just want to say that we needn't talk about it . . . what I mean is that I just wanted to say hello to you."

"Hello, Patrick. I'm well, thank you . . . I mean . . . you didn't ask me how I was, and so I didn't mean to answer a question you hadn't asked me . . . though that's how most conversations begin, and so I guess I was talking without paying attention, but, yes, you did mention that we needn't talk about it, so . . ."

At this point he tried to save me from making a complete ninny of myself.

"Are those grease stains I see on your hands, girl? Have you become a working woman then?"

"Oh, this . . ." I stammered, "no, it's not grease, it's ink. I'm helping Mr. Standemyre with the *Bulletin*." And then I was afraid I had given myself and Mr. Standemyre away. "I just help with the inking of the type, that's all."

"Let me look at those hands a little closer," and he walked up the last couple of steps from the dock. He took my hands in his and turned them over, rubbing his thumbs against my fingers. "Ink so it is," he said as he carefully lowered my hands back down to my sides. The skin of his hands was leather smooth and hard, and the press of his thumbs was like the weight of years that I had felt inside me these past few months. But it was a comfortable weight — like a ballast.

"And how are you, Patrick?"

I didn't know what else to say, but felt that I had to speak instead of just feel.

"Waiting for the stonehooking to start up again for the season."

Another awkward pause and looking about as if we didn't know where we were.

"Well, I should let you be on your way then. It was good to see you, Gretchen."

"And you, Patrick."

"Perhaps the next time you're out this way to help on the newspaper we could have a hot cider at Cotton's."

"Yes, I'd like that."

We stood there for yet another awkward moment.

"Well, I'll be on my way then. See you next week, Patrick."

"See you, Gretchen."

I walked home, with time now reassembled, but not moving quickly enough between now and next week.

It is odd not to have Gretchen at school with us. I notice how the other children have changed around us since then. First there was the story of Father, and now there is the story of Gretchen. I hear what the others say about her, and Victoria tells me the rest. It is not so bad. Gretchen was getting old enough not to have to go to school any more, and so it is not so bad. For a few hours each day now, I get to be the older sister instead of the middle sister; I think even Victoria feels she has moved up a space, even though she is still the youngest.

At home is different now than it used to be, too. For the first while we all moved around Father as if we were afraid of ourselves and what we might do, instead of being afraid of Father and what he might do. Mother says, though, that there is no reason to be afraid of things we don't know because there are lots of things we don't know and it makes more sense to try to understand than to just be afraid. "What good would it do to be afraid of the weather? We don't know what the weather will be next week."

I suppose now that we're all waiting for what we don't know instead of being afraid of what we don't know, and maybe this is a little easier to do.

Father's eyes don't seem to look at anything in particular any more. When he worked in the orchard he would look very intently at whatever he was doing. Even when he was in the house he would always seem to be staring. He would stare at his food when he ate, the same way that he would stare at the newspaper or the Bible when he was reading, or stare at us children when he talked to us, which was sometimes to ask us how our studies at school were going, but more often to scold us. Now his eyes wander around the room and over us without stopping anywhere except by accident. That's how it seems to me. Maybe his eyes are happier now because they get to do whatever they want.

Friday became the day of the week around which all the other days revolved. Friday was the day I went to work with Mr. Standemyre and then went to Cotton's to have hot cider with Patrick. For the first few Fridays, we met at Cotton's original store near Neeson's Hotel, and then, after the Easter Sunday fire, which consumed the whole block including the general store, we met at Cotton's new store, which was Clarkson's old store on Toronto Street, just past Elizabeth Street on the Canadian side of the river. It was slightly longer than it was wide and appeared even more so because the side walls were lined with shelves, and the main counter was along the right side. In the middle of the floor and towards the back was the stove, with enough room around it for people to gather and warm themselves in the winter months, either standing around the stove or sitting on crates. Cider and tea were served at the end of the long counter by the back of the store. By the time that I arrived to meet Patrick there were usually several people there, some to shop and some just to visit, so that we did not stand out too much from the rest.

Gradually, we were able to speak to each other without the awkward pauses. After the Easter Sunday fire we talked of that, and then we would talk of the weather and the water, of the river and the boats, of how April seemed reluctant to give way to May, of how May gracefully grew into June and the beginnings of summer. What I most wanted to tell him, though, was that I had written the report of the Easter Sunday fire for the *Bulletin*, but I remembered Mr. Standemyre's command and held to our pact. What I could tell him, though, was that since I helped at inking and proofing, Mr. Standemyre was considering expanding the *Bulletin* to four pages; what I couldn't tell him was that part of the reason for the expansion was that I would be contributing to the writing as well. Then I felt that I was talking too much about myself, so I asked Patrick if he was glad to be out on the lake stonehooking again.

"Yes, I am, indeed. There're those weeks between ice cutting and stonehooking where the restlessness gets hold of me and I get too tangled up in my thoughts. I'm much better when I can use my hands for something. So I'm glad to be moving about in a purposeful way again. I've been thinking, though, of working for the railroad. They'll be finishing this section of the line before next winter and they need some extra hands for the final push. The work would be harder, but the pay would be better, as well. I don't know, though. There's something about being out on the water."

"I think I would prefer stonehooking."

"You would, would you? You'd have to trade in your ink stains for blisters and callouses. I prefer your hands just the way they are. They're lady's hands."

"Even with all the ink," I laughed.

"Even with all the ink."

The tone in his voice had shifted into that place where I was made aware of him being a man and me being a girl — maybe even a woman, or a lady. It was the kind of talk in the kind of voice that, if I responded to it in kind, would so easily push us past our simple friendship and into a place I had often wondered about, but was not sure I was ready to go to.

"Do you think there's romance in stonehooking, then? Maybe inking type doesn't fetch your heart and soul as much as you'd like it to."

"Well, I . . ."

"I'm sorry. That was a sideways kind of a question."

"What do you mean by that?"

"I suppose I was trying to hide a question within a question."

"So why don't you just let the question out?"

I could hear my own voice sounding so cocky and brave, while my heart pounded in my chest in fear.

"Well now, you've got me backed into a corner and I'm not sure I know how to get out of it. It might be best to leave me there for a bit. Would you mind?"

"I don't mind. Besides, it's time I was making for home. There's not much sun left in the day."

"I'll walk you to the other side of the bridge, then."

With no more words we walked out into the late afternoon, with the sun still gloriously bright in the sky. Once on the street and walking towards the bridge we seemed unable to carry on with the ease we felt inside the store. I thought how much the world can change by simply moving from inside to outside. When we reached the far side of the bridge Patrick asked me if I was going to walk the road or the shoreline.

"I like the shoreline best."

"I'll walk you down to the shore, then."

"At this rate you'll be walking me all the way home."

"Would that be so bad an idea?"

Now he had me backed into a corner. I thought about arriving at my door and trying to explain Patrick being with me. What would Mother say? Would Father notice? Would Victoria giggle? And what then? It would be almost dark. Would I have to invite him in? Would I have to ask

Mother first? And what then? Would he stay for supper? And what . . .

That is when Patrick put his hand on my shoulder, leaned his face down and kissed me on the lips. I was so unprepared that I instinctively pulled myself back. Patrick, too, took a step back, as if he had been slapped in the face.

"I'm so sorry, Patrick . . . it's just that I didn't know . . . I mean, I wasn't ready . . . "

"Ready?" And with that he turned and walked quickly back to the road and across the bridge, never once looking back to where I stood, watching him until he was out of sight.

Walking back home along the shore I was all in my head and had no idea what my body was doing. I was content to let it take me home on its own. For the first long while I thought about Patrick's kiss. I couldn't even remember it, really. It happened so suddenly, that he could have kissed me on the shoulder for all the effect it now had on me. This was not how I imagined a first kiss would be, and now I wondered if I would get another chance, or if I deserved another chance after how I had reacted. How was I to be ready for such a thing?

I needed to distract myself from this creeping anxiety, so I thought about our conversation in Cotton's and about what Patrick had said about possibly working on the railroad, and that got me to thinking about Baketigweyaa and what he had said about the railroad that night. Why had he come to the shore by our house, and why so late in the night? Did he come especially to see me? How could he have known that I would even see him there or come out to see him, even if I did? All these questions seemed to serve no other purpose than to wear me down and confuse the little sense I tried to make of things.

And so I decided to stop pestering myself as if I were a crow cawing its annoyance at all the smaller birds around it. Just as I made that decision I looked up and saw that I was at Slade's marsh — almost home. As I reached the edge of our property Victoria came running down to meet me, waving her arms and shouting.

"Gretchen! Miss Jenkins called me up to her desk after school today and asked me to say hello to you."

"You make it sound as if this is the first time she's sent greetings since January."

"Yes, but this time she even said she misses you. What do you think about that? Isn't that very special, Gretchen? She misses you. I bet you miss her, too. I miss you at school, but I get to come home and you're here." And then she stopped to take a breath. "And guess what?"

"What?"

"She gave me this to give to you. It's a letter for you from Miss Jenkins. Did you ever get a letter before from anybody?"

"Well, there are the letters we get from Uncle Silas . . ."

"But they're to Mother."

"Yes, but we're all included."

"Still, this letter's for you and no one else. When are you going to read it?"

"After I've gotten into the house and had a chance to warm myself by the stove. Maybe even after I've had supper."

"How can you wait that long? Don't you want to know what's in the letter?"

"Sometimes, Victoria, waiting for something makes it better the longer you wait. The letter's not going to walk off by itself before I read it."

I walked the rest of the way to the house with Victoria running and dancing circles around me, as if I were a moving Maypole.

Finally, after eating supper, clearing the table, and washing the dishes I went up to my room to read Miss Jenkins' letter.

Dear Gretchen,

You have been much on my mind since Christmas. I hope you know that I have not purposefully ignored you these few months. I thought it best that you be able to come to terms with your sorrow and your fears on your own. It is a journey that can only be truly undertaken alone, as hard as that might be to understand or to accept. Since this is such a small village I have been able to hear bits of news about you, as I have tried not to pry into your affairs through your sisters at school, which would be inappropriate in that setting. I am glad for your situation with Mr. Standemyre at the Port Credit Bulletin. I am also to understand that you are doing more than helping to set and ink type. This is good news to me, indeed.

Still, it does feel strange to be in such close physical proximity to you and yet not actually see you and talk with you. I have missed your presence not only in the schoolroom, but in my own life as well. Let us meet some evening or Sunday afternoon, if only to go walking along the lake. As you may know, I am boarding these next two weeks with the Thorpes, but you might find it more comfortable to contact me at the school.

I look forward to your reply, and remain, as ever, your friend,
Cecilia Jenkins

I felt borne through a golden gateway into a marvellous new land — she had signed her letter "Cecilia." Could I dare to call her that name when we met? And when would we meet? Next week would be the end of classes before the summer break. I decided I would go to meet her at the school house on the last day.

She signed her letter "Cecilia."

Gretchen has gone upstairs to her room to read the letter Miss Jenkins sent with Victoria. Miss Jenkins had actually asked me first if I would deliver the letter, but I thought Victoria would enjoy it more if she could be the one to do it.

Since it's Friday evening and supper is done with I can play my fiddle without the bother of homework to do. I like to play in the evening when the sun has gone down and the house is quiet. The house is very quiet these evenings now that Father doesn't move around so much. He never did talk that much, except to say something to Mother about news he had heard from the village, but he would at least walk about in the house, going from the kitchen to the parlour, or upstairs and back down again, as if he was making sure that everything and everybody was in their proper place. But now he mostly sits in the same chair in the parlour and he seems to be content just to have Mother be in the same room with him, but I think he notices the rest of us, too.

About two months ago I decided to play my fiddle in the parlour one evening when Father was sitting in his chair. I wondered if he might like to hear me play, and maybe even like to watch me play, too. I stood over in the corner by the window so I didn't make it seem like I was playing especially for anybody, but just playing. I played a slow air because I thought that matched up best with the mood. Not because it was sad, but just because it was peaceful. I watched Father's reflection in the window to see if he would move in any way when I played, but he didn't. So I didn't know if he liked me playing in the same room or not. I decided that since he didn't move that at least he didn't not like me to play. So I kept playing for awhile. And now I play every Friday evening in the parlour.

Sometimes he looks slowly around the room, as if he is trying to see the notes of the music in the air. Maybe he can actually see them floating around the parlour like friendly spirits. That would make me happy if he could do that. I think it would make Mother happy, too. She is not so sad as she used to be, but she is not as happy as she used to be, either.

Tonight I will play a slow jig and see if Father's eyes dance a little bit when they try to follow the notes through the air. Maybe he could think of them as apples in the trees on a sunny, windy day in summer.

As I reached the mouth of the river the sun was gleaming off the surface of the lake, and every patch of green bud and leaf was sparkled into life. The tall, thin masts of the stonehookers stood in erect dignity, leaning stiffly back and forth, as if nodding to each other in wordless conversation. They were the only truly vertical lines in the otherwise softly flat landscape, rendered, in that particular spot, even flatter by the still surprising absence of buildings along Front Street. The blackened ruin left by the fire was gradually disappearing, like a scar that heals only with time. Once past the burnout I could get back to the banks of the river and begin following the well worn footpath.

It occurred to me how much I liked to walk next to water, and how many different kinds of water I have been blessed to be near — the lake, the creek, the marsh, and the river. Each has its own personality, and within each personality are all the various glories and oddities that make up that personality — stony stretches, grassy patches, sandy strips, trees leaning over into the water to see themselves, flowers like polka dots. The riverbank was the one I had travelled the least. Only a few times I have walked it as far as the Middle Road bridge, and only twice past that to Baketigweyaa's wigwam, which is past the rapids and just beyond the island where the river makes a sharp left turn before making its way in loops and curves up to Dundas Street. As I was leaving the village behind me I came immediately to the new railway trestle, over which the first train is to pass sometime this winter. I walked under it like some great span that connects worlds that I may never know, on either side of it, and then I was once again in the openness of river and field, and I, too, was opened up.

The smells of thawed earth and cold river water mixed together to make a strong aroma of hope out of hesitation;

all winter long we had waited for this return. And I, especially, had awaited it. I let all of my past trail behind me, like the ripple of my dress in the breeze. Something I did not want to let go of altogether, but something that I could put on and off as I needed to.

I heard the rapids before I could see them; I stopped and listened. I tried to imagine myself walking along this river bank for the first time, as a human who had never seen a river before, who had never seen rapids before. How would I have understood this sound? Would I have thought it was the wind? Or rain falling? And then I would have wondered how the sun could have shone and the rain could have fallen at the same time, how I could have seen and felt the one, but only have heard the other. Would the mystery of the sound have frightened me or filled me with reverence for that which I could not understand? There I stood with the new grass reaching for my knees, the sun warm on my back, and the sound of unknown river gods in my ears.

By the time I saw the small huddle of wigwams I felt I was ready to be with Baketigweyaa in spirit and in body. Two dogs chased each other in and out of the water, focused on nothing but themselves. If I was a stranger to them and to their territory they did not seem to be at all concerned. There were no children there, only a few elders who seemed to have escaped time and age; to me, they seemed to have always been elders, even though I did not know them and did not have any history with them.

His voice found me before I found him.

"Ah, my young friend, *aniish na?*"

He was seated on the ground a few feet from the river bank, his legs folded in front of him and his arms resting on his legs. He had a blanket around his shoulders.

"I'm fine, Baketigweyaa. I've missed you."

He motioned with his head for me to sit beside him. I tried to sit as he was sitting, but my dress and my legs wouldn't allow me to do it comfortably, so I leaned one hand on the ground, folded my legs underneath me, and sank myself down beside him.

"Tell me how you have been. Do you still enjoy skipping stones on the water?" He didn't wait for my answer, since we both knew what it would be.

"We don't have the right kind of stones here for skipping," he said, and shifted his head and his eyes, measuring the banks of the river, pointing out to me what he meant by "here."

The sound of the rapids came in and out of my awareness. They sounded different here than they did when I approached them from the other side. From here they were leaving; from where I stood to listen before, they were on their way to me. In the same way I seemed to drift in and out of awareness of where exactly I was. For a few moments I would be clearly present with Baketigweyaa, and then I would drift off to a place where everything and everyone around me seemed to fall away, like clothes falling to the floor.

"Can you hear the singing?"

"You mean the rapids?"

"No. Underneath that sound there is another sound. If you listen carefully, you can hear the singing. It comes from the deep pool between the fast water and the mouth of the river. It is the spirit Munedoo; a friend of the

Mississauga. My people say that he left there many years ago, but I can still hear him. Lately, I have even heard the beating of his drum. Only I can hear it; that is why I know it is a sign."

"Why did he leave the river?"

"He does not like your people. They took too many fish from the river; they did not need all those fish. Munedoo was angry. So he made the river greater than the banks, until nothing could hold it in. It rushed in a great wave to the lake. I think he wanted to drown all the white people, but it did not work. They are still there, and Munedoo has gone. That is the story."

I liked it when Baketigweyaa told me the stories of his people.

"You said that because you can still hear Munedoo that is a sign. A sign of what?"

"I will be passing on before the days begin to grow shorter again."

His left hand rose noiselessly from under the blanket and pushed his hair back from his cheek, and then it went back under the blanket, as if performing an action that had nothing to do with him and the rest of his body. I was trying to understand what he meant by "passing on." I wanted to ask him where he was going, but I didn't want to sound stupid. I thought it best to let him explain if he wanted to; if he didn't, then I would just have to figure it out on my own. But I couldn't help it; my voice spoke before I could stop it.

"Are you going to the Land of Souls?"

"Yes."

"But not in a dream?"

"No."

"So you're not taking your body with you?"

"No."

And then silence fell between us like the mist that night time leaves hanging over a river in the morning. There was the sun, and there was the river, and there was the mist between them as if to say that the light and the water should not come into contact with each other yet.

"There is something I want to give you."

His arms came up like spreading wings, and his blanket fell away from him. From a leather bag that hung around his shoulder he took out a small, flat stone that was just smaller than the size of his hand. Placing it in the palm of his right hand he bounced it a couple of times, as if testing it. "I think this is a good skipping stone." Then he reached out his hand for me to take the stone. It was warm from the heat of his hand and from being in the bag next to his body.

"Thank you."

The words felt so thin and poor, but I could not think of what else to say. I was filled with wonder and joy and sadness and confusion. Tears began to roll down my cheeks. Baketigweyaa put his hand on my shoulder and smiled at me.

"You will know when to skip it on the water."

We spent the rest of our time together in silence, sometimes looking up at the sun, sometimes looking at the river, sometimes looking at each other. By the time I rose to leave, the sun was almost at its highest point in the sky, a fierce button of yellow-white light in an azure boundlessness. I walked a few steps away from the camp, then turned and looked back at Baketigweyaa. His eyes were on me; he nodded his head slightly as if to say, "You'll be fine," and then he turned his gaze back to the river.

From that day on, I carried the stone in my pocket everywhere I went.

Going back, the river flowed with me until we both emptied into the lake. I turned towards home and put the sun in my face until I got to Slade's marsh. Finally, the hollow sounding stones of the shingle bar were making their muffled clinking beneath my feet, and I brought myself to a halt there with water on both sides of me — the lake on my left and the marsh on my right. The one calmly but persistently shushing up on the shingle, the other lying in perfect stillness. And my life in the balance between the two. I ducked through an opening in the poplars and chokecherry and climbing bittersweet, followed the sweep of bulrushes around the marsh to where the creek entered, then followed the creek bank until I found my spot. In the sand I wrote: *time, one world and another world, stones, hands, hearts.*

~

Sleep did not come easily that night. A dull echo of light seeped through my window and haunted the wall opposite my bed. If I stared at it long enough I could make it disappear and appear again; if I kept doing this long enough I would fall asleep. Instead, in that soft-edged frame I saw silhouettes — Patrick leaning over to kiss me; Baketigweyaa looking at us and nodding his head as if in recognition. Of what?

I wondered if Patrick would see me next Friday at Cotton's, after my awkward reaction to his kiss. Baketigweyaa said he would never see me again. I wanted to think about only one of these things, but they insisted on being tangled up with each other and tangling me up along with them. Why not just give myself up to my sleeplessness, get up, and go outside to stand by the water. But I could not risk it; I could not leave the house in the night for fear of what might happen to Father. I could not bear the responsibility. Pacing my room would have to do for now.

Standing by the window I erased the frame of light on the wall. The night was ragged with clouds, and there was either no moon or it was behind the house trying to get free. Beyond my window the landscape was a study in shades and shadows. Lake, horizon, shoreline, trees were all distinguished from one another only by tone, not by colour. What was it The Red had said—"You are haunted by colours. Colours will always trap you." The blue, the grey, and the red. The blue and the grey were in the stone — red, the blood, was somewhere else. What I was standing in the midst of here in my midnight room was beyond all colour; beyond even all time. This was a shadow of another world, in which I was being kept awake so that I might be shown the silhouettes that inhabited these shadows, so that I might understand what was at work on the edges of my life. Whatever was happening, I could not control it. It might be my life, but I was only a witness.

When I finally fell asleep I had the dream about the kite again. But this time the colour had been bled out of everything; this time I was drifting high above the lake and the marsh and the creek and the river, and I was attached to nothing that I could see. Instead of a string trailing from me there was a narrow band of light reaching down to the water — not to the ground, but to the water, and there were small, ghost-like boats bouncing on the surface of the lake and marsh and creek and river, like buttons, from which wispy threads were escaping into the air. These threads were the only things holding the button-boats to the water — they were like the light trailing from my kiteself. I was falling towards the water; the button-boats were floating up from the surface. We passed each other in such wonderful, slow motion, but the closer I got to the water, the farther away or deeper it got. It was a watery shadow of the sky from which I had come. I wished the others could have been there to sense all this with me. The others — I couldn't remember exactly who they were; I tried hard to remember, but I could not focus my energy into such a narrow concern. And then I remembered myself awake.

To see Father working out in the orchard you would never suspect that he was any different a man than he had always been. When he was with the trees he was somehow whole; when he stepped out of the orchard and into the house he stepped out of that capable and confident man into a man who did not seem to understand or to care that there was a world around him to which he belonged. Perhaps there were gods or spirits in the trees after all.

Mother seemed relieved that Father would still be able to provide for us, but I wondered if she, as his wife, felt provided for. What must it be like to be married to a man for so many years and then to have him leave you, even though he was still there? Mother had hardly left the property since Christmas, and hardly anyone had come to visit because no one was quite sure how to deal with

Father. I know she has sorely missed the company of friends.

"When your father is in the orchard he forgets that the rest of us are here — but that's a good thing. He needs to forget some things and to remember others. He remembers the apples."

We were both standing on the back porch, looking out at the apple trees, each of us trying to reel our own memories into the present.

"Your father has a story locked up inside him."

Mother turned to face me, but her eyes were aimed somewhere into the ground. "No, not this one . . . it's a story from before we met."

Then she looked up at me.

"I was not his first love."

She moved towards the end of the porch and leaned against the railing.

"He never spoke to me about . . . about her, and it was only through vague references that his mother made in unguarded moments that I was able to learn about that part of his life. All I know is that the attachment they had for one another ended badly."

She turned and walked back into the kitchen, and as she did so she seemed to leave the weight of her words on the porch behind her.

"Will you be around today, Gretchen? I'd like to visit Mrs. Lamer. I think your father won't miss me if I'm gone for a short spell during the day, but I'd like to know that you're here, just in case."

"Of course, I'll be here. I think it's a good idea for you to go out for a bit. Go out and have a visit, and don't worry about anything. I'll be here."

"Well, I've been thinking about Mrs. Lamer for a while now. Sally and the young Lamer boy have become such good friends, and it would be good for his mother and I to know one another better, too."

Mother left and I posted myself as temporary guardian of Father and the house. Although my promise was made to Mother without hesitation or trepidation, now that she had left I felt the weight of responsibility settle on my shoulders, like a dark and heavy blanket. I looked about me, but nothing had changed. The trees, the house, the rosebushes, the lake — none of these had taken on different colours or strange shapes. None of them noticed that Father was in the orchard, that I was on the porch, and that Mother was gone. But I sensed that there was an unseen shift that had taken place inside all these things, and especially inside me. Suddenly, any decision as to what to do — whether to stay standing on the porch, whether to walk around the yard, whether to go and help Father, or go into the house to write in my journal — had taken on grand consequences. This must have been what it was like to be Mother.

The world Mother saw was not the same one I saw. And what was the world that Father saw? I sat down right where I was on the edge of the porch, as if I had just had a conversion experience. How could I have not understood this before? I had always known that we were all individuals because we looked different from one another, we spoke differently, we had different fears and passions, but I had never understood how we were all looking at the same world and yet seeing very different worlds all at the same time.

I got up and walked slowly around the house and towards the lake. When Mother looked at this lake, what did she see? I spent some time with that. And then, when Father looked at this lake what did he see? And Sally, Victoria, Miss Jenkins, Patrick, Baketigweyaa — what did they see? I felt as if I had exploded into a hundred pieces, and yet each piece had all of me in it. For the rest of the day I walked around our property studying budding apples, blades of grass, rose thorns, swatches of clouds, and strands of my own hair; travelling in and out of world after world, without my feet ever leaving the ground.

∽

"Gretchen, if Sally ever decided to talk one day, what do you think she would say?"

"Well, Victoria, I'm not sure. What do you think she would say?"

"I think she would say she loves Tommy Lamer."

I was pushing Victoria on the swing we had hung from a branch of the maple tree. As I pushed her on her way up she would point her feet together into the air and lean her body as far back as her arms would let her go, and her head as far back as her neck would bend. She would speak to me on the arc she made coming back to me, where I would reach my hands up just as she stopped moving at the height of her swing and push her back again.

"Oh, and just why do you think she loves Tommy Lamer?"

"Because they look at each other all the time at recess, and even sometimes when Miss Jenkins turns her head away from us in the schoolroom they look at each other. That's all they ever do."

"Maybe they're just very good friends; maybe they understand each other in ways that the rest of us don't."

"I have lots of friends at school and we don't stare at each other all the time. So now everybody in this family is in love with boys except for me. But that's all right because I don't want to be."

"I'm not in love with anybody. And you don't have to be — you're much too young for that, anyway."

"You're in love with Patrick."

"I am not. I never said that — and don't you say it to anybody else, either."

"Gretchen and Patrick, Gretchen and Patrick," she sang out as I pushed her.

As soon as she came back down I grabbed onto the swing and stopped her dead. She jumped off the swing and backed a step or two away from me, with her head hanging down and her hands behind her back. She spoke to the ground, "I'm sorry, Gretchen. Did I make you mad?"

"No, I'm not mad," though I was a little bit. I felt sillier than she did for what had just happened. "I just don't have a boyfriend, that's all. I'm not in love with anybody."

"Well, is it all right for me to say that Sally loves Tommy Lamer?"

"I don't think that's a good idea, Victoria. You know how some of the kids tease her already. And I think Tommy gets his fair share of it, too, for his own reasons. You should just be pleased that Sally has such a good friend."

"He's adopted, you know."

I had heard the stories, too.

"Oh, and how do you know that?"

"Everybody knows that. His real mother was a Scotch lady and his real father was an Indian!"

We walked out to a sunny spot on the grass and sat down, picking at blades of grass. When she wasn't talking, Victoria was trying to blow through a blade of grass held between her two thumbs to make it whistle.

The story went like this. A young man came over from Scotland with his two young children and a governess to live in Erindale, north up the river from Port Credit. One day when they were picnicking by the river, near where the island and the rapids are, the governess was separated from the children and was captured by a young Indian. He kept her in a cave hidden in a high bank on the east side of the river for six months. No one knew where she was or what had happened to her. It was said that during that time the Indian loved the woman very much and had a medicine man marry them in the Indian way. Then, after six months there was a great storm which blew away the covering of the cave, and it was discovered by two villagers as they were rowing up the river. There they found the young woman and rescued her. Shortly after her rescue she gave birth to a baby boy, which she gave up for adoption, and immediately went to a convent where she still is. Tommy Lamer is supposed to be that boy. And that is why some of the ruder boys often taunt him by calling him Chief Tommyhawk and squawboy.

"You know, Victoria, you can't believe all the stories you hear."

"I know, but I like that story. I would like for Tommy Lamer to have a real Indian father. It would make him interesting."

"Can't he be interesting without being an Indian? Why can't he be interesting while being just like the rest of us, just like you and me?"

"I suppose he could. Do you think Sally likes him because he might be an Indian?"

"I think Sally doesn't pay attention to those kinds of things."

And then Victoria finally managed to make a grass blade whistle, and her thoughts were off in a new direction.

"I'm going to show Mother what I can do," she said as she jumped up and started running towards the house, with the blade of grass still between her thumbs.

I wondered if Baketigweyaa knew the story of the Indian and the Scotch governess. I wished that I had asked him. It was one of those questions that I had always thought to ask him one day, and now there were to be no more days.

Summer solstice was next week.

Chapter 2

THE APPLE BLOSSOMS HAD TURNED into small, hard, green eggs, ready to hatch all along the branches of the trees. There were hundreds and hundreds of them on each tree, so it promised to be a good crop this year. Perhaps that would lift Father's spirits. He was done his spring pruning, and the trees had flattened out, their branches pointing to each other instead of up to the sky. When Father walked from tree to tree and reached out his arm to check a branch here and there he was like one of those trees. No more pointing to heaven, but to what was closest to him here on earth. Then he saw me standing in the aisle among the trees and briefly pointed his arm towards me. Was he reaching for me? Could it be that he acknowledged me, there in the orchard where he felt so safe? But just as quickly his arm fell to his side, and he turned back to the row of trees, walking away from me and deeper into the orchard. What did he see when he looked at me?

From the other end of orchard I saw Mother step off the porch and begin to walk towards me. She was drying her hands on her apron, looking up at the sky, looking off to the barn, and then looking particularly at me.

"He seems so peaceful out here, as if the world has started all over with the new season of blossoms. Sometimes I try to feel the world like that, too."

She came up beside me and put her arm around my waist. I was a full head taller than her, and I almost felt as if I were the mother and she the daughter, sighing her resignation into my shoulder.

"It is a peaceful world sometimes, Mother."

That's all I could say. There was no use in letting words carry us any further into that place from which we could not escape, anyway. When you are standing in the pouring rain, rain so heavy that it becomes the physical weight of life, there is no need to remark that you are getting wet. Rain can be as peaceful as sunlight if you do not try to wish it away.

"Are you enjoying your work with Mr. Standemyre?"

"Yes, Mother, I am. It is a useful trade he is teaching me; one that will always serve me well."

"Do you not wish to be doing something more . . . I don't know . . . "

"Ladylike?"

"Well, if you want to put it that way, I suppose, yes."

"Mother, look at me. I am as tall as any man about. Why shouldn't I do man's work? It's not as if I am blistering my hands or risking my bones. Mr. Standemyre says I do good work, and I think I do good work. And I like it."

"I know you do, Gretchen. I know you do."

With that she let her arm slide off my body, took another look at the sky and at the orchard and barn and lake, and walked back to the house in the same attitude that she came out.

Did I truly like my work? Was I not in some ways afraid of being unladylike? Was I not risking creating a contrary reputation for myself that might once and for all define who I was in the eyes of not only the village people but in the eyes of those who forever after came to make my acquaintance? Would I become the talk of the village in the same way that Tommy Lamer was?

If I walked straight ahead I would be deep in the orchard; if I turned and walked towards the lake I would eventually find my feet swishing in the shallow water of the shore; if I turned farther around and walked back towards the house I would step up onto the porch and pass through into the kitchen and be in that space that, more than any other, had been so familiar to me since I was a child. If I stood there and never moved again, would I grow roots and branches and leaves? Would my family come out to water me every day and tend to my health? Would a robin come and build a nest in my hair, trusting that she was safer there than in any other tree?

Sometimes my thoughts are so clear they are like stars with bells in them, and I'm sure everyone can see them and hear them, even though I don't speak them. Other times I just feel like plain old Sally; not very special, but good enough to not be noticed as causing an unwelcome stir. I sometimes wonder how people can make such a fuss over me, when I am trying my best to not put myself in their way. I try to be like a tree or a rosebush or a simple wildflower in a field full of wildflowers, and yet some people will worry that I am not happy enough or paid attention to enough. That is why I like Tommy; he sees me like a wildflower.

Maybe I remind people of something they forgot to do and wish they had done but can't do for some reason. It hardly makes sense to me when I do try to make sense of it — at least when I try to think of it while I'm being plain old Sally. When I'm bright and ringing I don't notice that people are noticing me. Maybe I am two people and everybody else is two people, too. Maybe they, too, have their star and bell moments. I hope so.

Next month is my twelfth birthday, and I am thinking that I should begin to feel older. I'm not sure exactly what I will do to be older. Maybe if I watch Gretchen more closely I will get a better sense of what to do; or if I try to make myself even older than Victoria, more different than she is. Being stuck between the two of them puts me in the middle where I can't get out — not that it's their fault. And probably no one really notices it except for me. But I don't want to be in the middle any more, and since I can't make myself younger again, like Victoria, then I must simply be older, like Gretchen. Maybe I'll wait until I'm fifteen.

I had not been to the schoolhouse since before Christmas, and seeing it again after so much time had gone by and after so much life had been lived caught my breath and held it until finally, I let it out, almost in a sob. I was surprised at myself for how I was reacting. But then I was brought back to the present by the sound of children running from the schoolhouse, glad for the school year to be over — for this was the last day before summer break. I felt the slight breeze through the long, hanging branches of the weeping willow, and the sun warm on my cheek.

When it looked as if the last student had come out of the open door of the schoolhouse I walked in, and was seized by a momentary pang of nostalgia as I saw all the empty student desks, and Miss Jenkins standing behind her desk gathering some books and papers together.

"Gretchen! How lovely to see you."

She moved quickly from behind her desk and walked with great anticipation towards me, her legs swishing against the inside of her dress. She put her hands on my shoulders, kissed me on the cheek, and then decided to just give me a big hug. I could barely keep from crying.

"Victoria told me you would be coming this afternoon. Let's go out in the sun and sit on the bench — I could use the sitting down and the sun on my face."

Miss Jenkins kept the conversation going by herself, sensing that I needed to be eased into this new way of being with her. She talked of the sadness and excitement of the school year coming to an end, of how "delicious" it was to have a Wednesday be the end of the week and of the year, and then she mused about the state of the orchards and the hopes of a good harvest.

"I brought a picnic supper — I do hope you can celebrate with me. I thought that we could walk along the lake to the marsh — I'm sure you know some good spots for picnicking. And I've brought along a bit of a surprise."

I accepted her invitation, and, since we would be walking past our house on the way to the marsh, I could tell Mother of my plans with Miss Jenkins. I knew she wouldn't mind.

The sun was still high overhead when we reached the marsh. All life was in full bloom, and the normally muted colours of green, grey, and brown were ornamented here and there with waxy tufts of red clover, spikes of goldenrod, curled petals of wild blue flag; and near the edges of the marsh patches of purple duckweed, and the great whole of the landscape sharpened with the bright sunlight. I led the way around the marsh to the slope of Garter Snake Hill and then took the winding path up to the top, from where we could see the entire expanse of the marsh basin to our right, and the vastness of the lake ahead of us. We sat in the mottled shade of birch and oak, and Miss Jenkins began to unpack the picnic basket she had brought with her.

"I feel as if I could float off the top of this hill and look down upon God's creation and say, 'What a fine world it is.' Is it a fine world for you these days, Gretchen?" she asked me as she began to cut some slices from the loaf of bread and from the block of cheese. There was also a cucumber, a wonderfully huge red tomato, and two boiled eggs.

"I can't say for sure. There are mornings when I awake, and they are the same as the mornings I awoke when I was a child, and the world seemed so full of possibilities for joy, but I do have times when to walk out of my room to begin the day is to walk a gauntlet." I looked down at my hands in sudden embarrassment. "That sounds very dramatic, doesn't it."

"Life must be dramatic if it is to be lived properly." She handed me a small china plate with bread and cheese and slices of tomato and cucumber on it. "The dramatic parts are not usually the most enjoyable, as well you know, but they are necessary parts. Some of us girls are made to be women before our time; does it seem like that to you?"

"Yes, yes — that's exactly it." I had just taken a bite of bread and cheese, and almost spit them across the space between us as I blurted out my response. Once I composed myself, I asked her, "Do you mean to say, Miss Jenkins, that this kind of thing has happened to you?"

"Not in the same manner as it happened to you, but . . . yes. Let us save that story for after our meal. I'm sure we have many other stories to share. That is why," she said as she leaned over to the picnic basket, "I brought this along." She held out a small jar filled with a dark red liquid. "It's a 'spot of wine,' as Mrs. Thorpe would call it. Mr. Thorpe is quite liberal with his cider and wine and sees 'no harm in medicinal amounts every now and then to keep the vapours from invading these mortal shells of ours.' And so I have managed to bring just enough for a mouthful or two each." She must have noticed my look of astonishment, which I was not able to disguise, for she said, "Oh dear, Gretchen, I hope you are not offended, and I do hope you don't think me a debauchee, for, if truth be told, until my stay with the Thorpes I have only been known to have a glass of sherry at Christmas, and that poured very cautiously by my father. I just felt that today would be a very special day — I'm not even sure in what particular way." These last few words were spoken more as a pleading for approval than as a simple statement.

I couldn't say that I was uncomfortable, but I was truly surprised — mostly in a good way. I had never suspected this kind of behaviour of Miss Jenkins, but it was because I still could not see her being quite as human as the rest of us. To me she was first a teacher, a mature woman who . . . what? Who didn't eat food like the rest of us? Who didn't feel pain or joy like the rest of us? Even when she stayed with us during that horrible time before Christmas, I could see another side of her besides her teacher side, but what I saw was still a superior kind of human being who was above the petty circumstances of life, such as I and my family experienced them. Now, here she was offering me a chance to see her, and even know her, as a woman like any other woman. Like me.

My only response, then, was a smile that kept widening until I thought there would be no more room on my face for it.

"I'll take that as a sign that you are not disappointed in me," replied Miss Jenkins. She emptied the wine into two tiny glasses, and handed one to me, clinking it with hers and making a toast. "To Gretchen and Cecilia and this wonderful day."

And then I took the very first sip of wine in my life. The dark red colour did not suggest the bitter taste of it, and yet it was a pleasant, a stimulating kind of bitterness. A grown-up kind of bitterness. This, I thought, is what Eve must have felt like when she first bit into the apple; a sudden understanding — a knowing for the first time that life was not perfect, but that it was now hers to live. The joy and the pain would be hers by choice, and that would make all the difference.

For the next long while we just leaned against the trees and looked out over the lake, as satisfied with it all as if we ourselves had created it. I gloried in the presence of

Miss Jenkins — Cecilia, my teacher, my friend. My woman friend. Cecilia . . .

"Yes?"

"I'm sorry . . . " Her voice had shaken me from my reverie and I was afraid she had been speaking to me and I had not been aware of what she was saying.

"You spoke my name."

"Oh . . . I'm so sorry, I didn't realize I was talking out loud. I was just daydreaming and I didn't mean to . . . I'm sorry, Miss Jenkins."

"Please, Gretchen. You are no longer my student; I am no longer your teacher. I would very much appreciate it if you would call me by my first name. So please do."

"Thank you . . . Cecilia." What a beautiful sounding name.

"You're the first person in Merigold's Point to call me Cecilia; it sounds so refreshing. I feel as if I am me again. There is a certain distance put between the world and me when I am only Miss Jenkins; it's a distance I don't know that I will ever get used to." She slid away from the tree and lay on her side, leaning on her elbow. "I remember the first time I was addressed as Miss Jenkins by my first student. It was such a shock. I realized right then that I was no longer a girl — it had not occurred to me until that moment; and I'm not sure that I liked that sudden transition. It was unexpected — I was unprepared for it. I felt a sadness well up in me that I didn't know I would ever be able to overcome. Until you called me Cecilia just now I thought I had grown used to that formality, that distance. But I haven't. I don't know that I want to."

"You must have friends back home who call you by your first name."

"Yes, a few."

"Do you ever wish you didn't have to leave? Why did you go so far away?"

"I suppose it is time for a story." She shifted back up into a sitting position.

"I grew up in the Eastern Townships of Quebec — a small English speaking village surrounded by French speaking ones. My father was quite insistent about being of good Loyalist stock—'If I could hold my ground against the revolutionaries who wanted my forced allegiance I can damned well hold my English language against those who want me to trade it in for French.' I did, though, manage to surreptitiously learn French from some of my friends, though I had always to be on her guard at home to not let a French word slip into my conversation.

"My mother died when I was twelve, after which time my father became even more stern in the disciplining of me, his only daughter. It was his decision that I become a teacher, though I did not fight it overmuch because the vocation did appeal to me. It was also his decision, however, that I one day wed Timothy Stanton, the son of my father's business partner. Now that was a vocation that did not appeal to me. Not because I didn't ever want to get married, but because I didn't want to marry Timothy Stanton.

"And then, a few months before finishing my studies, I met Gilles Tournier. He could speak French like a Frenchman, and English like an Englishman. And he was so very handsome that it took three or four meetings with him before I could speak to him without blushing. Since we always had to meet secretly, and after dark, I don't think he ever noticed. Of course, there was no way that I could admit my attraction for Gilles to my father, and I could see no easy or proper way out of my predicament. So I heard about the teaching position at Merigold's Point and decided that the best thing to do was to come here — I would have employment, which would please my father, and I would have some time to myself, which he could tolerate. Timothy, too, could tolerate it. But not Gilles, and that I knew.

"The night before I was to leave, Gilles came to my house and threw stones at my window until I came down to see him. A strong wind was blowing, and I could tell there was a storm not far behind it. Every circumstance seemed to be pushing me into a smaller and smaller space from which I could not escape. I remember trying hard to hear Gilles' words above the wind, washing like great waves through the branches. Every few seconds a shush of branches would heave against my back and bend itself over my shoulder. Gilles grabbed my shoulders and shouted that he would not let me go. That's what he said: 'I will not let you go, Cecilia!' I was both frightened and angry, so I shouted back at him, 'You cannot stop me!' And then I felt a sharp sting on my face. It took me a second or two to realize that he had slapped me. And then he was gone."

Cecilia's silence at this point in her story was as sudden as the slap, and almost as disconcerting. She did not move, and I was afraid to break whatever spell it was she had cast upon the hill where we sat. Then, after many minutes, she reached across to the food by the picnic basket, picked up one of the boiled eggs and began to peel it.

"What happened when you went back for Christmas?" I asked.

"Gilles was nowhere to be found, and since neither my father nor Timothy knew anything about him, our Christmas was as stiffly normal as it had always been. I gave away nothing. I passed my time there waiting until I could return to Merigold's Point."

"And must you go back to your home now?"

"Right now, I must eat this egg."

And she laughed into the back of her hand, but her eyes did not laugh with the rest of her.

"Tell me about your love life, Gretchen. Victoria tells me you've met a boy from Port Credit."

"Victoria tells too many tales; but that is what makes her Victoria, I suppose."

"I didn't mean to betray her confidence . . . I didn't think you'd mind. And besides, a woman needs her share of gossip every now and then," she said with a sly smile.

"His name is Patrick Monaghan, and he tried to kiss me, but I made a botch of it. It was so sudden . . . I wasn't expecting it. But now I'm not sure if I would have kissed him back, even if I hadn't been so clumsy."

"Do you like him?"

"Now you *do* sound like Victoria." Words were now organizing themselves and making their way out of my mouth without me seeming to be a part of the process. "He is the first boy to ever pay me attention." I pulled myself up on my elbows and planted my chin in my hands. "I think I liked the attention."

"And?"

"Well, I think I liked the attention, as I said, but when he tried to kiss me, I all of a sudden felt that he wanted something from me, and even though I didn't know what it was, I felt that I couldn't or didn't want to give it to him. I felt I needed to protect myself. I know that that makes no sense, but I can find no other way to express it."

We ate in silence for a minute or so, digesting both our food and our thoughts.

"Sometimes, Gretchen, we want things and sometimes we need things."

"What is the difference?"

"You can live without the things you want. You can't live without the things you need."

"How do we know the difference?"

"We don't, always."

"Does it have to do with love?"

"It complicates love."

Then we put aside our words for a while, me leaning against the tree, and Cecilia on her side, propped up on one elbow.

"I suppose you'll be leaving soon, Cecilia?"

"Yes, I'm leaving on Sunday. I'll go back to be with my father for the summer. And then I'll return to Merigold's Point in September."

"Will Merigold's Point ever feel like home to you?"

"I don't know, Gretchen. I feel I am in between homes. So much of me has left Sherbrooke, and not enough of me has settled here. Sometimes I feel like a child's balloon, buffeted about by the wind, having no control over where I will land."

"Will you always be my friend?"

"Yes, I will, Gretchen."

"I'll miss you, Cecilia."

"And I you."

It was Friday, the day I would usually see Patrick after work. As I walked the shore of the lake to Port Credit my mind was awash with the debris of thoughts I had tried to toss away, but which kept returning, wave after wave. They were the thoughts of the people in my life, all of them — all of us — flailing about in a turbulence of emotions which we could neither control nor succumb to. I wondered what it was that Patrick had been thinking about since I saw him last; I wondered if he would want to see me or to speak to me again, or if he was dreading the possibility. Would he come at all? What would I do if he didn't come? Would I feel abandoned? Thrown over? Relieved?

I found a patch of sand within sight of the river mouth; I picked up a stick. I wrote: *Patrick, Baketigweyaa, Father, Mother, Cecilia, Gretchen* — all in a rough kind of circle so that each name could see every other name. Outside the circle I drew a heart. In the one place where no one was looking.

"Seems every second boat that puts into the harbour's carrying steel rails these days," mused Mr. Standemyre as I walked to the back of the room where he was already filling his stick with type. He spoke as much to the rows and boxes of type as he did to me. How he could manage to keep track of his metal sentences and his spoken sentences at the same time always amazed me, for he worked and spoke this way more often than not.

"I swear there are more men working on that railroad than there are actually living here and round about.

D'you know by the end of the year you'll be able to go all the way from Toronto to Windsor — two hundred miles and more — riding in the comfort of one of those train cars? That's a trip I'd like to make." He emptied the stick into the tray. "What about you, Gretchen? Think you'd like to go travelling down that line?"

"I don't know anybody at the other end, but I suppose it would be a fine thing to see all the country between here and there."

"Sure — you could just turn around and come back once you got there. No rule that says you have to stay at one end before you come back again. Course, I'm wondering what will happen to all those workers once the line is finished. I suppose they'll just keep following the tracks wherever the railroad bosses want them laid down. That's one way to see the country. Not the way I'd choose, though. Anyway, there's even going to be a station at Clarkson's Corners. Why, you might even be able to take the train to work by this time next year."

I couldn't imagine taking such a grand form of transportation just to get to the next village, which I could just as easily walk to, even if it did take me longer. To get on a train would be to make a great decision about your life, about leaving one part of it to find another part of it, though you had no idea exactly what that part might look like. If I did take the train to Windsor I would not simply turn around and come back, as Mr. Standemyre suggested. It would seem to me that the farther you travelled, the longer you must stay away. There must be some proportion of space to time. One day, if there were tracks all the way from here to New Brunswick, I could visit Uncle Silas, and maybe even all our distant relatives in

Concord, Massachusetts. I have often spoken that name out loud — Massachusetts — it is such a lovely and mysterious sounding word. I wonder if the land and the people there are also lovely and mysterious.

By just after noon we had the latest edition of *The Bulletin* printed and hung on the lines to dry.

"I guess that about wraps it up for today, Gretchen. Once the plates and type are clean you can mosey along."

I finished the cleaning in a little less than an hour — earlier than usual for a Friday. And then I began to think about Patrick. I had about an hour before the time we usually met at Cotton's General Store. An hour to wonder what my life would be like after my meeting with Patrick — if, indeed, he decided to come. I thought that it would be so much easier if he did not come; then my decision about him would be made for me. If he did come, I would have to make some sort of decision on my own, and as I stepped out onto the street to feel the sun full in my face, what troubled me was that I could not think of what to do. To kiss Patrick, or even to suggest by my behaviour that I would be willing for him to try to kiss me again, would change my whole life. Did I want my whole life to be changed this afternoon?

If only Cecilia were here now. She had her decision about love made for her, but I was sure that she would have been capable of making her own decision if she had to. What would she do in my position? Maybe I should talk to her before facing Patrick; maybe I could leave a note for Patrick and promise to see him tomorrow, when, after having talked with Cecilia, I would be better prepared. No, I was in this alone, much as I tried to wish otherwise.

This fretting and worrying had taken my mind off where I was, and the next thing I knew, I was standing on the edge of the water where the river met the lake. Away and up to my right was the bridge, partially obscured by the masts of the stonehookers; and leaning on the rail of the bridge, staring out at the lake, was Patrick. My first impulse was to hide myself, for I did not want to see him yet. He was not looking my way, however, and so I turned and walked calmly in the direction of the Government Inn, past one of the fishing huts, out of sight of the bridge.

That was my answer! It had to be my answer! If I had wanted to kiss Patrick my heart should have leapt at the sight of him; my body should have tingled in anticipation. But it didn't. And just as soon as I determined that this was my answer, I was overcome by an unexpected sadness. How could I hurt someone who had done me no harm, who had wanted to be close to me? How could I be so cruel?

"Are you all right there, young lady?"

I almost jumped out of my skin at the sound of the man's voice. He had a blue sailor's cap pulled down almost to his eyes and tilted to one side, and held a stubby pipe in his hand, as if he had just taken it out of his mouth in order to speak to me.

"Didn't mean to scare you . . . was just wonderin' if you was all right, is all . . . standin' there all alone with tears runnin' all down your face. You all right?"

"Yes . . . yes," I stammered. "I'm sorry, I was just . . . "

"You don't need to explain yourself to me. I was just passin' by. But if you're all right, why then I'll just be getting' along. So, you're all right then, are you?"

"Yes, I am. Thank you. I'll be fine now. Thank you. I'm sorry to have bothered you."

"Didn't look like you were botherin' nobody but yourself. Good day to you then."

With that he turned and walked off towards the street. I looked down at my clothes to see if they were shaking as hard as I was inside them. Where was I? I felt as if my mind and body had been separated and lost from each other. I tried to take a step, just to see if I still had some control of myself left. I watched my foot go out in front of me and place itself on the stones. I didn't fall; I could walk. I would be all right. But there was still Patrick up there on the bridge, and I could not escape what I had to do. So I wiped the tears from my cheeks, smoothed my hair, took two deep breaths, and walked back towards the bridge.

Once back on the street I tried as best I could to be natural. If I could not direct myself from my head, I would let my feet take care of things for a bit. They seemed to be doing a fine job so far. But now that I was on the street, should I make for Cotton's or for the bridge where Patrick was? This decision, at least, was made for me.

"Hello Gretchen."

It was Patrick.

"I thought I might sit down by the dock rather than at Cotton's."

He didn't wait for my answer; he just started walking towards the path to the harbour, and I followed him, though with what purpose in mind, I had no idea. Once at the path he turned to see if I was there, and then he just started talking as if we had no history at all. He talked of the weather and of what kind of a summer it might be.

He speculated on the profits of stonehooking for the new season and related some of the stories that were still going back and forth between the men about the Great Fire and about how all the boats had been saved, though some had to be scraped down and repainted.

I wondered at his apparent ability to erase our last meeting from his mind, for my mind was in turmoil, and I kept my face averted from his for fear that if our eyes met I would give way to my unstable emotions once again.

And then he said, "I've been talking to The Red."

The mention of her name suddenly shifted the conversation, one-sided though it was, and nudged me into a calmer, safer space; one in which I could more comfortably be a listener rather than a participant.

"When I say I've been talking to her it is more truth than lie, to be sure, for I don't know that she spoke a word the whole time I was there. She said she wanted to see me, and when I went there and sat with her by the fire, that's just what she did — see me, for it was I who did all the talking. Something like today."

Perhaps he meant this to be a joke to lighten the mood, which had become awkward and unforgiving, as was my reaction to his kiss.

"Well, you know how she is. I got to telling her things about myself that I had forgotten I knew — almost as if I was talking about someone else. Growing up in Clifden, in Connemara, I used to help my father dig peat out in the bogs. I think it was the first skill I ever learned. It was very much a routine — marking the rows, slicing the bricks, scooping them into a pile — so that your mind could wander wherever it wanted to, while your body did all the work. I can't say as I enjoyed the day after day of it the older I got, but I never felt like complaining about it, either."

We reached the end of the dock and sat down on the end of it, our feet hanging off the edge over the smooth surface of the river. As I looked down at the water below my feet it felt as if that water was the top of the world and I was floating above it, strangely unattached.

"I do remember, though, my first full summer of digging — I must have been seven years old — being left on my own for a hour or two while my father went back to the house to fetch something he had forgotten. Anyway, I was down near the bottom of a particular row when my shovel slid into something hard but spongy — not like peat at all. So I carefully dug around it. It was the body of a man - at least, I think it was a man — it could have been a woman, but judging by the clothes, for all the clothes were still fitted on him, I thought it was a man. The odd thing is that I was not afraid. More curious than afraid. There I was, standing deep enough into a peat bog so that I could barely see over the edge of the pit, and the body of a man lying at my feet. I remember leaning down and pressing my finger against his face — very carefully, you know — and it felt like soft leather. His eyes were closed and he looked to be quite peaceful in his death. I think part of the reason I wasn't afraid is that he seemed somehow familiar to me. I can't say what it was; it was just a kind of sensation I felt.

"When I saw my father coming back across the bog from our house I quickly covered the man up again. I don't know why. And I never told my father about it, nor anyone else until The Red. I don't know how she got it out of me. But the more she didn't speak, the more I could see that leathery face, just as if I was there again, just as if I was seven years old again. You'll think what I'm going to say next is the talk of a crazy man, but I think there was something that man had to say to me, and I didn't take the time to listen."

Patrick paused for a while, waiting, I suppose, to see if I did think he was crazy. I didn't; but then, I was not sure of my own stability, either.

"No, I don't think you're crazy. I would have been afraid, though. I could not have kept such a secret inside me for so long. Don't you feel blocked up by it?"

"I'm not sure if 'blocked up' is how I'd put it, but I do feel there is a line in me somewhere that has been broken and wants mending."

Then he looked at me so intensely that I could neither look away nor speak to break the trance I felt myself being drawn into. Finally, his eyes slid away from me and he sat with his hands hanging between his legs, staring into the river.

"That's it, then," he said. "I'll have to go back and find him. See what he has to say."

I wasn't sure if he was serious or if he was once again trying to ease some humour into our situation.

"Do you mean it?"

"Unless The Red forbids it."

"When will you go?"

"In a week or two, I expect."

I did not reply, for this was as unexpected, in its own way, as his kiss. When the silence began to hang between us like a curtain being drawn across a window, Patrick stood up and walked away. No matter how hard I tried to focus my eyes on the water or the boats or a particular cloud in the sky — anything at all except for Patrick walking wordlessly away from me, I could not keep the tears contained, and once I felt the moisture on my cheeks neither could I contain my sobs.

To celebrate school being over for the year Tommy Lamer and I decided to climb the tallest tree we could find down by Slade's marsh. We stood together on the shingle bar between the marsh and the lake, and looked across at the woods in front of us. As soon as I saw Garter Snake Hill it seemed to me that we had to choose a tree there because all the trees on the hill were higher than the trees down on the ground where we were standing. I tugged at Tommy's arm and pointed to the top of the hill.

"I think you're right, Sally. We'll have to go up there."

So we ran as fast as we could along to the hill and then up its side until we got to the top.

I like it when I run myself out of breath — it makes my head feel all light and open. I knelt down on the ground for a bit to let Tommy know that I needed to rest before we started climbing. He knelt down beside me. He always did things like that.

Once my breaths were easy to make again I jumped up and went searching for a good tree.

"There's one there that's got some branches low enough so we can get started. Here, I'll give you a lift up. Then you can grab onto my hand and help pull me up."

He locked his fingers together to make a stirrup. I put my foot into his hands, and my hands on his shoulders.

As soon as I was balanced he sprung me up till the first branch was right at my waist. I'm glad we chose an oak tree to climb. Whenever we climbed pine trees we got black smudges on our hands and clothes, and pine sap would stick our fingers together. This would be a much easier climb.

By the time we got as close to the top of the tree as we could get, we were out of breath again. But this was a different kind of being out of breath. This was a softer kind because my arm muscles and leg muscles were tired, too. Instead of just my head feeling light and open, my whole body felt like an angel's body must feel — as if it could float away on the tiniest breeze if it didn't hold on tight to something.

Where Tommy was sitting he could see out across the marsh; where I was sitting I could see out across the lake. We just sat there swinging our legs back and forth like scissors. And then I saw them — Gretchen and Miss Jenkins walking along the shore and coming towards the hill. Then I couldn't see them for awhile because of all the trees and their branches in the way. I hadn't seen them together since when Miss Jenkins stayed with us before and after the troubles with Father. Anyway, I forgot about them for a few minutes until I could hear their voices coming up towards our tree. And then there they were! Right below us and sitting down to have a picnic. Tommy touched my arm and pointed down at them and smiled at me and shrugged his shoulders. That meant that here we were up in the top of this tree and we wouldn't be able to climb down until they left, and wasn't that an interesting turn of events.

We stopped swinging our legs because we didn't want them to know we were up there spying on them. But we weren't really spying because we were there first. I guess we were spying, though, because we didn't tell them we were there. I didn't know if that was fair or not, but the longer we stayed still, the clearer it seemed to me that we had no choice but to keep staying still. All we could do was listen, even if we decided not to watch. But we watched, too. When Miss Jenkins took the wine from the basket I was so surprised. I could never have imagined her drinking wine — she was my school teacher. And I knew that Mother and Father especially would not be pleased if they knew that Gretchen was drinking wine. Such things were not allowed in our house.

After a while I was happy to see Gretchen and Miss Jenkins being so friendly because they were two of my favourite people in the whole world. Gretchen had not laughed like this for a long time. Then when Miss Jenkins let Gretchen call her Cecilia my face turned into one huge smile. As they ate more food I began to feel hungry, too, and wished that I could climb back down the tree and eat with them. I looked over at Tommy, and he rubbed his stomach with his hand to show that he was hungry, too. We both covered our mouths so we wouldn't laugh out loud.

When Miss Jenkins told Gretchen that Victoria had told her about Patrick, I thought how very like Victoria that was, to tell things she wasn't supposed to tell. But in a way I was glad she did, because now maybe I would find out something about Gretchen and Patrick that Gretchen would never tell me. Miss Jenkins' story about her boyfriend was so sad; I hoped Gretchen's story would not be the same. But after I listened to Gretchen talking about Patrick, I still wasn't sure if she really like him or not.

Miss Jenkins said a lot of things about love that I didn't understand, and then they said how much they would miss each other. I thought about how much I would miss Gretchen if she ever went away. After they walked down the hill, Tommy and I made our way back to the ground, but before we left I sat down and leaned against the tree where Gretchen had leaned against it. I wished I had my fiddle.

Cecilia, my friend, left today and I felt like a hollow tree standing in the forest, surrounded by green saplings and thriving, full-leafed oaks and birches and alders and maples. I, alone, had no life left in me. I wished that some solitary woodpecker would come and poke at me with his quick beak, so that at least I could feel recognized for the condition I was in.

It was the longest day of the year, and with the sun shining in a cloudless sky I decided that I would devote myself to it; I would spend the whole day where it could see me and warm my skin. And my heart as well. That place in my heart where I held Cecilia was a tender bruise now that she had left for the summer. That place where Patrick was, I had put behind a curtain and did not wish to look at. Nor did I wish to remember Baketigweyaa's words to me, "I will be passing on before the days begin to grow shorter again." This, the longest day of the year, could not last long enough.

How many people could one person hold in her heart? Was that what a heart was for — simply to hold others in? And if those people were sad, could her heart avoid being sad also? If those people went away, did they take their part of her heart with them? How many people could leave before there was not enough heart left for her to keep living? Was that how we would all die? I had always trusted that as I grew older I would have fewer questions and more answers, but I seemed to be moving backwards through life. I remembered as a very young child asking Father how apples grew on trees. All winter long the apples were not there, and then in the summer they were. He would just smile at me and say, "God makes them grow there," which I never found to be a satisfying answer. So I would ask him how God made them grow there. To which he would answer, "He just does. We don't question how God does things." And then I asked him, if we didn't pick the apples would they stay on the trees forever. He reminded me that apples fell from the tree if we didn't pick them. I thought about that, but I still wondered, if we didn't pick any of them at all, would only some fall off the tree and others remain? Would every single one of them fall off eventually? Father said that yes, they would. I figured that we could know for sure if one autumn we didn't pick any of the apples at all; we could just watch the trees and see if, indeed, all the apples would fall off the trees by themselves. Father said, "you're a silly girl, Gretchen."

Perhaps a heart was like an apple tree. That was where I could do my experiment.

But the only experiment I wanted to try today was to see if I could live forever inside this day, and make everyone else live forever inside it with me. So I brought the sun to all my favourite places to see if that would help. I went to the Butter apple orchard and walked the natural pathways among the trees. From there I walked back towards Russell Bush's Inn and went down the hill to the creek, and I followed the creek all the way to the marsh, walking in the water for as much of the time as I could. At the marsh I climbed Garter Snake Hill and looked out across the lake. I ran down the hill as fast as I could, daring myself to fall and tumble and break my bones. At the shingle bar I skipped stones until my arm was sore, and then I walked the shoreline to the mouth of the Credit River. I began to walk along the banks of the river under the new railway trestle.

I stopped. This was the way to where Baketigweyaa lived. If I kept walking I would find out if he had gone. I didn't want to know this. I couldn't know this. I turned to make my way back to the mouth of the river, but my legs all of a sudden lost their strength and I collapsed in a heap on the ground. No matter what I did, this day would not last forever. The sun would still shine on me all day long, and it would shine on me tomorrow; it would shine on all of us who were here. It would not notice those of us who were no longer here. I was angry at the sun, at the tall, green grass, at the peacefulness of the river, at the apples that would fill the trees in the orchards. They went on and on and on, and whether we were here or not mattered not a whit to them. Father could go mad, and they didn't care. Miss Jenkins and Patrick could leave, and they didn't care. Baketigweyaa could die.

So I didn't care if this day lasted forever or not. The sun would not be tempted by me; I would no longer let myself be tempted by it. I willed the strength back into my legs. I steadied myself, and I walked. My rebuke of the sun had caused it to be angry, for suddenly it disappeared from the sky and into the dark fluttering of a million wings.

∽

PORT CREDIT, June 23, 1855 — Residents of Streetsville, Oakville, Erindale, Merigold's Point, and Port Credit were astounded and frightened by the arrival of an enormous flock of wild pigeons into the region two days ago. The width of the several flocks stretched almost from horizon to horizon, and it took almost four hours to pass overhead, during which time the sun was blocked from view.

After their initial shock at the phenomenon many of the residents went out into the wooded groves at night, where the pigeons had settled, to capture and kill as many as they could, which they did by means of nets and clubs. Even the children took part and helped to knock the pigeons off the lower branches of trees. Many local families will be dining on roast breast of pigeon for many days to come.

Farmers are encouraging people to go out to hunt the pigeons; otherwise the pigeons will feed on their crops. It is hoped that whatever pigeons are not killed will be frightened off.

This bizarre invasion of wild pigeons overtook me immediately as I had picked myself up from the ground by the mouth of the river. At first, I was terribly frightened. Never before had I heard such a sound or seen such a sight. What this great visitation was, I could not tell for many minutes. I ran to the closest tree to hide myself, to protect myself. When finally I realized that what I was seeing and hearing was an unearthly large flock of wild pigeons I began to relax, but only a little, for though I was familiar with pigeons, I was in no way familiar with such a vastness of them. The flapping of wings sounded like a great wind that had been shattered into a million pieces, tumbling and grating upon each other. It was a sound that could have overwhelmed the voice of God if He had tried to speak. After fifteen minutes or so I began to wonder how there could be that many pigeons in one place at one time; and after what must have been at least an hour I could not imagine that there were that many pigeons in all the world. And still, it did not cease. I thought I would go mad — how could there be so many birds? I thought they could only be demons of my mind in the form of countless flocks of wild birds. Was I so removed from God and from His goodness that He would visit such a plague on me alone of all the people in my village? Or had I been transported directly to hell, without even the benefit of having died first?

And then, finally, the sky grew gradually light again, and all that was left of the wild birds was the echo of their wing beats. The quietness and the stillness settled back on the land as a great absence. The sun was much farther towards the western horizon, as if the birds had dragged it with them and only released it because they had taken pity on it. I had huddled myself so tightly to the trunk of the tree that when I tried to stand myself up again I could hardly loosen my muscles. It took several minutes before I could relax them enough to take a few wobbly steps out of the shade of the tree. I wondered if anyone saw me if they would see some mark on me indicating that I had been forsaken by God and so should therefore be forsaken by all who met me. But as I approached the harbour I could see and hear dozens of people talking loudly, every now and then gesticulating towards the sky and making a sweep of their arms that followed the path of the birds I had seen. I was not mad, then. I was not cursed; I had not been delivered into hell.

Turning away from the harbour and the mouth of the river, and beginning the long walk back home I was on the verge of exhaustion and feared that I might not be able to make it. So I retraced my steps and crossed the bridge into the village to knock on Mr. Standemyre's door.

"My dear girl, have you been out these four hours under those birds all by yourself?" cried Mrs. Standemyre as soon as she looked at me after opening the door.

I had no idea what a sight I must have presented. If I looked on the outside the way I felt on the inside, then I'm sure that her concern was in every way justified. Mr. Standemyre hitched his wagon and drove me home, where Mother and Sally and Victoria rushed out to greet me as if I were a resurrection. Over Mother's shoulder as she was hugging me I could see Father standing under an apple tree tapping the hard, green buds like tiny bells, listening for the ring of truth.

That night my body was so heavy that I lay myself down on my bed with great care, lest I break it with the force of my exhaustion. How could I feel so heavy and so emptied out all at the same time? I tried to keep my eyes shut, and draw sleep to me in that way, but my eyelids kept floating open; and when I tried to keep them open, they would fall shut. Back and forth I went, stepping up to the edge of sleep, then stepping back, playing a cruel kind of game with myself and with my sanity. For, indeed, I began to feel again as I did when the great flock of wild birds had taken over the heavens.

I don't know how long I continued in this state before I heard it. A high, thin melody that, for a minute or two, wove in and out of itself, originating I knew not where. Coming from inside my own head? A dream? Or drifting in from outside my window, the lonely voice of some ancient tree, or the heart of the great lake itself bleeding into the sand and rocks of the shoreline? And then I recognized the sound as that of Sally's fiddle; yet even then it made no sense to me because it was the middle of the night, and how could Sally be playing at such an hour? But it was her fiddle. I sat up in my bed, still heavy and weary; I stood up and walked to the window.

There, on the shore of the lake under a moon drenched sky, was the barely visible silhouette of Sally, her fiddle bow moving evenly back and forth, embroidering the dark cloth of the night with her strange melody. All of my senses gave themselves up to the single one of hearing; there was nothing left in the world except the song of Sally's instrument and my ability to hear it. When she lifted the bow from the strings and let her arm fall to her side, I thought I could see a heron lift off from the shore of the lake and slowly flap its great wings against the light of the moon.

I awoke well after the first rays of the new day had begun to shine in my window. I was on the floor beneath the window; someone had put a pillow under my head and a blanket over my body.

I play for Tommy, who is an Indian and who is not an Indian, but who is my friend and can hear my voice. I play for Mother, whose face smiles but her eyes can't. I play for Father, who wishes apples could talk, and maybe wishes that I would, too. I play for Gretchen, who is afraid she is being left behind. I play for Victoria, who saw me holding my fiddle in the dark and said, "Go ahead, Sally. Play it outside so the whole sky can hear." I play for Uncle Silas, who knew.

"Where were you, Gretchen, when the pigeons came?"

It was the question everyone asked as a greeting these days, sometimes before even saying hello. Patrick was leaning over the rail of the bridge watching the stone-hookers, and feeling, I was quite sure, a kind of sadness for not being out there on the water. I told him where I was, but not all the details of how I felt. Already I was feeling that he was moving away from me and that my words could not travel far enough and stay together long enough to reach him and make any sense to him.

"And where were you, Patrick?"

The sound of his name in my mouth was dry as a leaf fallen from a tree.

"I was with The Red. I thought for sure she had called the birds just to frighten me."

"Were you frightened?"

"I was unsettled, I think. I don't know how I would have felt if I hadn't been with The Red. I was just telling her that I had decided to go back home to see the buried man. And then the birds came, and I wondered if they were some sort of riddle she was giving me instead of an answer."

"Had you asked her blessing?"

"No, I hadn't asked any question at all, but it always seems that whatever she says is an answer to a question that I might not think to ask until the next day. And then I have to try to put them together."

"Do you think she wants you to go?"

"She didn't say I shouldn't."

He turned away from the lake and leaned his back against the rail, with his elbows on top of it so that his hands hung at chest level. I wondered how he could make his body look so relaxed. Did he feel so easy on the inside, as well?

"Anyway, I have my passages booked."

I wanted to ask him when, but I did not trust myself to speak the words. He was watching me, even though his head was not turned towards me.

"Monday morning I take the Telegraph Coach to Oakville, and from there the steamer *Magnet* to Lachine. Overland to Montreal and then steamship to England," he said. "I should make it to Connemara before the snow flies," he laughed half-heartedly.

I kept my eyes fixed on the lake, watching the stone-hookers, without really seeing them. I took a deep breath and made myself stiff and straight.

"I'll pray that the weather is with you all the way."

We stood there for a long while, facing away from each other, understanding that this could be the last time we ever saw each other.

"I don't want to leave any things unsaid before I go, Gretchen."

And then he shifted halfway back towards the lake so that he was facing me. Should I hold my position, or should I turn to face him? I reached inside me for every bit of courage I could find; I could think of nothing else to save it for. I turned to face him, saying nothing. Waiting for him to leave nothing unsaid.

"I know we haven't known each other long, but there's a strength of feeling between us that we haven't spoken about. It's what made me try to kiss you that afternoon. I allow that it might not have been thought out properly, but then sometimes we have to do things without thinking about them. I know that you're a thinking kind of a woman, and that perhaps it is that uneven ground we stand on that makes me into a clumsy man. But I want you to know that I have thought very long about all this that I'm saying to you now. So it's not that I'm not a thinking man. I want you to know that. I work with my arms and with my back, but I have thoughts just like you do. I don't have the words that you do, and so I don't speak of anything but which is easy to speak about. You are not easy to speak about, Gretchen — and I don't mean to say all this as if it was a failing on your part. All I mean to say to you, then, before I go, is that I recognize the strength of feeling between us, and I'm sure you do, as well. That, and a promise that I will hold you in my heart for as long as I can. I will bring that with me to Ireland. Some day, I may bring it back with me to this very bridge." He stood himself up straight and put his hands on the bridge railing, not so much to steady himself, it seemed, but to steady the world around him. "I would ask you to not push me out of your thoughts if ever I happen to arise in them."

I felt as if I had not taken a breath the whole time he spoke, and when he fell silent my chest heaved so that I almost made a sudden cry with my voice.

"I promise you that, Patrick."

Sunday morning, Father was out walking the orchard, where I hoped he could still find some remnant of the God he no longer went to church to worship. We, all of us in the family, had to try these days to find our connection to God everywhere we could, except in the church, where we were still too fragile to go regularly. So today I decided to wander the orchard with Father to see if we could find some bit of religious workings together.

If he noticed my presence, he did not acknowledge it, but even if I did not feel welcomed I at least did not feel rejected outright. He walked with his hands clasped behind his back, sometimes looking down at the ground, sometimes up at the sky, and sometimes at the trees themselves. I walked beside and a little behind him so as not to disturb his natural progression. Whenever I have spent such moments as these with Father I have done so in silence, feeling that since he did not speak, he would not hear me, either, if I spoke. But today I was speaking to him, and it felt like praying, not knowing if my words were heard by him to whom they were directed.

"Miss Jenkins has left for the summer, Father. We spent a wonderful evening together before she left, picnicking on Garter Snake Hill by Slade's marsh. Have you ever walked there? There is a good view of the marsh and the lake, the one like a child of the other, though the marsh is always still and the lake is more restless. I'll miss Cecilia — she has asked me to call her by her Christian name — more than I would like to think."

Father paused for a second or two, as if some errant thought had troubled his mind; or as if he recognized Miss Jenkins' name and was trying to recall her. I decided not to tell him about Baketigweyaa or Patrick.

"I left a copy of *The Bulletin* for you to read the other day. Did you read my piece on the pigeons? Have you ever seen anything like that in your life? I hope I never shall again, though I think that I would be better prepared for it now that I have experienced it the first time."

I followed Father as he turned, walked past a few trees, and then turned again to walk back towards the house and the lake.

"Would you like to walk down to the water with me? We can let the sun shine on our faces and just listen to the lapping of the waves for awhile. You could watch me skip stones."

I said this even though I knew he wouldn't go farther than the house. I had never seen him walk along the water all these months; he seemed to feel safer among the apple trees. So when we arrived at the side of the house by the porch I stopped, expecting him to do the same, but he kept on. I stood still where I was, but he didn't break stride and continued directly on towards the water. I wondered if he had been able to hear me all this time, if he was actually paying attention to me. Running to catch up to him I was so strangely excited that I passed him and ran all the way to the shore and waited for him there.

I watched his face as he came towards me, trying to see if there was any change there. Since that night before Christmas his face had been divided in two: his mouth and chin always seemed to be mulling something over — sometimes he pursed his lips and nodded his head up and down, as if agreeing with some invisible companion that the problem they had been talking about was indeed a difficult and interesting one; his eyes, on the other hand, never changed — they were caught in the middle distance somewhere.

Since I had offered to skip stones, and since he may have actually been expecting me to do so, I searched for some good, hand-sized ones and stacked them in a little pile beside me. Father was staring out at the lake and seemed to take no notice of my preparations. I threw the first stone. One ... two ... three ... and then it disappeared under the surface of the water. I tried another one. Five skips. After several tries, that was the best I could manage. As soon as I released my last stone I turned to look at Father. His head was cocked towards the water as if listening intently to the skipping stone instead of merely watching it. Once the stone sank below the surface, he looked down at the stones on the shore, then out at the water. He did this three times. Then he turned and walked back towards the house. After taking a few steps he stopped, as if he had forgotten something, twisted the upper part of his body to look back at the lake, then continued on towards the house.

"Thank you, Father," I called out to his back, behind which his hands were still clasped.

Father had disappeared around the edge of the house. I was still standing with my back to the water. For how long, I didn't know. Until a shy wave wet my heels. And longer still, until my feet were covered and the bottom of my dress floated and swirled about them, like the skin of a body that had lost its skeleton.

The colours of water: grey like a swimming stone; green like an eye reflected; brown like a drowned boot. And sometimes so transparent that it hardly seemed to exist at all.

I'm sorry, Father.

I rose from my bed with the dull light of a rainy morning, knowing that today was the day Patrick would take the Telegraph Coach to Oakville. I had not promised him to be there as he left Port Credit, perhaps forever, but I suspected that he would be disappointed if my hand was not one of those he saw waving him on his journey back home, his journey back to the bog to find the buried man.

I was too anxious to eat breakfast; the lump that I felt in my throat when I thought about never seeing Patrick again seemed to have spread itself into my stomach and even into my arms and legs. I didn't know how I would be able to walk myself all the way to the river, but I did not have enough time to let my worry delay me. Instead, I would use as much of the worry as I could to fuel my body and keep it moving. As for my mind, I had no control over it, nor the energy to battle with it. The best I could do was to not let it overwhelm me completely.

When I reached the mouth of the river, my boots were soaked through. Those parts of me that were not covered with my oilskin were heavy and cold with wetness. The walking had not tempered my anxiety, and I felt that I was no longer an independent being, but rather a mere witness to my own sorrow. Through the thousand lines of rain I could see four people standing under the veranda of the Commercial Hotel, waiting for the coach. One of them was Patrick. Before him, hiding his legs from the knees down, was a shapeless leather bag, which, I assumed, held all his earthly belongings. It was the sight of that bag that brought a sudden rush of tears to my eyes. To be able to gather all one's material possessions into such an insignificant bundle — how could one not feel ignored by the mercy of God. I thought of my own home, of my bed, my favourite chair in the parlour, our kitchen table, my dresses, even of the rose trellis and the worn steps to the back porch — how could I ever leave all those things and know that I might never see them again? How could I reduce my life to the contents of a single, rumpled bag?

As I stood in the rain, staring, I realized then that Patrick had probably arrived in Canada with no more than he was taking back with him. This tall, young man, whose hand once tingled my arm and who once tried to kiss me, stood so alone on this morning that I could hardly bear it. But I knew that I could not protect him, just as I knew that he sought no protection.

I could not move from where I stood; I could not make it across the distance between us to say something soothing to him because I did not know what to say. I could not put my hand on his arm because I would have been offering him a false promise. I could only stand there in the grey and the wet and the cold, and wish that none of this should ever happen.

But it did happen. The Telegraph Coach pulled up to the veranda and stopped in front of the four waiting passengers, blocking my view of them. This was not at all how I had imagined Patrick's leaving to be. I had imagined a sunny morning; I had imagined myself standing at the corner of the Hotel waving to Patrick as he leaned out the window of the coach. But now the coach was loaded and beginning to pull away, and Patrick had no idea that I was there. I wanted him to see me; I wanted him to know that I was there when he left, even if I could say nothing to him.

The horses jerked forward at the sound of the driver's voice, and the wheels of the coach groaned behind the clop of hooves. I ran towards the coach, praying that Patrick would look out the window and see me, but it drew so suddenly away from me. I waved at the back of it until it turned onto Toronto Street and made its way over the bridge. Where was my mercy when he needed it?

Every night before I closed my eyes and called for sleep to hold me in its arms I opened the drawer of my bed table and touched the two stones that lived there in the small, square darkness. One from the fire, and the other from the hand of Baketigweyaa; one guarding some secret of my life, the other waiting to disappear at last into the depths of some water of my choosing. Only this second one, which I put in my pocket each morning, was I able to control in some manner. "You will know when to skip it," he had said. How would I know? It was well past the summer solstice; well past the time when he had said he would have left behind his body to go to the Land of Souls. But had he? Did I not love and respect him enough to feel inside me somewhere the moment of his passing? He had taught me to smell storms; why could I not at least smell in the air his absence? I could make myself sure; I could walk up the river to his wigwam. I could see with my own eyes that he was there or that he was not there. And if he was not there I could ask, just to be sure. And what good would that do? There was a part of me that wanted to pretend the possibility of his still being alive in the midst of my own life. All I knew for sure right now was that it was not time to skip the stone. That time must make itself known to me so that I would have not the least hesitation in doing what I must do.

The apples were beginning to look like themselves. Perhaps they saw Father's hand rising towards them every day; perhaps they could feel the warmth of his touch and were beginning to shape themselves to his hand, knowing their purpose was to ripen and be harvested by their master. I missed his touch — though now that I thought on it, I did not remember it well. He was so sparing with the physicality of his emotions. I did not believe that he had no emotions, just that he did not know how to express them. I hoped that he was able to do that with Mother. I hoped that there was that part of him that still did it, even if only by the reflex of memory, when they lay beside each other in the darkness between the brightness of days.

Was it the nature of a woman's life to shape herself to the touch of a man, to be harvested by him? I wondered if that would be the shape of my life. Given how I had reacted with Patrick, I feared that I might not know how to be a woman. How many hands would reach out to me before none would ever reach out again? If only one, then there was the possibility that I had squandered the promise of my womanhood. What would Cecilia have thought about all this? I thought that she would not give herself to just any hand, and if the hands stopped reaching, she would still always be herself. That was how I must think about my life.

I touched the fired stone to my cheek. "The stone is grey. The fire has drawn blue lines like veins from deep inside it. But there is no blood in these veins. The blood is somewhere else." Where was the blood?

༄

"It's time you learned to use the composing stick. But first, the type-case."

With those words Mr. Standemyre put his hand on my shoulder and led me over to the cabinet where the type-cases were kept.

"Now, study this type-case well, Gretchen. You must come to memorize where the letters are — capitals and lower case — and where the punctuation and blanks are. The capital letters make up the right side of the case, in alphabetical order. But the lower case letters, over to the left here, are arranged by how often they're each used — the rare ones, like z's and x's and q's, as well as exclamation marks and questions marks are arranged vertically down the left side of the case. This will take some getting used to. Numbers are across the top." He indicated each section with a quick, short sweep of his hand.

"You must memorize where everything is so that you can reach for each slug you need without having to make your eyes travel the whole tray each time you reach your hand into it. As I said, that will come in time."

I looked at the type-case carefully for the very first time, and felt my stomach tighten. How would I ever memorize such an unusual ordering of type? Before I could slide too far into the possibilities of disaster awaiting me, however, Mr. Standemyre picked up the composing stick.

"Now, hold the stick in your left hand, so. Take a letter from the type-case with your right hand, and place it, nick up in the stick — the nick lets you know that you've placed the slug in the correct position. As you place each letter in the stick you use your thumb to push them solid against each other, like this. And remember, you're setting the type in the stick in reverse so that it reads upside down and backwards as you're looking at it. Don't forget to put a blank slug between each word and after each punctuation mark. Are you with me so far?" I nodded my head even though I felt completely at sea.

"Good. Now, you've set the sides of the stick to match the length of the line that will appear on the printed page. So, once you've completed your first line, you place one of these leads here — this thin strip — between this line and the next one that you'll begin right underneath it. The lead keeps the lines together. You're a good speller, so you shouldn't have to keep checking what you've done as you go along, as long as you remember that you're working backwards and upside down."

I looked up at him and was greatly relieved to see the hint of a smile on his lips and in his eyes.

When he finished his explanation I just stood there, not sure whether to wait for more instructions or to somehow begin a trial sentence or two.

"All right, Gretchen, here's the first bit of writing to be transferred to type. What you do is read a whole sentence at a time, not just one word. If you do that you're not thinking about the piece of writing as a series of connected thoughts, you're just putting down single words that have no relation to each other. It's very easy to make mistakes that way — mostly repeating or leaving out words. So get the full sentence in your head, then start transferring the slugs to the stick."

I looked at the first sentence, got it in my head, as he suggested, and then started to madly reach for letters from the type-case and put them in the stick. On my third thrust into the type-case I picked out the letter and as I was trying to place it in the stick, dropped it on the floor. When I leaned over to pick it up, I dumped the other two letters from the stick onto the floor as well.

"Whoa, there, young lady! Not so fast. Don't be expecting to do this as fast as I do on your first try. Take your time. Accuracy and attention are far more important than speed when you're beginning. It took me quite a long while before I got my speed up. Anyway, I'll leave you be for a bit, and you practise on this paragraph. Try to develop a rhythm — a nice, easy rhythm. You'll be fine." He patted me on the shoulder and left me to my own devices.

I had often watched him fill the composing stick — it seemed so effortless, as if anyone could do it. In just a matter of minutes, however, the distance between the doing and the succeeding had widened so that I could hardly see from one side to the other. I took a deep breath, told myself to relax, and began again. There were so many steps to become proficient at. I found I spent most of my time just looking for the right letters and punctuation marks. Then I had to pick the slug carefully from the type-case so that I didn't knock the other ones about in disarray. Then I had to drop the slug into the stick so that it didn't fall on its side.

Finally, I managed to fill the stick. Mr. Standemyre hadn't showed me how to empty it on the galley, but I had seen him do it a hundred times, and knew that I could at least handle this part of the operation on my own.

When he heard the metal type clattering onto the floor he came over to me and said, "And one more thing, Gretchen. Always ask to be shown how to do something before you attempt it on your own." At least he was still smiling.

"And now, my dear, tell me what it was that you put into the stick."

I looked at him with confusion in my eyes.

"Repeat the text back to me — what was the text about?"

I had put each individual sentence into my head, but as I tried to recall them, I found that I could not. What I had done was treat the sentences the way Mr. Standemyre had warned me not to treat the words — as disconnected fragments.

"Remember, Gretchen, you're working with thoughts and ideas and information here, not just slugs and cases and sticks and so on. But don't you worry, you'll catch on."

I think he threw everything at me all at once simply to temper my pride. I spent the rest of the afternoon trying to develop my own rhythm, and trying not to be frustrated by my inexperience. Mr. Standemyre had confidence in me; he was teaching me, a girl, a trade. I think I appreciated him more for that than for anything else. I knew I could write, and writing was not all that unusual a thing for a woman to do, even if she was expected to do it only in letters to family and friends. But to be a woman and to have an actual trade — Mr. Standemyre obviously did not see the world in quite the way that other men of position and consequence did. If I could not brag about the writing I did for *The Bulletin*, I could at least brag about being an apprentice typesetter.

But whom could I tell? Mother, I suppose; and Cecilia, when she returned from Sherbrooke. Patrick was gone. And so was Baketigweyaa. The realization suddenly entered my thoughts that I had no close friends in my life. Victoria had several playmates at school; Sally had Tommy Lamer. And I, though I did get on with my schoolmates when I was there, had not developed a close relationship during my years at school. I don't think I had ever missed such relationships until now, when I wanted to trumpet my accomplishments, or at least my potential for accomplishment, to someone of my own standing — that of a young woman no longer in school and not yet married, or even spoken for.

What had I done with all that time that others spent in social activity? I read and I wrote and I walked and I thought. How many hands of young men would reach for a young woman like me? I decided that since I had not been a girl like other girls, that I would not be a woman like other women. I would be like Cecilia — independent and confident. Still, I wanted to tell my decision to someone.

After supper that evening I asked Sally if she would like to go for a walk with me to the marsh. Just as we were about to leave the house, Victoria came running up.

"Where are you going? May I come, too?" As much as I thought that Victoria could not appreciate what I wanted to talk to Sally about, I could not refuse her.

I could tell that Gretchen didn't really want Victoria to come with us, but Gretchen can never say no to Victoria. She is a good older sister that way. I could also tell that Gretchen had something important she wanted to talk about. Whenever she is excited about something in this way she seems to try to stand taller than she already is — and she is very tall, already. But it's not like she's trying to be taller, it's more like she's trying to be straighter. As if the words she needs to say can only come out if she makes a straight path for them because there are so many of them and she wants to make sure they come out in the right order and don't get all jumbled up together.

"Mr. Standemyre is teaching me how to use the composing stick. I am going to be an apprentice typesetter. I am going to have a trade. I am going to be an independent woman."

Before Gretchen could get out any more sentences, Victoria jumped in. "What's a composing stick?"

Gretchen was very patient with Victoria, as she always is. But I was thinking it was a good thing Victoria asked the questions she did because I wasn't quite sure what Gretchen was talking about, either. All I knew was that it was very special to her. I was interested to know what an independent woman was because Gretchen said she was going to be one, but I always thought that she was, already. Only an independent woman could call Miss Jenkins Cecilia.

After Gretchen had explained to Victoria and me what a composing stick was and what a responsibility it was to be able to do typesetting, Victoria jumped in again, "Does that mean that you don't have to get married, then?"

As hard as she tried, I could tell that Gretchen was quite surprised by Victoria's question because her body stopped being so straight. It almost went back to its normal shape, but not quite. It wasn't so much that her words were starting to get jumbled; it was just that she didn't seem to be able to find the ones that she needed. So I stepped up to her and put my arms around her and just stood there and held onto her. And then Victoria did the same, and the three of us were just standing there like a tree whose trunk was divided into three.

June collapsed into July, as if it were out of breath, and each day of July took a deep breath of sun and measured it out into night, as if it were practising to dive into the water and swim across the lake to the far shore — a shore that was too far away to see from this side. And that's how I felt, too. Or maybe I was just treading water, far out in the middle of the lake, far from any shore, waiting for someone to come and pull me into a boat and row me back to the safety of land once again. Who would be at the oars, I wondered. Would it be Cecilia, rowing her way back to another school year at Merigold's Point, or would it be Patrick, navigating his way back from the bogs of Connemara? Who else was out there that could come to my aid? But then, if I truly were the independent woman I thought I was on my way to becoming, I should be able to get back to the shore on my own. I just wasn't sure at the moment which direction it lay in. Was this what independence meant — to struggle along on one's own, without ever really knowing what one was struggling for or where the struggles would land one in the end? This was not what I wanted independence to be. I wanted it to be a haven, not a confusion; I wanted it to be a place of strength, not a place of hesitation and worry.

Sally had just turned twelve, and all us of, especially Mother, wondered what would become of Sally as she grew older. If she ever left our home how would she make it in the world, with no voice? Here in Merigold's Point she was accepted as unique at best, and as a curiosity at worst. What would those who had no history of her think? I didn't think Sally would ever leave the Point; I didn't think Mother and Father had ever considered that she would. And as for me? Did they think I would one day go to live in a far off town or province, or even country? I could hardly imagine it myself. And yet, if I tried to look at Merigold's Point several years from now, I could not see myself anywhere in it — even though there was no other place I could see myself in. Perhaps that was simply because none of us could truly imagine the future; or because I had not yet seen the place I would be in, and so couldn't bring it to my mind's eye.

My fingers now had permanent ink stains on them, as if I had been marked by my decision to be an independent woman. Unless I kept my hands hidden from sight I could not hide my trade, nor could I present myself as a lady, for no lady would have such stained fingers as mine. I was reminded of the mark God put on Cain; I was both reprimanded and protected.

I had never understood the relationship between God and Cain and Abel. Abel was a keeper of sheep and Cain a tiller of the ground, and yet when each of them brought his offerings to God, God had regard for Abel's offering but not for Cain's. Why was that? I could not understand why God showed favouritism for no reason. And when He put his mark on Cain, He did it to protect him from being slain by those who condemned him for killing his brother. So, even though I had been taught that Cain had been marked to shame him forever, it seemed to me that the mark was to protect his life, not to harm it. Was this God's way of saying He was sorry for having shunned him in the first place? I wondered if Father looked at my hands and silently rebuked me for not accepting my condition as a woman, or if he thought that I was protecting myself from the necessary dependence on a man. I wondered, too, if I ever would have become a printer's apprentice if Father were still the man he used to be before that night.

I was now quite adept at using the composing stick and felt as capable and creative as a church organist. There may not have been much melody in what I did, but there was a rhythm and a cadence that I found pleasing to my ear as each slug clicked onto the stick. I thought that I was even happy when I worked. I didn't think that I had ever paid much attention to the very feeling of happiness, which was not to say that I had not been happy in my life. It was just that when I was younger happiness was not so much a feeling, as a condition. Now when I was happy I was aware of it as I was feeling it. Perhaps this was how Sally felt when she played her fiddle.

Sally and Victoria and Tommy were out in the yard playing on the swing. Sally and Tommy were doing most of the pushing, and Victoria was doing most of the swinging. As I watched them playing I had a sudden feeling of detachment, not from them, but from their abandon as they played. I felt that if I went out to join them they would not be as free with their joy. I knew that wasn't true, and I knew that whatever lack of ease there was rested only in me. This must be another sign of the shift from childhood to womanhood; the exchange of spontaneity for responsibility.

But today was not a day for being old and responsible; it was a day for walking and exploring the creek and the marsh. The bulrushes that ringed the marsh were now as tall as my hand could reach above my head, and when I stood in their midst there was nothing left of the world but the soft scraping of their leaves and the blue sky above me. I was lost in a feathery forest, safe from all eyes except those of the occasional red-winged blackbird singing for the simple joy of its own voice. Parting the bulrushes as I moved through them I lost all sense of direction; it was as if I were swimming through them, trusting them to hold me up, surrendering to whatever path they opened up for me. I would not have been surprised to trip over the baby Moses in his basket. Eventually, they released me back into the open space between the marsh and the woods, where the bright yellow of swamp candles competed for glory with the sun. On into the shade of the woods I passed the only blue beech that I had ever found in that area. The smooth, twisting trunk reminded me of the muscled arms of the sun-browned men who pulled the lead ropes of the boats at MacDonald's dock, tying them to their berths after a day's work on the lake.

It was the creek that I loved most of all. It wound through thickets of white willow, green ash, and riverbank grape; only here and there bold enough to escape into the full sunlight. The sound of its water was so delicate and shy that even a slight breeze through the leaves of the trees could overwhelm it. But where the leaves depended on the whimsical wind for their voice — and then I often wondered if it was the leaves or the wind that spoke — the creek was sufficient unto itself. Though it may not have been so powerful as the wind, it was more consistent and reliable. This, it occurred to me, was how Mother flowed through the alternating calm and clamour of our lives.

After I had walked along the creek for about an hour, the sun was high enough and I was warm enough to take off my shoes, pull my dress up above my knees, and wade in the creek, where it was shallow enough to do so. The sudden sensation of cool and wet sent shivers up my legs, until the heat of my blood and the cold of the water balanced each other. My toes pressed into the sandy bottom with each careful step, and the prints of my feet were quickly smoothed over behind me, as if the creek refused to remember any human presence. I was tolerated and even welcomed, but I was clearly other, and whatever pride of race I had was rendered as nothing in this pulsing of supremely natural life, which I felt most intensely as I stood in a bend of the creek where a miniature rapids beat against my white-skinned legs. I stood there for a long while, until I could no longer feel any separation between me and the water, between me and the trees and the grass and the stones.

 The longer I remained motionless the more I began to think of Baketigweyaa. In some ways I knew I had kept myself busy these past few weeks so that I would not have to think of him. Over and over in my mind had I turned and analyzed his last words to me, hoping to find another meaning to them from the one that I could not escape. For the first time since the summer solstice I was closing out the rest of the world so that I could concentrate on the memory of him. Or I was finally letting the whole world into me so that I could better remember him. Whatever it was, as I stood in that watery vein of nature I could feel his presence, without my sorrow. It was a feeling I was not familiar with, and for a few moments I was not sure that I was comfortable with it. But I forced myself to not move, to not think about anything else. To just let his spirit hover around me. And then I felt a calm, like a release that I could hardly explain. Everything between me and God had been removed, and for the first time I saw a clear path, where I had never considered the idea of a path at all. I held to my stillness now as a bird must hold open its wings to the wind; it was a matter of will and of surrender at the same time — these two ways of being that were supposed to contradict each other were locked in an awful embrace. I feared that if I so much as turned my head or moved my eyes I would fall from this space and never be able to find it again. I became rooted and weightless at the same time. You are the skipping stone and the water, said Baketigweyaa. That is the secret, he said.

My eyes opened slowly; they carefully re-introduced me into the physical world of the creek and the trees and the sky. The sun was setting and I was cold and shivering and disoriented. My legs awere numb, and as I turned, almost frantically, to step back towards the bank of the creek I fell like a chopped tree. Pulling myself up out of the water and onto the solid ground, I rolled over and over, trying to roll the blood back into my legs.

When finally I walked across the yard to the house, I passed the swing, hanging empty and in perfect stillness from the branch of the tree.

Victoria and Tommy and I stop swinging so that we can go with Mother to Port Credit to Cotton's store to see the telegraph machine. Gretchen has already seen it and says it is like magic. Mother calls it a talking wire. Half the people in the store are there to do their purchases and pick up their mail, but the other half are there just to watch the telegraph machine. Mr. Hamilton, who is the telegraph operator, sits very proudly at his desk, listening to the clicks from the machine and writing down words on a paper. I'm sure some people think he must be making up his own messages, because how could a bunch of clicks mean real words. Then he makes his own clicks by pushing a little lever with his finger, and he sends messages back to whoever is clicking at the other end of the wire somewhere in Toronto. Mr. Hamilton explains to us that the clicks are Morse Code and that there are short clicks and long clicks and that you can combine them in twos and threes and fours to make the letters of the alphabet. He shows us that a short click and a long click together make an A, and a long click and three short clicks make a B. Numbers have five clicks. He shows us all this on a piece of paper — a dot means a short click and a line means a long click. Tommy asks if he can write them down, and Mr. Hamilton lets him.

Three Indians came into the store while we were there. Mr. Hamilton was getting someone's mail, when the telegraph machine started to click. When the Indians saw the machine clicking all by itself, with no one around it, they got very scared. They said that only the devil could talk like that and they ran out of the store. No more Indians ever came into Cotton's store after that.

While Mother stayed in the store to make her purchases and talk with some people she knew, Tommy and Victoria and I went outside and walked down to the docks. Tommy made copies of the Morse Code for me and Victoria so that we could send messages to each other. We took turns knocking a stone against the wood to make the letters and see if the others could figure out what the message was. Tommy's message was, "Hello, my name is Tommy Lamer." Victoria's was, "This is fun." Mine was, "Do you like the sound of my voice," which made Tommy and Victoria laugh out loud. So now we all carry a stone in our pockets so we can send messages whenever we want.

When Mother was finished in Cotton's, Tommy helped her load the supplies on the buckboard. Tommy is always being helpful and makes me wonder what it would be like to have an older brother instead of just a father. But I just wonder about it; I don't really wish for it because Gretchen is as helpful to me as anyone in the world could be and I would never want a replacement for her. If she ever does accept some man's hand in marriage I would miss her more than she knows. Home could never be the same without her in it, but I suppose that one day that change will come. I don't really want to think about it now.

That night, after Victoria and I are in bed and Mother has tucked us in for the night, we take out our stones and try to tap messages to each other on the wall.

When I got home I felt as tired as if I had run all the way to Port Credit and back. My body felt almost distant to me; it was scolding me for ignoring it all that time I had stood in the creek. How odd it was that one's thoughts could become so intense that the body was completely forgotten. Did it mean that the body could live all on its own without my thoughts, or that I could keep thinking my thoughts without a body? Was Baketigweyaa still thinking even though he had left his body behind? Was I hearing his thoughts while I stood in the creek?

I was thinking about this as I tried to let my exhaustion change itself into sleep. I heard a muffled knocking on the wall by the head of my bed. Is that you, Baketigweyaa?

Fall — Winter 1855-56

CHAPTER 1

FOR THE FIRST SEPTEMBER since I was a very little girl I had not returned to school. Cecilia had returned to Merigold's Point, Sally and Victoria had returned to classes, the apples were once again ready for harvest, but I felt oddly out of time, as if the rest of the world had kept its circular motion, while I had spun off on a tangent leading to only God knows where. The closest I had come during this month to feeling part of the cycle that contained everyone and everything I knew had been the celebration of my sixteenth birthday.

At the end of that long day of celebration, with gifts and birthday cake and wishes and blowing out candles, when Sally and Victoria had gone up to their room and Father was taking his nightly walk through the orchard, Mother and I were left alone in the kitchen.

"You know, Gretchen, from the time you first learned to walk and then again when you tried out your first words, I knew . . . well, here you are, sixteen years of life behind you already. I feel so suddenly old."

Mother was holding both my hands in hers. I could see the tears begin to well up in her eyes, but she smiled them away as best she could.

"I know that being a printer's apprentice is not considered work for a woman, but I want you to know how very proud I am of you. And I am proud, too, of the stories you have written. You understand words, Gretchen. You understand how to connect yourself to the world. And to your sisters, especially. It's hard, sometimes, being the oldest child, I know. No one can teach you how to be the older sister. Sally and Victoria have always looked up to you, whether you wanted that attention or not, and you are, indeed, a good and loving sister to them."

Mother sat down on a kitchen chair by the table, and I sat down next to her, rather than across from her. I was afraid that to have the kitchen table between us would have broken the fragility of the words.

"Since the trouble with your father I have been able to depend on your judgment and wisdom to help keep the family together in those ways that are beyond the mere tasks and chores of our everyday lives. You have faith, Gretchen, and every night when I say my prayers I thank God for that. The greater part of my prayers, though, are for your father. There is a part of him that has left us, and I fear that it may never return, and . . ."

No longer could Mother hold back the tears with a forced smile.

"I am torn, Gretchen. I want you to some day have your own life, your own husband and children, but when I try to think of this house without you in it, and with your father still confused in his mind, I cannot imagine how I will carry on without you. I apologize for confessing my weakness to you, but I must confess it because I am so very close to not being able to carry on. There are matters concerning the relationship of a husband and wife that I could not explain to you, even if I had the courage to do so, and I just . . . I can't . . . I am so full of sorrow that I have almost no room left for love."

After those last words, Mother bowed her head and covered her face with her hands. Her whole body began to silently convulse, as if it would shatter and fall to pieces. To see her so desperately distraught scared me to my core. I did not know whether to try to soothe her with words or with my arms. I rose from my chair and as soon as I began to move towards her, she jumped up and threw herself into my arms, her crying now frighteningly audible.

We stood in this embrace for several minutes, neither of us knowing what to do next. Presently, Mother began to grow still, though she still held fast to me. And then, after many more minutes, she released me and sat back up on her chair.

"I watch your father preparing to harvest the apple crop and I know that there is something in him still that senses a responsibility to the work of supporting our household. But it is the harvest itself that drives me to the despair that I feel and cannot escape. This should be a time for celebration, for giving thanks for the bounty that God has provided us, but this bounty is not the one that can feed my soul. I am provided for in all except my soul. It is not enough. Damn this . . . this . . . it is not enough!"

I sat back down in my chair; I looked at Mother, at the table, the cupboards, the soft light of the lamp. I looked out across the porch to the orchard, still glowing in the disappearing light of the day. None of this could I reconcile with the words Mother had spoken to me, nor with the sorrow and the anger in which she had spoken them. Which of these two worlds did I belong to — the one with the orchard and sky, or the one with the kitchen and the chair in which sat the mother who had born me and nurtured me until this very day? Did God oversee both these worlds?

"Mother, please don't leave us."

"I could never leave this house."

She got up from her chair and began to walk out of the kitchen towards the parlour. Just before she was out of sight, she turned once more to me.

"You are a woman now, Gretchen."

Now, two weeks later, and tomorrow being the first of October, her words were still with me, as I felt they would be forever more. The composition of our household had changed. Where previously there had been a father and a mother and three daughters, there was now a man, two women, and two girls.

"Gretchen, what's it like to have a secret?"

I was sitting in a chair at the kitchen table, tipping and tailing a bowl filled with beans, and Victoria was dancing around me the whole time that she was talking.

"Victoria, I can't talk to you if you keep moving around me like a bee around a hive."

"Why do bees fly around a hive? Can't they find their way in?"

"Which of all these questions would you like me to answer?"

"The one about secrets. Do you have a secret?"

"I suppose everyone has secrets."

"I don't think I do."

"Isn't there something that you know or that you think about that you don't want to tell anyone else?"

That got her to stop her restless motion as she pulled at her bottom lip and began to think about her answer.

"Well, if there was, and if I told you what it was, then it wouldn't be a secret anymore, would it?"

"Then it would just be a secret between you and me."

"Really?" This seemed to add great value to the whole idea for her. "So, do you and Mother have a secret, then?"

"Yes, I suppose we do."

"Can we have one, too?"

"Sure. But you have to tell me something that no one else but you or I knows."

"Why can't you tell me something like that? You're older than me; you would have better secrets."

"This was your idea, Victoria, so you must go first. If you can come up with a secret, then I'll try to think of one, too."

Victoria sat down on the chair opposite me and began to run the fingers of one hand through the bowl of beans I had already tipped and tailed, while she leaned her head on her other hand. Her feet were swinging back and forth under the table.

"You know, you could help me with these beans while you're thinking."

She seemed not to hear what I had said, so fixed was she on trying to think of a secret.

"Gretchen, I think I do have a secret, but I don't know whether I should tell you or not. It's something I've never told anyone."

"Well then, you can always keep it to yourself. You know, you don't have to share every secret with someone else."

"But I think I want to tell you this one."

"All right then, why don't you tell me?"

"Why aren't my birthdays special, like yours and Sally's?"

"Whatever do you mean by that?"

"Well, Sally got a fiddle on one of her birthdays, and when you were eight years old, you told me Mother gave you a journal to write in, and she keeps giving you new ones all the time. I was eight years old in August, and Mother didn't give me a journal to write in."

"She gave you pretty barrettes for your hair, and she made you a beautiful dress, just like she did for my fifteenth birthday. I think those are very special gifts, don't you?"

"I guess so."

This clearly did not assuage her feelings of being somehow left out.

"Was that your secret?"

"I guess so."

I put down my knife, placed my hands on the table, and looked at Victoria until she stopped her restless stirring of the beans and looked back at me.

"You are just as much loved as any one in this family, Victoria. You should always know that. I don't want you to ever doubt that."

"But Sally plays the fiddle and you write and work for Mr. Standemyre, and I don't do anything special like that."

"What is it you would like to do?"

"I would like to have a little sister."

"I don't think there's anything we can do about that."

"Couldn't we ask Mother?"

"It's not that simple, Victoria."

"Is it because of Father?"

"Partly, yes."

Victoria got up out of her chair and began to walk aimlessly around the kitchen.

"Do you think Father will ever be like he used to be?"

"I don't know. I pray every night that he will."

"So do I. Do you think God will help us?"

"He will do what is best for us all, and sometimes we don't know what that is."

"But how can it be the best thing if he doesn't change back?"

I had no answer for her. As was her wont, she had backed me into a corner from which I could find no easy escape. Though I believed strongly that I should pray for Father, and though I believed that God would not forsake our family for no good reason, yet I did not have any optimism that my prayers would be answered. It seemed frighteningly clear to me that there was something faulty in the process, but I did not know what it was. The only answers that presented themselves to me were ones I did not want to contemplate.

"Well, if you are praying to God about Father, maybe I can pray to God for a baby sister, since we shouldn't ask

Mother because it's not simple enough to ask her. It would be simple for God, wouldn't it?"

"I suppose everything is simple for God, but that still doesn't mean it's simple for us, because we're still only humans. But before you pray to God for a baby sister, you should try to think if that is what Mother really wants, too. Just pray for what is best for each of us. Besides, having a baby sister wouldn't really change how you feel about yourself. It seems to me you're looking for something good that will come from inside you, not from outside you. My writing comes from inside me; Sally's fiddle tunes come from inside her."

"No they don't. They come from her fiddle."

"The fiddle is just Sally's way of speaking. Just as words come from inside you, melodies come from inside Sally; and just as you use your voice to speak your words, Sally uses her fiddle to play her melodies."

"I don't understand, Gretchen. I don't understand what's supposed to be inside me. I'm not as old as you are."

Victoria kicked her foot at the floor and twisted the top half of her body, as if she were trying to unscrew it from the bottom half. Then she walked out of the kitchen, onto the porch and into the back yard towards the orchard. Suddenly, I realized her dilemma — it was much the same as mine. Victoria wanted to be older, just as I wanted to be independent. Her whole family was older than she was, and she was beginning to feel left behind. To me, everyone else was independent, and I wanted to catch up; I wanted to find my balance. Was it, indeed, something that was somewhere inside me? What if it wasn't? Where, then, could it be?

The last week of September and the first week of October were the busiest ones for all of us, but especially for me. I divided my time between apprenticing with Mr. Standemyre and helping Father to harvest the apples. This year, Tommy Lamer had helped us with the buckwheat, cutting and binding it in sheaves, which we then took to the mill for grinding into flour. The garden vegetables were mostly left to Mother; Sally and Victoria helped out after school, sometimes in the garden, sometimes in the orchard. In the orchard we brought out the barrels on the back of the buckboard, and then carefully filled them, tree by tree. On the bottom of the barrel we put a layer of moss, and then the first layer of apples, close together and with their heads up. Then another layer of moss and another layer of apples, until the barrel was comfortably full. I remembered when I was very young Father tried using sand in the barrels to keep the apples settled, but the sand added too much weight and it made it difficult to move them. It was Sally's and Victoria's job now to gather the moss in the weeks before the harvest. Once the barrels were full we took them to the barn and lined them up in the corner closest to the root cellar. The apples we didn't send off to market were kept until the first snow came, then we took them down into the cellar for the winter. This year, for the first time, we were selling apples to Mr. Cook and Mr. Whitfield, who were cider makers. I wasn't sure why they all of a sudden had decided to purchase apples from us, when they had managed to be well supplied by other orchardists in the village, but I thought it had something to do with Father's condition. It was their way of helping us out.

Gestures such as these by certain of our neighbours and church acquaintances were evidence of the charity of fellow Christians, and though their actions did serve to keep us from the perceived possibility of destitution, yet they did not go any way towards resolving the disharmonious state of our family. It was not that I begrudged their aid; it was just that I wished for a release that they could not instigate. The harvest of crops and apples was a harvest of the fields of the earth only; I would have wished for a harvest of the soul. I prayed for faith and fortitude to grow inside us and to become ripe with the grace of time. But time was passing inside each one of us without, I feared, enough grace to save our souls. When I walked through the barn of an evening, the smell of apples filled me with both joy and sorrow. The joy came from the first time I could remember the smell of harvested apples and from the memory of all the autumns of my life; the sorrow from the fear that these autumns were now to be counted in ever smaller numbers. Still, I should have been thankful for what harvest there was, and I *was* thankful. I was just not so joyful anymore.

Once all the harvesting was done, Mother began canning the vegetables, and made more use of Sally's and Victoria's help, leaving me to spend more time simply being present to the family. I was not so sure that this was a good thing, however. It seemed that of late I had a growing tendency to brood. I once thought that this was reflection or contemplation, and perhaps it was, but now it had taken on a melancholy character that encouraged me to fret about a future which I could in no way understand the shape of, so full of absence as it was. Even Cecilia's return had not enkindled in me the sense of hope that I thought it would have. I had hoped that we would still carry within us the excitement and anticipation that we experienced on our picnic and in our exchange of letters.

"We are never the same in the present as we were in the past, Gretchen," Cecilia said to me one day shortly after her return. "But that is a good thing, not a bad one."

"If it be such a good thing, then why do I feel this weight in my heart?"

It was then that we talked once again about our relationships with those closest to us, except that we talked mostly of those we were separated from. Cecilia talked of Gilles and of her father; I spoke of Patrick and Baketigweyaa and of Father.

"Isn't it odd," I asked her, "we feel more strongly the force of those who are not with us than of those who are?"

"I don't know that I would use the word 'odd.' 'Ironic,' perhaps."

"What do you mean?"

"It means that what is most important to us is not what we think it is, or what we think it should be."

"Is there not a danger then of ignoring those we are with every day?"

"Yes, there is."

And that was the end of our conversation, for at that moment we both drifted off into our own thoughts about our own families and friends. We sat beside each other as two branches of the same apple tree, the wind blowing down the few stray apples that the hands and the eyes of the pickers had not been able to find.

Tommy and Victoria and I each picked an apple from the top of the barrel. We picked the roundest and biggest apples we could find. Then we took them and sat under the tree by the swing with pieces of cloth to shine them. We wanted to see who could end up with the shiniest apple. Tommy would spit on his and then polish it and then spit on it again and polish it again as if he were shining a boot. He always stuck out his tongue and pressed it to one side of his mouth while he was polishing. I liked to watch him because when he liked doing something he could make everything else around him disappear. That's how he would play with me and that's why I liked him so much.

Victoria sat on the ground with her legs straight out in front of her and sometimes used her dress instead of the piece of cloth to polish her apple. And then sometimes she would get up and forget about the apple for awhile and sit on the swing. I think she did that hoping that we would put our apples aside, too, and give her a push. But eventually she would go back to her apple because we didn't pay any attention to her.

I liked to wrap my apple up in the cloth and then turn it round and round inside the cloth. I would do that for a few minutes and then take out the apple to see how shiny it had become. Then I would do it again. I always looked forward to seeing how much new shine I had put on the apple each time. I would also smell it each time before I wrapped it up in the cloth again. It was very hard not to bite into it, it looked so good.

After we had spent a long time polishing our apples we put them beside each other to see which one was the shiniest. We each thought our own apple was the shiniest, so we decided to take them to Gretchen and make her decide whose apple was the best one. We all knew, though, that Gretchen would not choose a winner because she didn't want to play favourites. She tried to tell us that each apple was different, and that even though all apples looked the same you couldn't find two that were, no matter how hard you tried. So she said that each apple had its own best shine. We went back out into the yard then, and ate our apples, trying to see who could eat most of the apple and leave hardly any core. Tommy was always the best at this part. He would even eat the seeds. Victoria warned him that an apple tree would grow in his stomach.

I held the letter in my hand, as if it were an object so strange that no one had ever seen its like before. I certainly had not. In some ways it resembled the letters I received from Cecilia — it was much the same shape, being slightly more rectangular than square; and it was made of paper, with more paper inside it. And sure enough, it was my name that was on the front of it, but where Cecilia's rendering of my name was in a thin and almost dancing script, here my name was printed in thick, bold letters as if, having to travel so far, they might somehow disappear before the folded and enveloped paper reached me. I held it in both hands and rubbed my thumbs slowly and gently across its surface to see if I could feel the weathering of its long journey. I held it up to my face and smelled it to see if I could smell Ireland and the Atlantic Ocean on its dull white and creased skin. Then I carried it up to my room, not taking my eyes off it the whole time.

How long I sat on the corner of my bed trying to imagine what words Patrick had written me, before actually opening the letter to read his own words, I did not know. Would he chastize me? Would he appeal to me? When finally I tore open the envelope and took out the single rough piece of paper I felt as if I had been through a long and tiring journey myself just to get this far. Patrick's handwriting was curiously unslanted — it did not lean to the right as my own did or as Cecilia's did. Each letter seemed laboured and not sure of how to join itself to the letters on either side of it. The whole was written on the one side of the page, in a heavy, dark pencil, which smudged a bit when I rubbed it.

Dear Gretchen,

I am now truly very far away from you and stonehookers and Corktown. Sometimes I don't really know if I have just arrived back home or if I have just left my home. I have not yet gone out to see if I can still find the bog where the man is buried. I hope I can find the exact spot. I don't know how much patience I will have if I can't find it right away, but I guess I know that I won't be able to leave this place until I do. I hope you are well and that your family is well. I hope you are still enjoying being a lady typesetter.

Your friend,
Patrick Monaghan

I felt disappointed at such a short communication. Surely a letter that had to travel as far as this one did should be required to have more substance to it; surely it should take several minutes to read, not what seemed to me barely a single breath. What had his passage been like? Was the ocean calm or disturbed? Did he feel the time pass slowly or quickly? He did mention that he was confused about where his real home was, but he did not say more than that — I wanted so much more than that. As soon as my hand fell to my lap, still holding the letter too tightly, I was transported back to the bridge and our failed kiss.

I realized then that my feelings for Patrick were so unresolved as to be fluttering about like a flock of birds around a tree, not sure if they should land on its branches; having been in flight for so long that they could not remember even how to land. This was not at all what I wanted to feel; it was certainly not how I had expected to feel. But I could not escape it; I could only suffer it.

Suffering. I was barely sixteen years old and still lived in the house of my mother and father. Dared I suffer?

For months now people in Merigold's Point and in Port Credit have talked of almost nothing but the new railroad that will pass through our villages to connect Toronto to Hamilton, which is already connected to Niagara, London, and Windsor. For some time there had been a discussion as to whether the railroad should go along the lakeshore, through Port Credit and Clarkson's Corners, or whether it should follow a route north of here, through Streetsville and Milton. The editor of the *Streetsville Review* was obviously in favour of this latter route, arguing that it would pass through more manufacturing areas and larger farm areas, thus making more efficient feeders to the main rail line. Mr. Standemyre argued that the lakeshore route was more favourable for two reasons: it was a shorter distance between Toronto and Hamilton, and the bridges would be easier to build because they would have to span only the mouths of rivers and creeks, whereas on the northern route they would have to span much deeper and wider ravines. So, in the end, and much to Mr. Standemyre's great satisfaction, the lakeshore route was chosen.

Since the early spring, when the snow was just beginning to thin, the workers have been crowding into all the available rooms in the hotels and inns in Port Credit, and even into Russell Bush's Inn, though Captain Sutherland has since purchased it and turned it into a country home for himself and his family. So it is Port Credit that has become the centre for much rowdiness and uncontrolled behaviour, especially on a Saturday evening.

We have been able to measure the approach of the railroad itself by the dim orange glow of the great log fires that have bled like wounds into the night sky. As each long, thin mile of forest was cleared, the bodies and bones of the trees would be piled and burned, for there was no other way to quickly and efficiently remove them. This iron line would connect one end of space to another, but would divide its left from its right like a river keeping two banks apart.

I spent many of my spare hours during the mid and later summer observing the construction of the bridge over the mouth of the Credit River. Compared to the simple and mean affair that carries foot and wagon traffic, the railroad bridge is quite the grand structure, with its trestlework seeming to hang like a spider's web from some invisible support in the air. The rails themselves creep up to and away from the trestle in perfectly straight and parallel silver lines, which seem to grow closer and closer together the farther away they stretch from the eye.

Mother and I even took Father for a long walk up to Clarkson's Corners to see this marvel of progress. Since that awful night of his breakdown, Father had walked no farther on his own than the orchard, and had once accompanied me to the shore of the lake by the house. Still, Mother wanted to get him to venture beyond the bounds of our property. She felt that if the three of us just began walking, Father would somehow find it natural and comfortable to accompany us, and not feel threatened by what might have now become unfamiliar to him. And so it was that the three of us made it as far as the new railway.

Father said nothing, but I watched his face to see if I could catch something of what he might be thinking. I could see his eyes squint as they followed the rail bed towards the horizon, and then slowly unsquint as they followed it right back to where he was standing. Sometimes he nodded his head ever so slightly up and down, and sometimes from side to side, as if to say, "Yes, yes," or "It's hard to believe." And all the time, his hands were clasped behind his back, like a schoolmaster perusing the work of a student.

When Sally and Victoria and I went to look at the rail line, the reactions were quite different.

"Miss Jenkins says the Indians call the train an iron horse. Does it really look like a horse?"

"No, Victoria," I answered, "they call it that because the horse is the fastest means of transportation they know, and because we are now about to replace the horse with the steam engine. And I suppose, from what I've heard, and from the pictures that Mr. Standemyre has shown me, that when the engine starts to move very fast the long bar that connects the front and back wheels of the engine and makes the wheels turn looks like the legs of a horse when it runs really fast."

As I was explaining this to Victoria, Sally began to move her arms in the same kind of motion the bars connecting the wheels would make, and then started to run in ever faster circles around us, until she ran out of breath and collapsed on the ground, at which point Victoria, giggling madly, fell on top of her, and the two of them rolled around in the tall grass. Once they had regained their composure, Victoria asked me more questions.

"Gretchen, will we ever go on the train?"

"Oh, I'm sure we will, eventually."

"Where would we go?"

"Well, I suppose we could go wherever the train goes — to Toronto or Hamilton, even to Windsor. And once in Windsor you could go almost anywhere into the United States. Even to visit our relatives in New England."

"Is that very far away?"

"It would probably take a few days, at least, to get there."

"What kind of relatives do we have there? Are they like Uncle Silas?"

"I think they would be distant cousins of some sort. I'm not even sure if they know who we are. Neither Mother nor Father has ever really spoken of them. Still, it would be interesting to meet them some day, don't you think?"

Victoria did not answer this question right away. Instead, she tilted her head to one side and looked in an angled way up at the sky.

"I didn't think that was such a difficult question to answer, Victoria."

"I'm trying to figure out what they look like. And how many of them there are. And whether they would want to play with me or not. If they would like to play with me, then I think I would like to meet them. Why don't we write them a letter and find out who they are?"

I had never given the idea much serious thought before, but just as the railroad was opening up vast new territories to the traveller, so it was opening up new possibilities in my mind. Where would I travel to if I could?

In the damp early autumn sand by the creek, where it curved between a willow that not only wept but sighed, and a black oak that held its leaves into autumn and winter longer than any tree by the marsh, I stood, stiller than these trees, with a long stick in my hand. I was waiting, but for what, I did not know. I drew the stick across the sand, like a fish through the water: the word *train*; two lines running from it into a wavy-edged circle (that was the ocean); two other lines running from it in a different direction, and bumping against the word *Concord*, and this word ornamented with question marks, like petals on a flower; away from the train and the lines and the ocean and the flower of Concord an oval flitting across the sand as far as the stick would reach from where I stood (that was a stone skipping across some body of water I didn't quite recognize).

"Gretchen, you must read this!"

Cecilia had walked Sally and Victoria home after school, without even straightening out her things on her desk before leaving — this she told me later — and arrived at the back porch of the house quite out of breath. When she first cried out that I must read this — she had not yet even said hello — I could not see what object she was talking about, because her arms and hands were hidden underneath her shawl.

"Read what, Cecilia?"

At hearing me call Miss Jenkins Cecilia, which was still a novelty to me, Victoria giggled, with her hands covering her mouth, and Sally gave me a broad smile, as if she was breathing a sigh of relief for me.

"This, oh this!"

She could barely contain herself, but she did manage to at least bring a book out from underneath her shawl. With her other hand she grabbed me by the wrist and led me as quickly as she could towards the tree where the swing was hanging from its great branch.

"Listen to this, Gretchen."

She paused to take a deep breath, and then another one, and then set herself on the ground and took another breath. She opened the book to its first pages and read.

"Here are his very first words: *I celebrate myself* —I celebrate myself! What other poet has ever been so bold!"

She then quickly ran her finger down the page.

"And here — listen to this:

Stop this day and night with me and you shall possess the origin of all poems,

You shall possess the good of the earth and the sun . . . there are millions of suns left, —is that not the most wonderful of invitations?"

She paused, and looked at nothing particular in the distance, then came back to herself, and to me.

"I received this book last evening and have spent more hours than I can count reading its pages. Indeed, I hardly slept at all last night, and today I'm not sure what my students thought of me — I'm sure I was not wholly present to them for most of the day."

The book had a green cloth cover, and on it was the title *Leaves of Grass,* the letters like the tendrils of a plant growing out of the cover itself.

"Received this book from where? From whom?"

"From a cousin of my father's whom I hardly knew existed. She lives in New York and is, according to my father, quite liberal in her views. Apparently word has traveled through various family members to the effect that I, too, again according to my father, am 'a little too well read in modern texts.' So she sent the book to Sherbrooke and it has been forwarded directly to me. I am quite sure that my father did not peruse the contents; otherwise, he may not have been such an amenable go-between. It seems that not many readers know what to make of it, but my father's cousin was sure that I would be able 'to decipher it.' Decipher it! Can you imagine? Is it not so absolutely clear? Is it not so full of earth and ether?"

I did not know what to make of it myself; nor was I quite sure what to make of Cecilia. I was almost intimidated by her joy.

"Who is the author?"

"Walt Whitman. Look, here is an engraving of him on the frontispiece."

He stood there, his head confidently cocked to one side and sporting a wideawake, which emphasized the posture. A neat beard adorned his daring face. He wore an open collared shirt, his left hand in his trouser pocket, his right hand on his hip. Yet all this confidence his picture exuded never tumbled over into arrogance; it was more sureness, a certainty, which he seemed to dare me, the reader, to find in myself.

"Is he a famous writer?"

"This is apparently his first published work. Can you imagine it?"

Never before had I seen Cecilia so unrestrained. I must admit that I looked back at the house to make sure that Mother was not a witness to her outflow of emotion. Cecilia saw me glancing at the house.

"Oh, Gretchen, I haven't embarrassed you, have I? I must seem quite beside myself. I'm sorry."

"You must never apologize to me, Cecilia. Certainly not for feeling so full of wonder and joy as you seem to be. It's just that I feel . . . well, overwhelmed. I must admit that I can hardly remember any of the words you read, so overtaken was I by your very reading of them. Would you read the passage again?"

And so she did, and more.

Though I paid more attention to the words this time, I still could not quite find my balance amongst them. I recognized them all, and I thought I could understand their basic meaning, but I did not know whether this was poetry or prose. There was neither rhyme nor meter that I could identify, and yet there was a lyric quality that was beyond the simple telling of a story or relation of a feeling.

"Isn't it so perfectly disconcerting?"

With these words, Cecilia stood up and began pacing in irregular circles around me, unable to find a comfortable rhythm into which to settle herself.

"What are the titles of the poems you just read?" I asked.

"They have no individual titles — they are all *Leaves of Grass*. Here, let me read you another passage:
There was never any more inception than there is now,
Nor any more youth or age than there is now;
And will never be any more perfection than there is now,
Nor any more heaven or hell than there is now.
Does this not turn the world on its head? It is so frightening and so demanding and so encouraging all at the same time. Gretchen, I have already written directly to the publisher to request another copy, so that you may have one. It will be a gift from me to you."

The rest of my time with Cecilia that afternoon was, as she said, perfectly disconcerting. I tried, after she left and after dinner was over and after the day was done, to make sense of Mr. Whitman's "poetry," for Cecilia convinced me that it was, indeed, a book of poetry. This was as far removed from John Donne as the moon was from the earth. Mr. Whitman seemed to be so completely in the present moment, acknowledging the past and the future only as poor cousins to the inescapable present. How long can one be loyal to the present, and not be seduced by either side of it?

I fell asleep in my own bed, wondering if I, too, had a poet's mind, and how it might grow.

∾

Dear Patrick,

Last night was the first soft snow of the winter. The flakes fell like powder sifted from the light of the stars. The snow is early this year, as it is not yet Halloween. The cold has been with us for several days now, but not yet enough to freeze the river or the shores of the lake. Still, the stonehookers are now tucked away in the harbour for another season.

What is winter like in Ireland? You never really spoke about your home such that I could get a picture of it in my mind. I do remember, though, you telling me about digging peat in the bogs, and so I suppose I have imagined some sort of landscape. It is one that is all sky and horizon, with you and your father close against the long line of the earth, almost imperceptible except for the movement of your arms as you swing spadefuls of peat onto an ever-growing pile. Is it anything like that? I imagine that if I stood in the middle of Ireland I would be able to see the edges of the island in every direction, though I know that it is not really so.

I wonder if, as I write this letter to you, you have already found your buried man. That is something that I cannot picture in my mind. I hope that you will describe it to me in great detail. I hope that you will tell me what it feels like. I hope that finding the buried man will in some way tell you where your home is, and that you will be satisfied to be wherever that is.

The railroad will soon be completed, and will bring people who have never been here before, and it will take people away from here, some of whom will never come back again. Perhaps home will become something we carry with us instead of being somewhere that holds us firmly to one spot.

Your friend,
Gretchen

Chapter 2

TWO LINES OF MR. WHITMAN'S POEM had decided to take up residence in a corner of my mind, where nothing else seemed to want to live, and they troubled my sleep for much of the night: *There will never be any more perfection than there is now, Nor any more heaven or hell than there is now.* But where was this heaven and hell for Mr. Whitman? There was something not quite Christian in his view of the world; I did not think that the heaven and hell to which he referred were places which awaited us at our death. And when I rose from my bed to look out my window upon the new winter's day to see Father standing and staring out at the lake as if he were waiting for some phantasmal ship to come and rescue him from his silence, I wondered if hell might not be frozen rather than burning with flames, and if it might not be lying in wait in some deep recess of our minds rather than somewhere deep in the pit of the earth. And though I cannot explain the source of the sensation, I felt as if I were one of a series of beads on a string that had been unknotted — one bead was the phantasmal ship, the next was Father, the next me, and behind me, God. And all of us were about to slide off the open end of the string.

Everyone was talking about how early the snow was this year, and how they were sure that the ground would be white now until the spring. Some of those gathered around the stove in Cotton's General Store thought this an early gift of peacefulness and looked forward to evenings around the hearth, with hot apple cider and biscuits — these were mostly the women; others were taken by surprise and had not yet properly organized their winter stores. As for me, I liked the snow well enough, especially if it was cold enough to feel the crunch under my boots when I went walking. This afternoon, as I was helping Mr. Standemyre set the print for the next *Bulletin*, he suggested that there was enough space in the following issue for me to write a piece on winter — anything about winter that I wished to say.

"If it's a good piece, I'll put your name on it. What do you think about that?"

I honestly did not know what to think about that, for it was not something that had been at all on my mind. I was quite content to be able to write the occasional report anonymously, being thankful that I had the opportunity to write at all. But to think of having my name in the *Bulletin* for all to see! As I let the idea sink in, I became more apprehensive than excited, and was not sure that I could do it. The expression on my face must have betrayed my inner confusion.

"I wouldn't suggest this to you, Gretchen, if I didn't think I would be proud to have your name attached to the *Bulletin*. Think it over for a while."

He turned and began to walk back to his desk, then stopped, and turned once again towards me.

"Never be afraid to let the world know who you are. And if you're thinking to yourself that you don't quite know who that is yet, then maybe this will help you come clear about it."

For the rest of the day I performed my tasks as if in a dream. How could I be overwhelmed by such a silly little thing? The silly little thing, of course, was who is Gretchen Williamson? If that was not enough to keep me tilting just off centre for the day, when I left Mr. Standemyre's shop to begin my walk home, and was just about to cross the bridge, I felt a hand touch my elbow and turned to see The Red standing there, as still and secure as if she had lived her whole life on that very spot. I had not seen The Red since last Halloween, and now, as the sun was slipping below the horizon, with still the echo of daylight left, there she was before me like an echo of an echo. Her unmoving eye was fixed on me, as if I had been in her sight all the time since last I saw her.

"The evening after All Hallows. Bring the stone. And the other stone."

With those words, she turned and walked back towards the village, waiting for no response. I had been summoned.

Tonight I felt like a cloud in a windstorm, unable to hold my shape in the face of the elements over which I had no control.

It was not until I woke up the next morning that I realized The Red knew about the stone Baketigweyaa gave me — at least she knew that I had another stone. I opened the drawer of my night table and took the stones out, one at a time, and laid them beside me on the bed. The grey stone with the blue veins running through it, and the small, flat stone from Baketigweyaa, which I carried with me every day but put in my night table while I slept. I picked this one up. I bounced it in my hand, testing it for the skipping stone that it was. The only other hand to ever hold this stone was Baketigweyaa's, and as I felt the weight of the stone fall back into my hand again and again I sensed that he was standing somewhere behind me, waiting. I turned to look, just in case.

Sally was standing in the doorway, watching me with her mouth almost in the shape of a smile. It was a smile of understanding. Her fiddle was hanging from one hand, and the bow from the other. Then she raised the one to her chin, and the other to hover above the strings. Like an autumn leaf settling lightly on the lap of the earth, her bow met the string, and just as lightly began to stroke the string, making it sigh a whispery tone into the expectant space between and around us. Another, higher tone slid over the first one, and the two of them together created a harmony that almost lifted me off my feet. Out of this vibrating ether rose a melody that spiralled around itself, and I was broken. So beautifully and perfectly broken. And then the melody rose higher and higher until the pieces of me were drawn back together again, but in a different arrangement than I had ever been.

When Sally let the bow float off and away from the strings, and dropped her fiddle to her side, she stepped towards me, then rose on her toes and kissed my forehead.

In the barn, Father walked among the barrels of apples, pausing now before one barrel, now before another, as if trying to choose among them. He found one that was suitable and bent over it, always with his hands behind his back. After a minute or so, he brought one hand slowly up to the barrel and began to tap the apples one at a time. For a brief moment I was reminded of how he would lean towards Victoria when she was still a baby and sitting in her high chair at supper. He would softly tap her tummy, and she would giggle and move her arms and legs in that jerking motion that only tiny babies can make. I didn't recall Father ever laughing, but I remembered that when he poked his finger into Victoria's tummy his smile was as broad as I had ever seen it.

I watched Father for a long time, so contentedly tapping the apples. His apples, from his trees that he loved so much. In the midst of his tapping, he turned his head to look at me, standing behind him, and without missing a beat of his finger on the apples, he fixed his eye on me and smiled. My bones turned to jelly. What was it that drew up the corners of his mouth? What was it that made him rise each morning and put on his clothes for another day? What was it that passed between us in that very moment? I didn't know if his gaze was truly attached to what was inside him, if he saw me as I was at that very moment or if he saw only a figure that was familiar to him, but in a way that he could no longer grasp hold of.

"He's just like God in the Garden of Eden when it's winter."

Victoria's voice knocked me rudely out of my troubled reverie. She was standing behind me and to me left, just by the barn door.

"What did you say?"

"I said Father looks like God. In the Garden of Eden maybe God picked all the apples from the Tree of Knowledge and saved them up in case He needed them later. Then, when He needed to know something, He would go to the barrel with the right apples in it and He could find out."

I was often taken aback at the leaps of imagination by means of which Victoria would manage to navigate herself into points of religion and philosophy that not even a Minister would think to ponder. I could not respond to her; I could only try to enjoy being in that world of hers for as long as I could. Which was not for long.

"Gretchen, will you pull me on the sleigh?"

"Only if we take turns and you promise to pull me, too."

"I can't pull you, you're older than me."

"Just because I'm older, you can't pull me? That hardly seems fair."

"But you're bigger than me."

"Oh, well that's different."

"How is it different?"

"Older is not the same as bigger."

"Yes it is. You're older than me, so you're bigger than me."

"What if I were a midget?"

"Then I would pull you on the sleigh because I would feel sorry for you."

"And just why would you feel sorry for me?"

"Because older people should always be bigger than younger people."

"But what if God decided that some older people should be smaller than some younger people? God makes midgets, the same way that He makes you and me. You shouldn't feel sorry for someone because of the way God made him, should you?"

"I suppose not."

"All right, I'll pull you on the sleigh."

"Gretchen, what if I never grow any more? Will I be a midget?"

"You're not a midget, Victoria."

"But how do you know for sure?"

"You'll have to trust me, Victoria."

"Well then, maybe I'm a dwarf."

"And maybe I am Snow White."

"But Snow White had black hair. Yours is brown — no, it's yellow — no, it's in between yellow and brown. Anyway, it's not black, so you can't be Snow White."

"Then you can't be a dwarf."

"You're trying to trick me."

"Perhaps. I'll tell you what — I'll pull you in the sleigh if you promise never to let me eat a poison apple."

"I would never let you eat a poison apple. Besides, all our apples are only good apples because Father grew them. He would never let you eat a poison apple."

"You're right, Victoria. He never would. Now, run and get the sleigh before I change my mind."

༄

This Halloween night was white and silver, not at all like last year when there was not yet any snow on the ground. All day long I had been thinking and wondering if I should go back to the same spot that I had gone to last Halloween night. But this time The Red had not directed me to find another stone and to build another fire. Should I do it on my own? I decided not to choose another stone and not to build another fire. But just as the sun was going down I walked along the lakeshore to the marsh, followed the curve of it to the creek, and traced the meandering line of the creek to the place I had built my fire exactly one year ago.

The tall, thin spire of the birch tree rose out of the snow, and the last ray of the day's sun was sliding up off the top of the tree, as if the lungs of evening were taking a deep breath before letting out the soft darkness of night over the slowly turning earth.

The colours of evening: red, like the new growth on a rosebush in spring; orange, like the eyebrow of a varied thrush; purple, like ink and blood mixed together.

And then, just as evening was about to give way to night, time hovered, as when a great bird holds its wings wide and still just before it lands. I felt myself caught between earth and sky, my body more shadow than substance. The birch tree, which I tried to hold on to for support, became as transparent as my body, and we seeped into each other. It swelled with breath, as I did; I became a hundred arms and a thousand fingers reaching at the sky, as it did. We rose up to see the fire in the eye of God, as it stared us out of ourselves. The unblinking eye of eternity that saw us as we were, as we always had been. I tried to keep my eyes wide and wider open. But I blinked. I hit the ground like a stone dropped from a hand. The next thing I remembered was waking up in my bed.

∽

When I got to Corktown, at first I couldn't remember the street The Red lived on. When I recognized the street — I had only ever been down this way the year before with

Patrick — I then couldn't remember which dwelling was The Red's. I was standing part way down the street, turning in one direction and then the next, trying to make my eyes remember the door, and the whole time feeling the weight of the stones in my pocket.

"You'd be looking for The Red, if I'm not much mistaken."

The voice came from a face on which the sun seemed to have burned in the grime of long days of hard labour. A lopsided cap covered the man's head and spilled out over the tops of his ears, so that the part of his face I could see was lit only by the glow of the stubby, short-stemmed pipe that hung from the corner of his mouth.

"Yes, I am . . . how did you . . . "

"I've a memory for a pretty face. You were trailing Patrick this time last year. Yes, I've a memory for a face like yours. The door you're looking for is directly in front of you," he said, taking the pipe from his mouth and pointing it across the street. "Now, *your* memory . . . " He finished his sentence with a wink and walked off towards the lake.

I knocked on the weathered wood of the door and waited. When the door creaked open, as if on its own, I realized I had been holding my breath in anticipation. I had to consciously will myself to breathe in a normal fashion, as The Red stood to one side and motioned me towards the fire with one hand while holding the door with the other.

"Welcome, my young willow."

She closed the door behind me and motioned me to the chair by the fire. When she took her place across from me and fixed her eye on me, it felt as if I had been here only yesterday, and yet a whole lifetime ago. We sat in silence for a few minutes, she as still as a bridge across a river, her face changing shape as the firelight flickered shadows across it, and I trying to copy her stillness and her gaze, but unable to keep my eyes from wandering around the small room, though they could not resist returning to her face. Finally, she held out her hand to me.

"The stones," she said.

I reached into the pocket of my cloak and lifted the stones out, one at a time. The first one, the one from last Halloween, I placed in The Red's hand. She turned it over and over, as she had done the first time, nodded her head, and then placed the stone in her lap. Again, she reached out her hand.

"The other stone."

This one she did not turn over in her hand as she had the first one. Instead, she seemed to massage it with her thumbs, and then she raised it towards her face, her head leaning down to meet it halfway. She pressed it against her cheek.

"He is in the other world. The one who gave you this stone is on the other side."

"Yes, he is."

"You are supposed to do something with this stone, but it is not time yet. Soon, it will be time. When this time comes, you will do what the stone does."

For a long time, she did not speak, and I did not know if she was waiting for me to say something, or if I was supposed to simply listen, even if it was only silence I was listening to. And then, "This stone from the fire," she said, resting her hand on the stone in her lap, "you will have to wait much longer for this stone. But its time will come, too."

More silence. The only sounds the crackling of the fire and the muffled noise from the street outside the door. And my breathing, which seemed to be fighting with my body.

"Breathe like the white tree, my young willow, breathe like the white tree."

I felt as if her one, unmoving eye could see me standing by the birch tree last night; as if she had been there, watching me, as she was watching me now.

"Would you like some tea?"

She stood up from her chair and moved towards the kettle and a small teapot that were sitting on a large, flat stone by the fire, not waiting for my answer. Carefully pouring out two cups of tea, she swivelled her body towards me, one arm outstretched, a cup in the hand at the end of it. Then she sat back down in her chair, saying no more. We sat in silence once again.

Her gaze was almost more than I could bear. I could not help but fidget, both in body and in mind. I felt as if I were being probed, as if her eyes had their own body, separate from the body that sat in front of me, and this other body was walking around inside my head, poking at one part of my brain and then at another, not looking for anything in particular, but just curious to see what was there. For how long we sat in this way, I cannot tell. There were only two sentences we spoke somewhere in that drifting silence, before I left.

"How do you know the things you know?" I asked her.

"The same way you know them."

When I was not trying to solve the riddle of The Red's last words to me, I was worrying myself about the article that Mr. Standemyre had asked — had challenged — me to write. Anything about winter that I wished to say. I could think of everything, and therefore of nothing, to say. Where was I to begin? With snow? With the season itself? With my experiences of it? With the particular winters of Merigold's Point or of Port Credit?

"Do not try to think in such broad terms," Cecilia advised me. "Choose a specific moment or a particular place or thing. You could write an entire piece about a single snowflake if you wanted."

"If I could, you mean."

"Of course you can. Didn't you try to catch snowflakes on your tongue when you were a very young girl? What did they feel like? What did they taste like?"

"Like the sky."

"Well, now, that was an answer I didn't expect. And that's why it's a good answer. And that's why you will be able to write a wonderful piece about winter. There's a bit of Mr. Whitman in you, I think. Shall I read you another of his verses to inspire you?"

"Or frighten me away from ever putting pen to paper again. I know you mean well, Cecilia, but my skills are not of the same measure as Mr. Whitman's."

"You don't have to write like Mr. Whitman; you just have to open yourself to what is around you — the way that he does. You could do with snow what he does with grass. Here, listen to this."

Cecilia sat us both down on the sofa by the window. Father was wandering the skeletal forms of the orchard, Mother was busy in the kitchen, and Sally and Victoria were off playing somewhere, so we had the room to ourselves.

"*A child said, What is the grass? fetching it to me with full hands.*

He goes on to answer:

I guess it must be the flag of my disposition, out of hopeful green stuff woven.

Or I guess it is the handkerchief of the Lord,

A scented gift and remembrancer designedly dropped,

and then,

Or I guess the grass is itself a child . . . the produced babe of the vegetation. And I especially like this image:

And now it seems to me the beautiful uncut hair of graves."

If Mr. Whitman can find all that in a single blade of grass, even as he says he knows no more what it is than a child, what might you not find in a single, glorious snowflake, so much closer to your own childhood than he was when he wrote that verse?"

"He seems to have so much more experience of the world than I."

"He was thirty-seven years old when he wrote those words. And yet for that, I think his wide world exists within his breast. Inspire the world into your lungs, Gretchen."

Like the white tree. A white tree, rising from the white snow, standing against a white sky. White — the colour that holds all the other colours inside itself. The white world that waits to shine through the prism of my life.

∽

In two weeks, the first train to travel the new railroad would leave Toronto for Hamilton. Mr. Standemyre, as well as many of the villagers in Merigold's Point and especially Port Credit, had been able to talk of almost nothing else. Today, he was taking me by coach to Toronto to see the new locomotive that would lead the train on its first journey.

"You won't ever have to make this trip again in such a bumpy and incommodious fashion. The passenger cars on the train will have comfortable seats, aisles to walk up and down if you want to stretch your legs, and stoves to warm you in cold weather. It will make people want to travel longer distances, and more often. Families that have been separated east and west will be brought closer together. Yes, the Indians think this some sort of miracle, but I can tell you that there is many a white man who agrees with them. The world beyond our village has been changing at a great pace, and now that change is coming to gather us up in its great movement forward. In my lifetime I have seen the Lakeshore Road and Centre Road go from corduroy to planks to macadam. And now there is the railroad. This is an exciting time to be alive, young lady, believe me. It's an exciting time to be alive."

I had never thought about life, my life, in that way. Was this time, this very time, an exciting one to be alive in? How could I know, for it was the only time that I would ever experience. I supposed that Mr. Standemyre was comparing this time to times past and that he preferred to be alive now rather than any time before now. I wondered if he thought about this in the same way that I thought about the life of General Wolfe or Joan of Arc, or about Grey's "Elegy."

The locomotive was certainly an impressive "piece of machinery," as Mr. Standemyre called it. The body of it was a shining, dark green, as if velvet had been turned into metal. The trimmings were all of brass, and even if this machine could do nothing more than sit where it was for the rest of its days, it was a beautiful sight to behold. Its shape was like nothing else I could think of. At the front end of the locomotive was a tall, funnel-shaped smokestack, where the steam vapour would pour out once the engine was ignited. Two great wheels were positioned towards the back end, the second of them just below the square cabin where the engineer would stand to control the various levers.

"To think that that enormous engine is powered by steam, the very same that comes out of your kettle when you cook water for a pot of tea. It's steam that will turn those wheels and drive that engine, pulling several passenger cars, mind you, up to fifteen miles an hour."

"Have you ever ridden on a train, Mr. Standemyre?"

"Me? No, though I have had the opportunity. I could have travelled from Niagara Falls to Windsor last year — being a journalist and the owner of a newspaper and all, but I decided to wait for the railroad to come to me. I decided I wanted to walk to the end of the street and board a train, right in my own village."

"Somewhat like Muhammad waiting for the mountain to come to him?"

"Now where did you learn that expression? Surely they aren't teaching Muhammadism in Methodist schools these days."

"I read it in a book of world religions. I like to read about how other people understand God. You don't think I'm being heretical, do you, Mr. Standemyre?"

"Surely you're teasing me. I know you have wits enough about you to be seriously, and not frivolously, curious about the world around you. The best way to understand yourself is to see how others do it. We're all pretty much made of the same stuff, in the end. 'All roads lead to Rome,' as they say. Do you know that one?"

"No one method is better than another?"

"Yes, that's the gist of it, but where does the saying come from?"

"Didn't the Romans build so many roads and connect them all in such a way that no matter which road you took you would eventually end up in Rome?"

"That's it. And do you know where the saying about Muhammad comes from?"

"When Muhammad brought his message about Allah to the Arabs, they didn't believe him, and wanted some sort of proof of his powers as a prophet. So, he ordered Mount Safa to move. That's the mountain coming to Muhammad."

"Ah, yes, but did the mountain come to Muhammad?"

"No, but he said that God wouldn't let the mountain move because it would have fallen on the people and killed them all."

"Very good. Now, I'm going to let you in on a little secret — I didn't know that part of the story. So, do you think that by waiting for the railroad to come to me, it will somehow fall on me or on all of Port Credit?"

By his mischievous wink and nudge, I understood that I was spared having to try to respond.

But all the way back on the coach ride from Toronto to Port Credit, I thought about Muhammad and the mountain. If we didn't get what we wished for, did we then get God's mercy instead? Could we only get God's mercy if we didn't get what we wished for? If Father never came back to our family the way he used to be, did that mean that God was having mercy on us?

"I baptize you with water for repentance," said John to the Pharisees and Sadducees. "He who is coming after me will baptize you with the Holy Spirit and with fire," he said.

In winter, I say, God baptizes us with snow.

When all the earth is bleak and barren and brown, snow infuses darkness with light. So bright is it that even the midnight cannot extinguish its glow. It is the clean slate upon which a new spring will write another chapter of the descendants of Eden — we who plant the seeds and harvest them, as God has planted us here and will one day harvest all our souls.

When I catch a snowflake on my tongue, I am branded with the love of God. I am set in that place of anticipation, where hope hovers over the landscape. Like snow.

No single snowflake can be placed on another, and not leave a part of it uncovered, or cover more than is there. No one person can hold another and say, "I hold all of you." No one person can speak to another and say, "I love all of you." God can do this; that is what we have been taught. God can cover us over with His love, leaving no part uncovered, yet covering only what is there. Like the snow covers the earth — it can only cover what is there, and no more.

Winter is a sacred place that must be entered with faith and with intention.

Thus much had I written about winter, but it was no longer for Mr. Standemyre or for the *Bulletin*.

༄

Today, Cecilia delivered my own copy of Mr. Whitman's *Leaves of Grass*. I held the book in my hands and felt the weight of all the words that were contained therein.

"Cecilia, do you think you will show the book to anyone else in Merigold's Point besides me?"

"I can't think of anyone at the moment. And you?"

"I had never thought about it, but just as you asked the question, the answer seemed to arrive in my head at the same time. I think I would like to show it to Mother, though I must be mad to believe that she would read it with any favour."

"Do you often share such things with your mother?"

"Such things?"

"I mean thoughts or ideas that have nothing to do with she and you being mother and daughter, that have nothing to do with Mr. Williamson being her husband and your father."

"Is it possible to escape such attachments?"

"Not escape them, perhaps, but step outside them, as one would leave the house to go outside. It does not mean that you intend to abandon your house, for you know you will always come back to it. Sometimes you need to breathe different air into your lungs."

"That is the second time you have used that image."

"Yes, I have been thinking a great deal about breath and breathing these past weeks. Do you feel how the air in winter seems to invigorate your lungs in a way that it does not in any other season. I think it is because the winter air is nothing but itself. In all the other seasons there are the fragrances of living things — flowers and trees and grass and the very earth itself — that saturate it. The winter air is like a horse without a rider or a destination."

"But Cecilia! That's it! That's how I feel when I read Mr. Whitman's poems. I feel like a wild horse, but my wildness is foreign to me. If someone were watching me from afar he would marvel at how I displayed my wild nature in running freely across the fields, but he would not know how I was helplessly subject to my own wildness. If only I could explain this to Mother."

"Have you ever tried?"

"I have never talked this way with anyone before now."

"Give her the benefit of the doubt, Gretchen. She is your mother, after all."

"But that is exactly the problem."

Sometimes, when I looked at Mother, I wondered if she was moving only by habit rather than by desire, but if I watched long enough I could see that there was a conscious will that propelled her, and though there may not have been any joy visible on her face, she was, nevertheless, a woman still in control of her fate. And so I wondered, as I prepared to show her some of Mr. Whitman's poetry, if this might not unsettle her just enough that she would be forced to struggle with herself, and with me as the "bringer" of the poems, in order to maintain the equilibrium she had so carefully nurtured. But then I thought again, and I chastised myself for considering her as some sort of invalid. I should show the same trust and confidence in her as she always had in me. Still, I would choose carefully which of Mr. Whitman's poems to share with her.

I chose, also, a brilliant, sunny Saturday afternoon to suggest that we sit down at the kitchen table and I would make us both a pot of tea. It was simple gestures of that sort that could bring a smile to her lips, and almost to her eyes.

"I've been reading poetry these last few days. I thought you might like me to read some of it to you."

"You are always reading so much."

Mother seemed suddenly to not know what to say next, as if she were out of practice. She was almost embarrassed, I think, as she fiddled with her tea cup and looked away from me.

"I like it that you read so much. I liked reading very much when I was your age."

And then she laughed.

"I make myself sound like a grandmother rather than a mother. I don't mean to complain about the years. There are years we treasure, and years we simply survive, and all those years together make us who we are. So, tell me, is there a poem in one of your books there that would be suitable to a cup of tea on a day such as this, in such a year as this?"

I had brought with me a volume of Wordsworth, as well as Whitman. It was only as I reached my hand down that I lost my courage and took from the chair beside me the Wordsworth instead of the Whitman. I could not risk Mother's unhappiness. I had to choose between offering her the melancholy of regret or the brute force of an unbridled nature; the one familiar, the other disruptive.

As she saw me open the cover of the Wordsworth, she asked me, "I seem to remember a poem by Mr. Wordsworth that was about a snowdrop. I know I shouldn't have spring so much on my mind, since winter has hardly begun, but still, I especially remember the last few lines about the jonquils:

Blue-eyed May
Shall soon behold this border thickly set
With bright jonquils, their odours lavishing
On the soft west-wind and his frolic peers;
Nor will I then thy modest grace forget,
Chaste Snowdrop, venturous harbinger of Spring,
And pensive monitor of fleeting years!'

I like the way he has of describing the flowers. I often watch them myself, you know — when I need reminding of the beauty that God has laid out all around me. It will be good to see the green stems come up out of the ground once again. I never tire of seeing the seeds come up . . ."

And then her voice and her thoughts trailed away into a silence where I could not follow her.

༄

The afternoon was cloudy, the sky trying, but not succeeding in reflecting the snowy white of the ground. The weather was just the lower side of freezing, so that the stomping and shuffling of the many boots did not manage to make slush and mud underfoot. Most of the villagers lined the tracks at Clarkson's Corners, looking eastward, waiting for the first train to come steaming in from Port Credit on its way to Hamilton. A smaller group of people were gathered around Mr. Carthew, who was putting the finishing touches to a barrier of logs he had built across the rails and secured with posts driven deep into the ground. The railroad ran through his property, as it did through many properties of farmers and landowners in Port Credit, Merigold's Point, and Oakville. Once the government had decided on the route for the rail line, it offered what it thought was fair market price for the land it expropriated, but expropriation it was, which meant that the farmers and landowners had no choice in the matter. Mr. Carthew was the most resistant and disgruntled of those who were dispossessed of pieces of their land, and so he felt he was left with no other means of protest but to block the train from proceeding through his property.

Mr. Standemyre had gotten wind of Mr. Carthew's plans for the blockade and had asked me to interview him with the purpose of reporting his views in the *Bulletin*. I did go to his house, and he did agree to speak to me, but only on the condition that I not publish what he had to say.

"There's a principle here, which no one but me seems to want to stand by, and that is the principle of private property. Now, I bought this land from the government, fair and square; I bought the title, and by rights I should be the one who decides if I want to give up all or some of that title. I'm not saying I'm opposed to the railroad, though I don't agree with your Mr. Standemyre and all the others about the best route for it; what I am saying is that I should be asked for my opinion and not told what it is. So, the government has decided to take away my voice, but I've one last thing to say to them, and if you want to know what it is, you be out at Clarkson's Corners on December 3 when that first train tries to pass by here."

And so it was that there was double the excitement at Clarkson's Corners than at Stavebank Road in Port Credit.

Indeed, I thought ours was the only village to have a tempered reaction to the new rail line. At fifteen miles an hour we wondered if the locomotive would be able to apply its brakes in time to avoid crashing into Mr. Carthew's barrier, but it seemed the engineer had been given plenty of warning. As it was, the train, blowing its whistle loud and long as it approached the crowd of villagers, had to slow to allow for the various dignitaries to lean out of the passenger car doors and wave, and eventually to stop to deposit some of them, like cavalry generals offering blankets to the Indians as a gesture of good will from the government.

First, there was the cheering, the raising of arms, the holding of babies at shoulder height so that they, too, could witness the festive occasion; then there were the "oohs" and "ahs" as the train crept by us; and finally a few sporadic cheers and shouted comments as the train halted before Mr. Carthew's barrier. Some of these last cheers were for Mr. Carthew, and some were for the fact that his barrier was about to be dismantled. Mr. Carthew himself was arrested and bundled on to the train, so as to minimize any kind of demonstration, for or against, that might ensue.

So, here was the magnificent train at last. And how oddly disappointing it was. The actual arrival of the mighty locomotive could not equal the anticipation of it; nor could the physical presence of engine and passenger cars match the imagination of them. It should have been more momentous; there should have been some celestial acknowledgement of the event — a rearrangement of the constellations, a differently coloured or newly shaped moon. I should have been transported spiritually, as I might, one day, be transported bodily by this marvel of human engineering. The only true moment of significance for me was when Father, his hands clasped behind his back, as usual, looked at the train as it came to a halt, looked carefully at me, looked back at the train, then squinted his eyes and nodded his head, as if he recognized some connection between me and the train. I had tried to impart Mr. Standemyre's admiration for the technology to Father, and perhaps that was what he was remembering.

Mother stared at Father more than she looked at the train, wondering, if this new and spectacular event in the life of our village might not occasion a shift in the event of their lives. Victoria was as quiet as I had ever seen her, which was a great surprise to me. I had expected her to be uncontrollably delighted with the spectacle of it all. She was more subdued than outwardly stirred, and I wondered if she was not, for some reason, afraid of it all — of the crowd of people and the almost monstrous size of the locomotive. As for Sally, I could see new fiddle tunes dancing behind her eyes, and could hardly wait to get home to hear her translate this glory of technology into the sweetness of melody.

Soon, Mr. Carthew's barrier had been cleared, and the train steamed up again to continue its journey on to Hamilton. We all stood where we were until the train was well out of sight, and the stillness of the night, having previously retreated in annoyance, no doubt, from the frenzy of noise, settled back down upon us. The presence of the train was echoed back to us by the steam whistle which moaned a curious lament into the darkness. I was suddenly and unexpectedly overcome by a deep sense of melancholy. Was that steam whistle the ghost of something that had died, but whose death none of us could yet recognize? Though something wondrous had been given to us, had not something else, something more lasting been taken from us?

As we made our way home, I thought of Baketigweyaa.

∽

With all the anticipation of the first train coming through the village, we had almost forgotten about how close Christmas was. In our family, especially, we had welcomed the diversion, for Christmas now is an anniversary of another sort. This would be the second one since that night when Father had changed. I was not sure if Father even knew what Christmas was any more. I didn't know whether giving him a gift would mean anything to him. And what gift could I give him? I would have liked to give his spirit back to him. I would have liked to give us back to him. I would have liked to take away that night from our lives, but I could just as easily have taken the Big Dipper out of the sky, never to be seen again.

I sat on the edge of my bed, trying to want to get in it and go to sleep, but my mind was taken over by the memory of that night, and by my strange meeting with Baketigweyaa. I could use his presence now. I wanted him to be able to say something wise, something that would shine a clear ray of light into the darkness of my family. If I closed my eyes tightly and concentrated very hard I might be able to call his spirit to me. So I tried. But it was no use, for I did not believe strongly enough in the power of his spirit to make itself known to me. It wasn't that I didn't want to believe, because I did want to. I just couldn't make myself do it. It was then that another realization hit me, like a sudden gust of cold, wintry air: just as I could not will myself to put enough faith into my connection with Baketigweyaa's spirit, neither could I summon enough faith in my connection with God. When had I lost this faith? How long had I been rudderless in this vast ocean of life?

I felt dizzy from the loss of my certainty about God — dizzy not from the loss so much as from the realization of it. Had I taken my faith so much for granted that I had never truly had it? I had never questioned it. If I had, I would have come face to face with the consequences of the answer that much sooner. For most of my life, I had simply followed Father's faith in God, a faith that was never really discussed so much as it was merely accepted, in the same way that all of us accepted Father's authority as head of the family.

And yet . . . and yet, there was Baketigweyaa. Father never did condone my friendship with him. He feared it as much as he disliked it. Did he fear Baketigweyaa's Indian faith? Did he fear that I would run off with the Indians and abandon my family? Abandon him, my father?

I could no longer stay in my room and pretend that I could rest this night, so I went quietly down the stairs and towards the kitchen. There were no lamps lit, yet I could hear a steady pacing on the kitchen floorboards. For a moment I was frozen in my tracks, so unexpected was the presence of someone else down there in the darkness, when I believed everyone else to be in bed. As I stood there for long minute or two, my eyes adjusted themselves to the absence of light. Then I proceeded carefully towards the kitchen, where I could make out the dim, but unmistakable shape of Father moving back and forth down the length of the room.

"Father?"

He very calmly came to a stop, paused, with his hands clasped behind his back, and then turned to where my voice had come from. There was just enough moonlight glinting off the snow that it lent a dim light to his eyes as they focused themselves on my face. He said nothing, of course. Where once I would have feared to be confronted by him in such a manner, tonight I was only curious. As always, I wondered what was going through his mind; I wondered if he recognized me. I wanted to talk to him, but I wasn't sure exactly whom I would be addressing if I did choose to speak.

"Father, I am troubled because . . . I am troubled because I . . . "

I could not finish the sentence because I did not know how to articulate my confusion. The reflected light of his eyes did not waver from their focus on me, and I felt that I was being bored into by some slow, spinning drill. I felt as if I, too, were beginning to spin around the point of that light.

"Do you still love me, Father?"

Though his eyes did not change their position, as his body did not change its position, his arms dropped from behind his back and fell to his sides. Both of us stood there, unmoving, expectant, waiting. At least, I was waiting; I did not know what Father was experiencing. If he was even breathing at all, there was no sign of it, for there was no discernible rise and fall of his chest, and since I was holding my own breath, I listened for his, but could not hear it. For a moment it seemed that we were caught in that same terrible limbo that we had been hurled into a year ago after he shouted out my name for the last time.

Finally, I could stand it no longer and turned and walked deliberately out of the kitchen and back up the stairs to my room, where I fell onto my bed and began to shake uncontrollably until I exhausted myself into sleep.

On the last day of school before Christmas, Tommy Lamer brought me a Christmas present. When lessons were finished for the day, he took me by the hand and walked me around behind the schoolhouse. Then he made me close my eyes and hold out my hand. I felt something very light and very smooth and round in the palm of my hand. Then I opened my eyes and looked down at it.

"It's a killdeer egg," he said.

It was so tiny and so perfect. It was greyish-white with black speckles all over it. If I couldn't feel how soft and light it was in my hand I would have thought it was a stone, like the ones you find on the beach down by the marsh.

"Don't worry," Tommy said, "I didn't steal it from a nest. Killdeer don't have nests anyway. I found it on the shingle bar just a few days ago. That's where killdeer lay their eggs, you know. Anyway, it must have got left behind and it never hatched. But it's very beautiful, don't you think?"

I nodded my head. I wondered how I would keep such a delicate thing safe from being broken. I was even afraid to hold it in my hand, even though there wasn't anything alive inside it anymore. But the shell was still very beautiful, and the way it felt in my hand I could tell that the shell was still alive in its own way.

Tommy walked me home, but I don't remember much of what he said because I was concentrating on holding onto my egg, but not too hard. I made my hand into a nest, and my eyes into a big, leafy tree.

Sometimes there were events or moments in our lives that did not achieve their full weight until days, weeks, or years after they had visited us. At the time of their occurrence they may have seemed rather ordinary, or their true import may have been obvious only to others. Such, I was beginning to think, had been the arrival of the train in our village. When I witnessed it I was certainly aware of its magnificence, of its great size and noise and power, but these things were not of my inner world, so much as they were of the world of those around me, outside me. What was becoming clearer to me now was what the train represented, rather than what it was. And rather like the Indians than my own people, I had come to see it as a living thing which had the power to invade and to take away. A week after the train had begun its regular journeying back and forth between Toronto and Hamilton, I overheard Mr. Standemyre telling a group of men around the stove at Cotton's General Store of an Indian woman who, when she disembarked from the train at Stavebank Road, fell to the ground as if in a swoon. When someone came over to her to ask if she was all right, she answered that she was waiting for her soul to catch up to her.

I understood what she meant. She had been taken out of herself by a force over which she had no control; she could only wait for it to disgorge her, and then wait for the rest of her — her soul — to find its way back into her body. How frightened she must have been. And yet, to hear Mr. Standemyre and the others talk about it, the train was simply a faster and more comfortable coach, with no horses to have to feed and groom and give rest to. They spoke of it mostly in terms of commerce and business, though they did admit to it bringing distant relatives closer to home.

That's what the train was — a shortcut through time and space. A disturber of equilibrium. And yet, I was intrigued. I was more than intrigued. I was embarrassed to say that when I thought of the train now, I could compare it to no other sensation than when Patrick had first put his hand on my arm. There was that same sense that one part of me was recognizing something that the rest of me could not make head nor tail of. And it was more than recognizing — it was desiring. This was what embarrassed me.

"So what part of you do you think is doing the desiring?" Cecilia asked me when I tried to explain it to her, as we walked arm in arm along the shore towards the marsh.

There had been a minor thaw over the last two days, and so, though the snow melted off a bit, there was still enough of it left to keep the land coated in soft curves of white, with the dark trunks of the trees rising out of it, like dead scraps of lightning. The creek was a sinewy black line running through it all, and it was this that we followed after we turned away from the lakeshore.

"All I know is that it's a part of me that I can't control. You know how when you get out of your bed on a winter's morning and the air in the house is cold, and your body shivers of its own nature? It's like that."

"That's what would be called an involuntary reaction as opposed to a voluntary reaction. Do you remember me teaching you that in school when we studied the muscles of the body?"

"Yes, I do — and that's exactly it. It's as if my body is reacting to the temperature around it, but in another way it's not like that at all, for it's not simply my body that is reacting; it's — and this may sound as if I'm living on the moon, but it's my soul, too."

"Your soul?"

"Yes . . . I think. I've never felt my soul before. Is this a proper kind of feeling for a soul?"

"Well, the soul is that part of us that is in touch with God; it is that part of us which serves as a pathway between us and God. He sends His love to us through our souls, and we glorify Him through our souls. Remember when Mary was visited by Gabriel, and he said to her, 'Hail, O favoured one, the Lord is with you,' and 'The Holy Spirit will come upon you.' And when she went to visit Elisabeth, she said, 'My soul magnifies the Lord.'"

"I'm afraid I don't understand you at all, Cecilia. I may be a virgin, but I don't believe that I'm about to conceive the son of God."

We stopped our aimless wandering along the creek, and Cecilia turned to face me directly.

"Don't take the meaning so literally, Gretchen. You must understand these words for what they point to, beyond the mere event. Your soul can hear things before you can. When Mary said that her soul magnified the Lord, she meant that she had been opened to a grace that she could receive only by surrendering herself to a power that was so much greater than she was. By doing so, her life became that power."

"Are you saying that she became God?"

"No, no . . . or maybe, yes."

"You certainly never taught us that in school."

As soon as the words were out of my mouth I realized I had inadvertently made light of what she was trying to tell me, and all at once, I also realized that I had done this through my own discomfort with what she was saying. I could tell immediately, by how she lowered her head and pressed her lips together that she felt as if I had struck her a thoughtless blow. And so I had.

"Please forgive me, Cecilia. Oh, please do," and I hugged her to me and held her against me. "I'm so afraid."

There it was. I had not understood it before, but now a sense of fear came rushing over me, from whence, I had no earthly idea. And this added uncertainty only made it more frightening.

"It's time for you to go, Gretchen."

"Oh, please don't say so."

"You know it, Gretchen. You've known it for some time, now. It's time to surrender."

"How can I do it? How can I ever leave Mother, with Father the way he is, and Sally and Victoria so young? How can such a thing be surrender, when it feels so cruel and insensitive? Who will look after them all?"

"They are all stronger than you think. You must allow them their own strength. And you must allow yourself yours."

"But where am I to go?"

"You will know."

"When will I know?"

"I can't tell you that, Gretchen. It is not for me to say."

"Please don't be so distant with your words; I cannot bear it."

It was Cecilia's turn to hug me to her, but the closer she held me to her, the farther away I felt myself, as if my soul were already departing, and leaving my body behind as a keepsake for those who loved me and would miss me.

"They are only words, Gretchen. It is I — it is all of us — who holds you. Remember that."

That night in my room, when everyone else had gone to bed, I was once again restless and at loose ends. Other than Cecilia I did not know to whom I could turn for advice or solace, so I was left only with my books. I thought the *Holy Sonnets* of John Donne would be particularly suitable to my condition this night, reeking, as they did, of equal measures of devotion and despair for this earthly life, but I could not find the volume. I turned, then, to my Bible to find the rest of the verses of Luke, which Cecilia had quoted to me.

And Mary said, "My soul magnifies the Lord, and my spirit rejoices in God my Saviour, for he has regarded the low estate of his handmaiden . . . He has exalted those of low degree; he has filled the hungry with good things, and the rich he has sent empty away."

Where once these were words I could have read as simple statements of truth, or at least of God, they now spattered against my ears and my heart like so many raindrops from clouds that blocked me from the light and heat of the sun. What was I to make of these words — they are only words, Cecilia said — in my state of confusion? I could understand myself as being of low estate and of low degree, but what were the great things He had done for me, and how had He filled my hunger with good things? What good things? And was I not sacrilegious for trying to fit myself into the spiritual shape of Mary?

As I went to place my Bible back on my night table, I realized that it had been sitting on top of Mr. Whitman's *Leaves of Grass*. I put the Bible back on top of it, but then slid it aside and picked up the volume of poetry. What now was the difference between sacrilege and hope, if I pretended to look to Mr. Whitman for guidance where I could not find it in scripture? Still, I could not resist, so desperate was I for any kind of direction out of my despair. I opened the pages and read:

People I meet . . . the effect upon me of my early life . . .
The real or fancied indifference of some man or woman I love . . .
They come to me days and nights and go from me again,
But they are not the Me myself.

I read the words over and over again, until I almost came to believe that some part of me had written them and had given them over to someone else to release on to the page, to protect me from my own thoughts.

Moving my chair to the window, I stared those thoughts into the muted glare of the white landscape, into the dark, yawning waters of the lake, until the blood of the new day began to rise to the surface of water and sky and bleed respite into my exhausted Me myself.

Chapter 3

CHRISTMAS HAD PASSED, like a visitor who had come to our door and knocked, only to find no one at home. As a reminder of his attempted visit, he had left behind some knitted scarves and bonnets, needlework cushion covers, landscapes painted on heavy paper, and the echo of Bible passages and fiddle tunes. A week later it was 1856.

I had been trying to write a piece on winter, as Mr. Standemyre had challenged me to do, but my mind had been so occupied with everything else that was my life. We had not talked of it since the day he had mentioned it, and I thought he was being polite enough not to remind me of it, for fear that he might provoke more frustration than excitement in me. He was usually aware of my moods, and he certainly tempered his relationship with me by his understanding of my family situation; he was careful not to speak of Father, unless it was in a very general way that included the rest of my family as well.

I had begun to think of winter as a soporific God gave the earth and the people and plants and living things on it as a respite from the sheer business of being alive. I knew there were places on this earth where the cold never came, but probably the people who lived there were somehow more adept at balancing their daily concerns than we were. Perhaps they did not need to "get a living" in the same way that we did. Perhaps God gave us winter because we had not yet learned how to live properly and evenly throughout the year.

But something was happening to me that was very unwinter like, for I did not feel at all drugged in my spirit or in my body; quite the contrary, I felt my blood was roiled and turbulent. With each new day I seemed to become more and more restless.

Today, as I looked to the books on my night table, I thought instead of the stone in the drawer and the stone in my pocket. I took them both out and placed them on the bed beside me. They lay there like the fossilized hearts of an earth that humans could not remember. Placing one in each hand, I could feel the weight of time pressing against my palms, and at the same time I could feel the counterweight of timelessness. Just then, Victoria walked into my room.

"Gretchen, why do you keep those stones?"

I felt I needed to give an answer that was not the true one, both because I wasn't sure I knew what the true answer was, and because I didn't think Victoria could understand, even if I could articulate that unformed truth.

"I just like them, that's all."

"I have some stones, too, but they're just tiny ones — they're not as big as the ones you have."

"Yes, I saw them in a little bowl of water when I was staying in your room. And why do you keep your stones?"

"Because they're pretty colours when they're wet. I just like to look at them."

"That's a good thing to do."

"Do you really think so?"

"Yes, I really think so."

"Why do you think so?"

"Because sometimes we need beautiful things to help slow us down. The more beautiful things there are, the more we take the time to notice them, and the more we notice them, the more we feel good."

"Do you want to come down to the lake and put my stones in the real water and look at them for a while?"

"Yes, Victoria, I think that would be lovely."

"I haven't ever asked anybody else to look at my stones with me, you know."

"Well, then, I am honoured to be asked."

As soon as the words were out of my mouth, Victoria was running to her room to collect her stones.

Once bundled up in our coats and scarves and mittens, we walked down to the shore of the lake. The afternoon sun was not so much a round ball of light as it was a drop of yellow, dropped into a much vaster bowl of blue and grey water, its edges not clear enough to discern. A bit of wind was soughing in the pine trees and stirring up small waves on the lake.

"You know, Victoria, I think we'll get our boots and our feet wet if we try to put your stones in the lake. Maybe we should go down to the creek, instead."

"All right, let's go."

Victoria grabbed my hand and began pulling me along the shoreline towards the marsh. As we reached the shingle bar and were about to turn away from the lake and follow the curve of Garter Snake Hill towards the creek I heard a *kill-deeah* . . . *kill-deah* . . . *dee* . . . *dee* . . . *dee* rise into the air behind us. It was a familiar bird sound, but it seemed out of place for some reason. Before I could think much about it, Victoria was once again pulling me along towards the creek.

"We need to find a place where it's not too deep and where there's sun on the creek so we can see the colours when I put the stones in the water," said Victoria, almost out of breath, more from trying to pull me along, I'm sure, than from running. "Here! Here's a good spot! Look, the sun's shining right on the water and it's hardly deep at all."

Victoria squatted as close to the water as she could, then took off one of her mittens and reached as deep as she could into her coat pocket to find her stones. She brought out one handful, carefully dumped them into her other hand, after pulling the mitten off it with her teeth, then pushed into her pocket to retrieve the remainder of the stones. She laid them on one of her mittens on the ground and then, one by one, very deliberately, she held each stone just at the surface of the water, before dropping it in.

"I like this one the best," she said, without taking her eyes off the stones in the water, and while pointing her finger at one of the stones. "When it's not in the water it's only kind of grey, but in the water it turns green and you can see little white stripes across it. And this one, too, it turns red — well, not really red, but I can't think of another colour to call it, because it's not really brown or purple, either. And this bright green one — I really like that one, too. I think it's a piece of bottle glass, but I still like it, anyway. Which one is your favourite one?"

I squatted down next to her so that we were touching shoulders.

"I think I like that one that's really black. It looks like a weasel's eye, don't you think?"

"When have you ever seen a weasel?"

"Once or twice on the far side of the marsh. Have you never seen one?"

"I don't know. I've seen some tiny animals that I don't know the names of. Maybe I have seen a weasel."

"Well, it's long and thin — less than a foot long and the size of your forearm, and it's very sleek."

"I've seen animals like that."

"Well, then, you've probably seen a weasel."

"And its eyes look like that stone?"

"That's what that stone reminds me of."

"What if all these stones were eyes — then they'd be looking at us right now."

"Yes, they would. You could say that the creek was looking at us while we're looking at it."

"And then I could take the eyes and put them somewhere else, and wherever I put them, that place would be looking at us."

"That's a wonderful idea."

"I like that idea, Gretchen. What do you think the creek sees when it's looking at us right now?"

"Well, I think it sees two very pretty girls, and it wishes it could look at us all the time."

Victoria giggled and put her hands over her face. Then she turned to musing, with her head tilted slightly to one side, away from me.

"So if I take the stones out of the creek, then it won't be able to see us anymore?"

"I don't know. I think the creek can always see us; it's just that when you put your pretty stones into the water, it helps the creek see better."

"Can the trees see us, too? And the marsh and the hill, too?"

"I like to think so, sometimes. Sometimes it gives me comfort to know that I'm being watched over."

"Me, too. I like to be watched over."

With those words, Victoria leaned against me and rested her head on my shoulder. This, all this, was what I would be leaving behind.

The letter looked as if it had traveled several times around the world and had adventures that could be told only by the stains of time and weather on it, and by the wearing down of its original shape and firmness. I could even believe, before I opened it, that Patrick, and even I, had somehow shared the length and breadth of the experience, so worn was his printing of my name on the paper. I carried it from the post office in the pocket of my coat, and kept it pressed into my hand the whole way home. With brief greetings to Mother and to Sally and Victoria, I made straight for my room, where I could finally open the letter and find what news there was for me from Patrick.

Dear Gretchen,

I have found the man in the bog. I set out early each day to look for the spot where I had first found him. How many days it took, I don't remember. I was not truly sure that it was the right spot until I had carefully dug down through a layer of peat that had already been dug and replaced by me so long ago. When I had uncovered him once again, it was early afternoon of a cold cloudy day. The sleet was turning to snow and back again. He lay there as if he was sleeping the peace of an old and contented man. I just knelt there beside him, staring at his leathered face so long that it seemed to begin to change shape. And then I seemed to lose my bearings. I felt as if I had never left Ireland, and yet I remembered Canada and you as if somehow I was still there. I felt as if the man lying in the bog before me was staring me into all this confusion, even though his eyes were well and truly closed in death. And then I could hardly see him at all because darkness had overtaken me unawares. When I came back to myself there was a thin layer of snow over everything and over me too. When I tried to move I could hardly feel my body at all, I was so numb from the cold.

I've told you this story because you may be the only one who could understand it. And maybe you can now also understand why I will stay here in Ireland.

Your friend,
Patrick Monaghan

I shivered as I realized that night had fallen on me, too, and that I had lost Patrick to another world. I unlocked my fingers from his letter, curling and uncurling them to force the blood back into them. Then I lifted my arm, and then I stood up. More than anything, I felt a strange sadness and disappointment. And just as I could feel the blood moving through my finger joints again, the image of Father flashed quickly before my eyes.

In my dusty white sand journal, blessed by the presence of the creek, the distant hum of lake water, the silent torpor of snakes somewhere in the gut of Garter

Snake Hill, and the hope of a summer sun that would rise high and higher above the trees: a tiny circle with four lines, like spokes, wandering into four circles, and from each of these circles a wavy line that had nothing at its end. In amongst these circles and lines, the words *now* and *here* and *blue* and *red* and *grey* and *me* and *myself*. A constellation visible only from the point of a stick that was once a branch that was once part of a tree that was once a seed dropped from the beak of some bird that was not from this land, and who passed through without a human eye to see it.

Winter gathered all the force it had left and grasped Merigold's Point in its icy fist for the last week of February, then it seemed to let out all its breath and collapse into March and the first thaws of an early spring. Like the frozen earth, I, too, felt that I was waiting for release, for some infusion of new energy so that I could step forward into the next stage of my life. This next stage, I knew and I feared, would not be in Merigold's Point; everything in my body and spirit was preparing itself to leave.

I needed a destination. I needed to be able to say to Mother that I wished to travel to a particular place, and she would need to know that it was a safe place, a place where there was someone other than God to look over me. For though we had never spoken of it directly, I was sure that Mother and I had the same sense of God's ability to look after us, even though my faith in him had wavered. Perhaps He could take care of our souls, because only He knew what souls really were, and, therefore, only He would know how to look after them. So, I needed to choose a destination where a greater human being than myself could look out for me.

The only possibilities, then, were New Brunswick and Massachusetts: there was uncle Silas in Kingsclear, and some Talbots in Concord, though they probably had no idea who I was. I was sure of only two things: that Mother must be able to rely on my being in safe hands at journey's end, and that once I got on that train I was probably not going to arrive at the destination Mother thought I was. I could tell no one, not even Cecilia, what I was up to, for I did not truly know, myself. I could end up in Kingsclear or Concord or Ireland, or none of those places, depending on how long my meagre funds would support me. I did not know where I was going or for how long I would be gone; I knew only that those things did not matter in the end, and that no matter how afraid I was, my resolve would not waver, at least not in the beginning.

"Mother, what would you think of my going out to visit Uncle Silas?"

Her hands, which had been sliding knitting needles quickly and easily in and out of a line of wool that was slowly becoming a sock, fell to her knees, as if the weight of them had become too great for her arms to support. Her eyes looked up from her knitting, but not at me; they were aimed into the distance, as if they were too tired to focus on any particular thing.

"A girl needs to see more than her own small part of the world," she said. I didn't know if she was speaking of me or of her younger self. "You should see where your family came from."

"I know you would miss me, and I would miss you, but . . ."

"We would all miss you. Your father would miss you."

There was the sentence that was a regret, a pleading, and a weapon, all at once; we both knew it. The pain and the sorrow, both present and anticipated, left no room for further words. But words had been few between us for all these years; we did not need them. We understood the turn of a head, the movement of a hand, the speed and rhythm of the breath, the weight of feet across the floor. Still, at this moment, I could not bear the silence.

"I would not be gone for long."

I had never so intentionally and so carefully lied to Mother before. For a brief moment I thought she might stand up and slap my face for having so cruelly shattered the trust between us. But nothing happened; neither of us moved or even changed expression. I could only guess what turmoil I had stirred up in her heart. Could I dare to go through with my plan? Could I hurt so many people?

"You will never be gone in spirit, my dear. This will always be your home, and by leaving it you will come to know the truth of that deeper in your heart than you can know it now."

She reached out her hand. I walked over and knelt under it, letting it rest on my head, as my head rested on her lap. In this way, she blessed me; she blessed everything that I was, forever.

Cecilia cried as she tried to turn her smile into a joyful laugh. She hugged her love into me, and held me long enough for it not to leak out once she let go of me.

Victoria looked as deep as she could into my eyes to find out if I would still love her and be her big sister while

I was away. More than anything, she wanted to trust that we would never lose each other.

Sally's eyes smiled, while the rest of her face settled into a kind of serenity that I remembered feeling on my own face at times of great peacefulness that came from a place I could never understand, but could always feel safe in.

Father's hand, which hung by his side, seemed to struggle to find its way towards me, but could not remember how to get there. His eyes grew suddenly watery, but the tears, like his hand, could not find their way.

The lake tossed a gentle wave at my feet; it flowed up and around my boots, as if to trace my footprints into the skin of the shoreline, to be saved until I returned.

The creek sang me a vesper as it seduced the last rays of the sun and the red blood of my heart into the marrow of its liquid bones.

The marsh was still and alive as an egg in a nest.

The stones of the shingle bar echoed the depths of my being across the lake and into the sky.

Letters were written to New Brunswick; letters came back from New Brunswick. Train schedules were pored over; tickets were purchased. Time rushed away from us in all directions.

Day by day, I set aside certain things, besides the obvious clothes and toiletries, I wished to take with me: a box of writing paper for letters, a clothbound journal, several pencils and a sharpener — ink would not serve on a train — my Wordsworth, and my copy of Mr. Whitman's *Leaves of Grass*. I thought about Donne's *Holy Sonnets*, but still could not find them. Since I was not committed to bringing them with me, I did not search as hard as I might have for them.

When I went to bed that night, I was restless and knew that I would not be able to fall asleep easily. I tried going through my mind to find what it was that was at the core of my disturbed state, and when I had rummaged through all my thoughts, I was left with a strange disquiet about not being able to find my book of Donne's *Holy Sonnets*. This surprised me, because there were so many other concerns in my present condition that were of far more importance. Still, I could not get the temporary loss of this book out of my mind. So, I decided to get up and look for the book.

I looked as quietly as I could — for everyone had retired to bed — into every corner of my room, without success. Then I tiptoed down the stairs in the dark, went into the kitchen, found a candle and lit it, in order to continue my search there and then in the parlour.

Just as I lit the candle, my eyes happened to pass over the window that looked out into the orchard. Something in the bare skeletons of the trees caught my eye, but I couldn't tell what it was. I decided it was nothing, and turned back towards the doorway to the parlour, when I stopped and looked out the window again. I cupped my hand around the candle, to erase its glare from the glass of the window so that I might see better into the darkness. I still could not see clearly what it was I was trying to look at. I blew the candle out. Whatever it was, I would not be able to determine it without going outside, which I was very hesitant to do, because it would mean going back up to my room to dress myself against the cold.

Before I could make a rational decision as to what to do, I found myself standing out on the porch, still staring into the orchard. The night air was cool and moist; one could almost hear the newly thawed earth relaxing into friable soil once again. I walked slowly and carefully into the orchard towards one of the trees that was not shaped like the others. Just as I was about to come up to it, my slippered foot knocked against something on the ground. I leaned over to see what it was. Picking it up I could tell that it was a book. A sudden gust of wind came up, and something knocked against my shoulder. Instinctively, I tried to push it away with my hand. It was heavy, and swung away from me, then back into my shoulder. It was Father's leg.

I felt like that Indian woman did when she got off the train and fell to the ground, waiting for her soul to catch up with her, except that it was I who was trying to catch up to wherever my soul had gone. I stood there, unable to move, unable to force my mind back into the flow of time, from which it had detached itself. I existed neither in the present nor the past nor the future. I existed, yet did not exist, at the same time.

I don't know how long it was before I went back into the house. I did not run, I did not shout; I walked back in the same manner in which I walked out. I climbed the stairs to my parents' bedroom. The door was open, and against the dull light of the window, I could see Mother sitting on the edge of the bed, as if waiting for me. As if she knew the news I brought from the dark body of the orchard. When I sat down beside her and put my hand on her knee, I was suddenly catapulted back into time;

my soul was hurled back into my body. But I did not cry. I felt abandoned by my own tears.

"Mother?"

She tilted her face towards me, her eyes glistening in the muted light.

"Mother? You know?"

"I have cried all my tears each night for this past year and more. I have tried to cry life back into him every night for all this time, fearing each time that I might cry my own life out of me, and then where would we be? He could not come back. I want to believe that somewhere deep inside him, where we could not see, he was trying to come back. And now..."

Now. What did that word mean? What other words were in it, and which words did it reject? Did it have anything to do with time anymore? Did it include absence? Did it allow for pain? Did it hold all of us in its great hand, or did it break each of us off like brittle fingers, thus destroying itself and leaving us to the world, bereft of all essential connection?

"And now, we must bring him in, Gretchen."

We put on warm clothes and boots and made our way into the orchard, and up to the tree, where he hung like a shadow that had lost its owner. We wrapped our arms around his legs, but we had not the strength nor the wherewithal to shift him. I climbed into the tree to try to loosen his neck from the noose of the rope, while Mother held him and tried to push him back up towards the sky, but we could not do it. I edged myself back down the tree and went to the barn to get the axe. Back at the tree, I handed the axe to Mother, and climbed back into the tree. Mother reached the axe up to me, and I began to chop at the branch. I couldn't position myself well enough to bring enough force down with each swing, and so it took me several minutes worth of short, feeble strikes of the axe before the branch was severed, and with a sound like the heart of a tree being torn from its trunk, Father fell back to earth, into the arms of Mother.

∾

All of Merigold's Point, all of the parishioners of our church who had been so awkward in their reaction to Father's predicament for the past year, and in their reaction to our family, came out to the funeral. As they had not found a comfortable manner in which to address Father's "madness," neither could they now find a way to understand his suicide. Some of the eyes into which I glanced during the service were filled with confusion, some with pity, and some with outright condemnation.

There were still two weeks remaining until my departure, and though Mother, Sally, Victoria, and I had not spoken about it, we were all keenly aware of it, as one is aware of a wave rolling inexorably towards the shore. Though I did not wish to take the bandage from a wound before it was healed, it was still clear to me that not even Father's death could deter me from my chosen path. I did not know how long I would be gone; nor did I wish to fix the length of my absence. Whatever was to happen to me once I boarded the train was in the hands of some power beyond my own.

Fear had not invaded our lives, as many thought it would on the death of Father, and this surprised everyone, including ourselves. Some part of me felt that I should fear for Mother, for Sally, and for Victoria — what would they do without my support in this difficult time? Whether we spoke it or not, we all knew that we had been thrust into our own versions of independence, ready or not. I thought Mother had been prepared for this for a long time; sometimes I even believed that there was a certain anticipation of her own future, for now it depended on no one but herself. I thought even that she was thankful for my leaving, so that she could prove herself. And I would prove myself.

The book I had stumbled on as I found Father hanging in the apple tree was my copy of Donne's *Holy Sonnets*. Father must have carried it out to his final moment on this earth. The pages of the book are now stained with the dampness of that night and with the odour of thaw. They are thick with time, stiff and wavy like an arthritic wave. I decided to take it with me, anyway.

It was not until the second last night before my departure that I noticed a marker in the book, a marker not my own. As I opened the book to the page at which it was inserted, I realized that the marker was Father's favourite one, one I had often seen him place in his Bible. This, at least, explained why I could not find the book when I had searched for it before. The poem which was marked was "A Hymne to God the Father," and it was the final stanza that closed its fingers around my heart:

I have a sinne of feare, that when I have spunne
My last thred, I shall perish on the shore;
Sweare by thy selfe, that at my death thy sonne
Shall shine as he shines now, and heretofore;
And, having done that, Thou hast done,
I feare no more.

I wondered if Father feared no more as he prepared his own death in the orchard he loved so much. Perhaps his love for the trees and the apples was the only love he could understand and rely on in the end. Could such a love truly transcend fear, even fear of death?

But there was something else about the poem. About the second stanza:

Wilt thou forgive that sinne by which I'have wonne
Others to sinne? and, made my sinne their doore?
Wilt thou forgive that sinne which I did shunne
A yeare, or two: but wallowed in, a score?
When thou hast done, thou hast not done,
For, I have more.

Next to this stanza were two stars drawn in pencil. They could only have been drawn there by Father.

I took the book and went to Mother's room. She was sitting on the edge of the bed, as if it were a place she could no longer recognize. I sat down beside her in silence. After a few minutes, I opened the book to Donne's poem, to the two pencilled stars beside it.

"Do you know what this means, Mother?"

She looked at the page, and if she could not recognize her bed without her husband in it, she clearly recognized the drawing next to the poem.

"That was her name."

I looked at Mother, not understanding what she meant.

"That was her name — Two Stars."

Back in my room, sitting alone on the edge of my own bed, I no longer felt that in leaving Merigold's Point I was about to leave a part of my world behind, for it had already left me without having said goodbye. And I realized that I could not now take this book with me. More than a remembrance of Father's death it was a remembrance of his tragedy. These holy sonnets were too taken up with the fear of God rather than with the love of God, even if the words seemed to tempt the reader with the opposite understanding. I did not want to regret anything I ever did. Perhaps I was too susceptible to the boundlessness of Mr. Whitman's view of the world, but if I was going to suffer fear, it would be fear of possibility rather than fear of stricture.

I went to sleep that night no longer knowing how to pray.

The sun rose, severe and confident, on my last full day in my parents' house. This day was the day of stones. I rose with the sun, and shivered with the excitement and apprehension of my trip I knew I would not be able to eat breakfast. Instead I prepared myself for a long walk. I pulled open the drawer of my night table and took out both stones this time. The grey one with the veins of blue running through it, I would take with me on my journey, to see if I could find the red in it; Baketigweyaa's stone, it was time to skip across the water.

I set out along the lakeshore to the river at Port Credit. All the way there, the sun burned into my cheeks, as if branding me so that I might not be lost, no matter where I traveled. And all the way there, the stone in my pocket insinuated itself into my very being. It was the counterweight to my own existence, it was the solid expression of all those parts of me that could be articulated in no other way.

At the river, I crossed the bridge and found my way down to the mouth of the river, where it exhausted itself into the great lake. I chose a spot, still on the river bank, but close to where it turned in a wide sweep to become the shore of the lake. Reaching into my pocket, I took out my stone. I bounced it a couple of times in my hand, feeling not only the weight of the stone, but the weight of my memory of Baketigweyaa. Of Father. Of my life at Merigold's Point. Then, measuring the distance, I threw the stone, as hard as I could, across the surface of the water. It skipped across the last few feet of the river and out across the surface of the lake, until I lost it in the glare of the sun on the water. I looked back over my shoulder and shouted towards the land, towards that place I had come from, towards all those who had birthed me.

"Did you hear that?"

ABOUT THE AUTHOR

Matthew Manera has extensive literary magazine and journal publishing credits for his poetry and fiction, including *Canadian Literature, Grain, Dandelion,* the *New Quarterly, Arc* and the *Atlanta Review.* He is a recent winner of the Cecilia Lamont Literary Contest (BC). *A Stone in My Pocket* is Manera's debut novel. He lives in Victoria and teaches at the University of Victoria.